The Peterloo Affair

A Tale of the St. Peter's Fields Massacre

Lucinda Elliot

THE PETERLOO AFFAIR

First Edition

Although this novel is a work of fiction, the historical references are accurate, and extensive research has been made to render the situation as authentically as possible. The real names of historical figures have been used, as far as their documented contributions to the eventual disaster are concerned.

The book is sold subject to the condition that it shall not by way of trade or otherwise, be lent, resold, hired out, or otherwise circulated without the writer's prior consent, electronically or in any form of binding or cover other than the form in which it is published and without a similar condition including this condition being imposed on the subsequent purchaser. Replication or distribution of any part is strictly prohibited without the written permission of the copyright holder.

Copyright © 2018 Lucinda Elliot
All rights reserved.

ISBN: 9781730789632

Book layout by ebooklaunch.com

To Liese Szwann with Love

Acknowledgments

I want to thank Robert Wingfield, RL, JD, all my writer friends, the historians Peter Foden and Dr Kevin Linch for their invaluable advice, and also Dominic Butler of the Lancashire Infantry Museum, the staff at the People's History Museum in Manchester, and all those who have helped me in writing this book.

1.

Fine Schemes

Lancashire, England 1819

The idea came into Joan's head as perfect and as ready to see the world as a full term baby. It took her breath away, sending tingles through her.

"Marcie, we must get a group of lasses and women together, and march with the men to that great meeting on St Peter's Field."

She rushed on. "Those women in Middleton and other places are in the right of it."

Marcie turned, her sweeping dark eyebrows up at their highest. She could put you down with a lift of those eyebrows. Yet, Joan knew that should Marcie laugh at her, she would stick by what she said anyway.

It meant that much to her. Maybe it was a bit like the falling in love those stories went on about.

Joan had fallen in love with an idea, in the same way as she'd fallen in love with the their plan to escape from growing up to turn into her mother or Marcie's, and this wish wasn't different, at that. It was somehow part of it.

Marcie nodded. "You're right. You know, I've been weak and let myself be put off speaking up to say the same, thinking of the men joking and Mam scolding."

That was typical of Marcie; she was more unsparing on herself than on anyone else.

"We must tell them we want to join now." Joan turned to where the sounds of the tramp of the men's feet on the dry earth, and the shouted orders of those acting as drill sergeants, or whatever they called them, came through the copse of trees fringing the side of the meadow.

When caught by an idea, Joan tended to act before thinking things out. Marcie took her arm. "We need more of us. They'll only laugh at two. If we had some of the matrons in with us, say, they might take notice. We must try to win Widow Hobson over, besides."

Joan groaned. That terrible old woman wasn't a Methodist[1] but she argued like one, knowing the Bible like the back of her hand and using chapter and verse against anyone who did things she didn't think fitting—most of all wenches. "You could do it," she urged.

Marcie had a knack for that when she put her mind to it. Joan got heated when disputing things. Marcie had a way of getting people on her side before they knew it, as when she talked their parents into letting them go along with their brothers to the fair a couple of years since.

Marcie winked, as they both did, though winking and whistling were seen as improper in a female, like most things that were fun. "We'll start tomorrow."

Now, the loud clapping the marchers made when they stood at ease, which they joked was rifle fire, sounded in their ears.

She and Marcie shouldn't be lingering out here in the fields so late. All about them, the colours faded into grey, with only the sky bright pink in the west. The blackbirds and thrushes still sang on high, though now bats flitted, soon to darken the sky in their thousands.

The air might be the sweeter after that day in the workroom by the looms, full of dust from the cotton waste, but there was work waiting. There always was. Besides, their mothers held that only flighty wenches stayed out after dark.

They were only allowed out now because they were supposed to be finding edible plants, and maybe some herbs for their medical potions. During this August drought, they foraged ever further from the village to get any dry dandelion leaves, plantain or anything edible. At least this made a good excuse for staying out so long.

"Right wheel!"

---

[1] Methodists, while maintaining spiritual equality between rich and poor, held that it was a Christian duty to comply humbly with the position in life to which one had been allocated.

That was Joan's brother Tom's voice. He was one of those who led the men, being a veteran from the late wars against Napoleon Bonaparte, or 'Boney' as they liked to dub him, half jeering and half admiring.

Now Tom had to shout that order again. That showed he had 'Daffy Danny' in his lot, as the poor fellow couldn't fathom which side was which. Tom tied some cotton waste onto his right arm as a guide, but it didn't seem to help.

The girls followed the sounds, drawn towards that air of excitement that the marchers gave out. It was as if, at last, after failed petitions to the Prince Regent and his government, here was an answer to being unseen and unheard.

There was a great meeting planned, with half the people who worked in cotton in the towns and the villages hereabouts marching into Manchester to hear the famed speaker, Henry Hunt. He was called 'Orator' Hunt[2] for his fine speeches, and was one of the few wealthy folk on their side.

Marcie and Joan came up to the trees and shrubs which lined the edge of the field, and looked on the men and lads, training. Not only young men, but older men too, such as Marcie's father. Mr. Wright, Joan's father, led his own file of men.

He marched with head held high, a strutting bantam cock of a man. Hunger might be using them all up, draining the play out of the children, the colour from their cheeks of the girls, and the spring from the legs of the lads; worry might have turned Joan's mother's once near gold hair mostly silver, but what it couldn't do was bend the back of her father.

He'd always had strong ideas about how working men should have the vote, not only those with land. He was quick to follow Samuel Bamford's[3] example, and with the help of army veterans like

---

[2] Henry Hunt (1773-1835) was a landowner and supporter of parliamentary reform, noted for his vigorous speechmaking and known as 'Orator Hunt'.

[3] Samuel Bamford (1788-1872) was a leading Radical. A weaver and self-educated man from Middleton, he advocated agitation in support of calls for parliamentary reform.

his son, get a troop of men ready to march to this planned great meeting, as disciplined as soldiers.

That cousin or second cousin—whatever he was—of the Ridleys' led his own file of men. He was a veteran from the French Wars too. Seán McGilroy, that was his name, as Irish as could be, though he was only half Irish from his father. Most agreed he was a fine, strong, handsome lad, tall and lean as he was, with longish black hair curling almost into ringlets, and bright blue, wide set eyes. Not light blue, like Joan's own, but near as blue as cornflowers.

Joan was annoyed at how the girls hereabouts were acting silly over him. She didn't know why that vexed her. Maybe it was because before him, her brother Tom was the dashing veteran soldier they'd all been making cows' eyes at.

Marcie said that Tom's golden mop was like a girl's, while Joan said she thought McGilroy's made him look like one of those daffy water spaniels she'd seen once. There was talk about him as a roving, ne'er-do-well type with a bad name as a light o' love, but that didn't seem to put off his Ridley girl cousins.

Joan's younger brothers were both in Tom's group of a dozen men, a squadron, or whatever they called it. They looked as solemn as if they were in chapel. More so; in chapel they tickled each other.

Joan thought that Marcie made a point of not looking at Tom, for all—maybe because—he did look rather fine. She said instead, "They say there's thousands about yon drilling practice, in Middleton, Oldham—you name it."

Then she broke off as they saw someone else watching the marching. He was crouched behind a sapling. Joan nudged Marcie, putting a finger to her lips. Together, they tiptoed towards the man.

He was counting out loud, using his fingers, and mixing up numbers now and then. "Seventy…Nought and seventy…" He was in too much difficulty to hear them come up.

"Neddy Pritchard—what are you about?" Joan spoke suddenly and loudly.

He whirled round. As they broke out laughing, his drawn face twitched. "What d'you mean by it, you bloody sluts? Be off with you. You both need a whipping, that you do."

Marcie snorted. "Careful, Joan, he's a 'Waterloo hero', remember."

Neddy Pritchard was forever talking about his fine deeds in the late French wars. He might boast of how he'd acted the hero then, but Joan had never seen him do anything for anyone in civilian life. He was even said to raise a hand to his mother.

Now, he looked as if he wanted to do the same by them. Remembering Tom saying once how war did things to men, so that sometimes they couldn't stand being surprised from behind, Joan felt sorry for him. Whatever Ned may have done in the wars, though still under thirty, he came back to the village as winkled and dried up as a prune.

"We didn't mean to give you a turn. It was only a jest…" She broke off, remembering some talk about Ned Pritchard being in the Deputy Constable's pay. Maybe it wasn't fair to believe it, though. With all the paid spying going on these days, rumours were as common as flies, and trust half gone.

Marcie said, "Why don't you join them at drilling, if you're so interested?"

Neddy started towards them. They tensed, but held their ground. He passed by, throwing over his shoulder, "The pair o' you foolish wenches needs to learn some respect for a real soldier as knows about drilling, unlike that lot of fools led by trouble-making radicals like thy masters, as never fought a real battle in their lives."

"You sneaking old rascal, a deal of those lads were in the French Wars and all," Marcie rapped out. "You'd lead them all to gaol for a farthing."

"You sluts aren't worth wrangling with." Scowling, he stumped off.

They went on through the shrubs at the edge of the field. "It's ugly to think how many others there must be, running tales to earn a crust from that Deputy Constable Nadin[4] and those who would keep us down," Marcie murmured.

There were perhaps two hundred of the local men at the drilling, aged between thirteen and fifty.

---

[4] Both Joseph Nadin, appointed Deputy Constable of Manchester since 1803, and the Magistrates who employed him made heavy use of paid informers. He was much hated for his brutal practices.

Tom, as he led his group, was as lively as if he'd been living on meat every day these last months. A couple of years since, when he came back to the village, having turned into a man and lost the pimples he'd gone out with, he'd caused as much of a stir among the lasses as his friend Seán McGilroy did now. Tom, though, only admired Marcie. Poor Tom: Joan saw that no one else would do for him, and Marcie would have none of him, or any man.

That was because she and Joan had it all worked out between themselves that they wouldn't be wives and mothers. Instead, they were going to escape out into the wide world. They hoped to learn enough to get a living from working on doctoring and healing.

They were even saving up. Marcie had two crowns[5] and Joan had three from presents in better days from those they'd healed with their herbal cures.

Close behind Tom, Timothy Yorke was drilling, as solemn, from the look of him, as Joan's younger brothers. Unlike the others, the Yorkes had done well enough since the Corn Laws[6], running a bakery as they did, for all they moaned of people never paying their bills.

Joan was glad enough that he had joined in the drilling, seeing he was the sort of fellow who said if you strived to get on in life, you could, no matter where you started out from, even the workhouse. Joan thought it showed the strength of feeling against how they were all being treated, that he was marching too.

Now the drilling was over. The men were gathering about the centre of the field for some speeches. Joan knew that sometimes some well-known man from a neighbouring town, like Samuel Bamford himself, came to give a speech. Still, there had been no sign of a stranger today.

Hulking Jimmy Thribble called out, "You going to do the honours instead, Tom, my lad?"

Tom slapped McGilroy on the back. "McGilroy's got the gift of the gab: he can do it."

---

[5] A crown was five old shillings.

[6] The Corn Laws (1815) imposed tariffs on imported grain to keep prices high.

Then Joan's father got up on the old short legged wooden stool he took as a platform. He shouted for quiet with a voice more suited to a giant, powerful even after this long time of scarce food. Recently, when she and Marcie were out late gathering the foodstuffs, they'd heard him holding forth. He never did anything by halves. When he told a story, he put his heart and soul into it, and when he sang a song, he raised the roofs.

"Friends," he threw out his voice as he must when he was a lad calling in the cows, "It's a fine idea that we hear McGilroy, seeing the man we had coming isn't here by whatever cause. This lad is one of us now, as you know, living and working with his uncle Ridley's family, and he can give us an outsider's view of things."

"Full of fine lasses, that's the view for him," a voice called, and there were some coarser jibes and whistles as Joan's father jumped down and McGilroy took his place.

There were shouts for and against his speaking, and he flashed his white teeth at them in the dusk as if he enjoyed it, and went on regardless.

Joan had to admit it, this McGilroy was a likely looking man, tall, spare and upright as he was, and dark to the point of being swarthy, with those black ringlets and olive skin. The Ridleys said his father had been 'Black Irish', whatever that meant.

He had a pleasing voice with a sort of lilt to it, from his dead father, she supposed, but mostly he sounded as Lancashire as the rest of them.

"My lads! Maybe it's forward of me to stand up here when I've only been living and working with you for a short time…"

Somebody's voice shouted, "Hear, Hear!"

"That's right enough," McGilroy continued with a grin, "but I've been staying with my Uncle Ridley on and off since I was a bairn, so I'm no stranger for all that.

"I saw how things were then, when a weaver could bring in two pounds a week by himself. Most of t'houses were full of fine things, with roasts on the table. That's all changed since the wars. When I came back this time, even with all of us at it, and the extra looms and all, we still can't get a proper living. T'only way to get meat is to trap a rabbit. All above board, of course, for any spies harkening."

He winked when he said that. Joan remembered the talk that nobody was so bold a poacher as he, sallying into the squire's grounds with never a care for the gamekeeper or his traps.

There were shouts of agreement. Joan sighed, remembering those past meat dinners.

McGilroy went on, "I know that Master Wright was one of those who signed that petition to the Prince Regent and his government. That was only one that was sent and turned away, for the government reckons there is nowt to be done. They can say so easy enough, when it's not their families clemmed[7], and we don't have the vote to make our voices heard".

"We've got some of the landed men with a say in the running of the country with us; still, there's not enough of them for the rest to take heed. There's many who put their faith before in those men doing something for us, who say now how we must do something for ourselves. And that's why we must all go to this great meeting at St Peter's Field: that's why all of us who can go, ought to go."

There was a shout. That was something on which the men all agreed. McGilroy lowered his voice. "What I see all around makes me riled, and I've only had weeks of it, while most of you have had a bellyful of it long since—and that's the only way anyone here's had a full belly lately."

A few of the lads laughed, but not many. Jimmy Thribble was one and Jack Hoper another, but Joan thought they would laugh on the way to their own funerals.

"Aye, it makes me want to fight it out with some of those in charge, and some of you must want that a bloody sight more and all."

Joan knew many of the men must be gripping those stout sticks they carried harder, and her father would be clenching his fists, even thinking of it.

"Still, that's not the way. We don't have the troops, and those Yeomanry Cavalry part time soldiers on our side, while all those special

---

[7] Dialect for 'going hungry'.

constables they're signing up have been told we're going to swarm into town with no more order and thought among us than so many rats.

"So, we're going to take them by surprise. Right enough, there's many of us, enough to confound 'em—even if they've got the troops. But we're not going there to riot—that's the last thing we want to do. Yon magistrates are only waiting for an excuse to break up the meeting. It will only take one brawl to do that, and we don't want the troops sent in[8]. We've got to keep orderly and quiet. We'll march in files, with our music and our banners, more of us than they've ever seen joined together.

"We want to show that we're open to reason, yet at the same time, we want something done. It may be that this Henry Hunt and these others have a good plan about how to get that something done. We need to go and hear 'em and judge.

"And we won't if we give any chance for those magistrates to break up the meeting as a riot before it's even started. So that's why we've got to keep calm, like a troop with discipline, staying out of trouble, so those who are against us see how we are all joined."

He grinned round at them, and Joan thought that it was hard not to like him when he smiled like that. "That's all I've got to say, though I'm guessing Master Wright has summat to add to it. I give you thanks for hearing me."

"That was a fine speech, and I've nothing to add tonight," said Joan's father.

There was an outburst of clapping and cheering, while Daffy Danny, who was hard by the edge of the meadow near Joan and Marcie, put up a hand, like in Sunday School. They saw he was trying to say something, but whatever he was saying was lost in the noise.

• • •

Joan caught at Marcie's arm. "We've got to ask them now, when they're all het up from the talk. If there's ever a time they'll say aye to us, it's now."

---

[8] In this time before a police force, if a disorderly crowd gathered, first the 'Riot Act' was read, and an hour later troops were sent in to disperse it.

Without waiting for Marcie's reply, acting as if driven by something outside of her, she walked forwards, clapping too. For once, Marcie followed.

2.

Sean McGilroy

Those men nearest them span round as if shot. Most of the others didn't take note of the girls' approach, and began trooping off the meadow. Joan walked boldly up to the speaker's group, even as McGilroy jumped down from the wobbly stool.

Whenever Joan ran into him since his return to the village, he'd looked amazed, as if she shouldn't be there. Whatever that was about, it was nothing to how he looked now, eyes dilated, weight dropping automatically, as if crouched for a fight. Maybe there was something in what folks said about the Irish always being ready for a scrap.

Then he laughed. "It's all right: it's only two of our lasses, as pretty as pictures. And us all thinking you were some of Nardy Joe's[9] lot, eh, fellows?"

"Joan!" Mr. Wright glared at them. "What are you doing out at this hour? Your Mam will be all of a tizzy."

Joan knew that part of what he said was for the others. He couldn't be seen as a man who let his wenches traipse about half the night. Now she saw Marcie's father coming over, shaking his head and clicking his tongue at the girls. They might have been ten years old, sticking their fingers in the pies in the sweetmeats shop.

"We were waiting for you to stop marching, to tell you how there's a deal of lasses who want to drill along of you, and Marcie and me at the fore." Joan's words came out in a rush. She saw if anything came of this, she'd have to find all these make believe lasses and quick about it.

---

[9] 'Nardy Joe' was the nickname for the hated Deputy Constable Joseph Nadin.

The girls' fathers and McGilroy tensed up again. Luckily, most of the other fellows went on trooping off the field, not interested in listening to fathers scolding their daughters for being out late. But those near enough to catch Joan's words, including her brother Tom, stopped dead, looking as if a lightning bolt had opened up a ravine by their toes. Timothy Yorke came over too.

"After all, there's young lasses and married women and all, drilling in yon Oldham and Middleton and places else," Joan went on. "And you said the more who go, the better. Half of those can make the walk are female, and why not have all of us march, instead of the women trailing along out of step?"

Marcie backed her up. "That way, we really show them that all of us are behind this, men and women alike. It's only the same as the women are doing in other places, and we don't want to seem timid beside them."

Joan smiled at her friend. Marcie could simply reach into her head for the best argument, and pluck it out. Both Mr. Wright and Mr. Royce looked put upon, as well as shocked. They always did when Marcie or Joan was too smart for them.

Mr. Royce spoke slowly and importantly, "We'll see, lass, we'll see. Thy master and I must talk this over with your mothers."

Joan knew what that meant, too well, and so did Marcie. It meant their mothers would say, 'Not my lass; only over my dead body.' Then their fathers, not wanting to be thought henpecked, though dreading strife, would take the easy way out of giving no clear yea or nay for as long as they could. The drilling practice would be put off forever.

But now, Tom spoke up, and Joan had never been so fond of him. "They're in the right of it." He smiled at Marcie like a flash of sunshine in the dusk. "I'd be happy to teach them how to drill."

Seán McGilroy nodded. "I wouldn't hold with females marching, in the normal way, but this is different. As these lasses say, we need to show we're all in this together. The women slaved over these fine banners to take on the march. It's only fair they should march under 'em, and not out of step, neither, Miss Joan. I'll speak to the rest of the lads myself."

The couple of men standing near walked off, looking scornful of such nonsense, though not willing to argue with the leaders.

Timothy Yorke shook his head, but Joan didn't care about that. A year or so since, Timothy started sidling up to Joan with a smile on his face to say something that had nothing to do with anything. At last she saw that he had a fancy for her.

To make things worse, Joan's father had noticed Timothy Yorke's interest in her and he sometimes teased her about it, and his teasing was about as subtle as a dig in the ribs from one of the Ridley girls. Joan's mother said that he was a nice lad. The way Joan saw it, Timothy Yorke could be a nice lad and she'd like him for it, so long as he didn't pester her.

"We won't say aught about it till we've made sure of the others." Marcie was as quick thinking as ever.

"Thy mother will be riled enough at your staying out to watch us, leave alone all this copying of those wayward females in t'other towns," grumbled Mr. Royce to Marcie. "Lord knows what she'll say about thou setting thyself up to act so unwomanly. They say the most part of those drilling females are harridans."

Joan had an answer for that. "Mam's for clemming[10] all dignified at home, but you're not, are you, Father?"

"I'm not for that," Mr. Wright admitted, "But this needs some talking over, as Mr. Royce says."

They set off home, with the fathers walking ahead, talking about the boring things older men wanted to talk about. Joan and Marcie followed behind, flanked by Tom and Seán McGilroy on one side, and Timothy Yorke on the other, with Joan's younger brothers Nat and Ben dodging all about, wanting to chase each other, but knowing that they must act like men.

That great yellow harvest moon was up now, lighting their way. Maybe by the light of it, Marcie's own brother was still working in the fields on the farm where he went to help out most years. It gave Joan a funny feeling, to think of all the places she had never seen, and folks thinking thoughts in them, not knowing about this one.

---

[10] Starving, as in note 6 on 'clemmed'.

For sure, what went on among them here would never make the grand newspapers. They only wrote of the balls at Carlton House[11] and so.

Ben ran up to his father. "Father, you're never going to let the wenches join in, are you? That'll spoil everything."

Joan and Marcie had to laugh. Marcie said, "This is no game we're playing, my lad. This is our whole future at stake. That's why females have got to be part of it."

Mr. Wright nodded. "Thou has a point, lass. We're all in this together, Ben."

Meanwhile, Nat—who'd been full of talk about joining the forces since he'd attended the drilling—was pestering Tom. "Go on, tell us more about what you did in t'wars, Tom, for once. You keep all sorts back."

Tom smiled. "I've told thee many times and oft, Nat. I got wet feet, and blisters from my boots rubbing. And I said then, 'If ever I get out of this, I'm going to look after my feet for the rest of my days'. Don't go joining the army: it's not worth it."

"Ah, come on!" Nat pleaded. "I know you saw a lot. You'll tell us, won't you, McGilroy? I bet you killed some of Boney's lot."

McGilroy laughed. "Not me, youngster, thou'rt out there. Every time I saw a Frenchman, I scampered off quick as a startled rat. That's the way to come out of a war unscathed." He winked at Joan.

He was so forward, that she tried to stop laughing. After all, lads always took that for encouragement.

Still, she'd seen his look before he made that quip, clear in the silvery light. It had been sort of—what was that grand word which Nancy Ridley read out from one of her novels she'd been reading as they sewed? 'Tormented', that was it, and Nancy told them that it meant somebody being so upset about something that he or she couldn't forget about it ever after.

That happened a lot to the heroes in those stories. They went round brooding about some foolishness they'd done years since. That made Joan giggle. A fine lot those gentlemen had to fret over, with their grand houses and loaded tables.

Then, McGilroy was anguished about something.

---

[11] The London residence of the Prince Regent.

And so he ought to be, if only half of the stories of his playing false with wenches are true.

Ben groaned his disappointment. "When I grow up I'm going to sea, straight from Liverpool, the port as Father went to once. I'm not hanging about here, working an old loom. And when I come back I'll have some fine tales."

"You do that, lad." McGilroy smiled on him, then turned to Joan, speaking to her very formally. "Miss Wright, we haven't talked since I came back. I mind as a young wench you had pluck, and would climb a tree as high as any lad: well, you've not changed, coming here for t'other lasses to speak up about joining in the marching."

Joan didn't want to take credit as the supposed leader of a made up hoard of lasses, all pushing and shoving to join in the drilling. "I had Marcie along with me," she pointed out.

It seemed to her that you couldn't want for anything better than Marcie as an ally to face life's hardships. Lasses like the Ridleys were always going on about getting a man to look out for them. It seemed to Joan that a female friend was a deal better, though so many of the wenches would fall out over silly lads, turning on each other and running each other down and showing themselves up.

That was how a lot of them were acting over this McGilroy. She told herself that he could keep his dusky ringlets and fine swagger, though she did like a fellow who could make a joke about himself.

A cloud came over the moon, blotting out half the light. McGilroy took hold of her arm, as natural as could be, gently, but she could feel the strength. "Take care, there's a dip here."

She laughed at him. "I'd be a dafty if I didn't know this path, living here all my life. As I'm to join you drilling here, I'll have to take care of myself."

"I don't see why he won't talk about t'wars," Nat cut in.

McGilroy looked round at him as if he'd forgotten he was there. "Frenchies have all got two heads; that's why they don't take much heed of the guillotine; they've always got one to spare. Comes in handy during a war, as you can look all round at once."

Nat snorted. "Aye, and there's a man living in yon moon."

That bright moon was peeping out again from behind the cloud, as if it had heard them. Walking along in that strange light that changed everything, Joan felt a surge of joy. They'd be allowed to join in the drilling, her and Marcie, so long as they could get some other girls interested.

Of course, it must be argued out with their mothers. Still, Marcie's mother always gave in to her in the end, while her own made a big thing of the man being the 'master of the house', so the thing would be to get her father to hold out against her scolding.

Joan envied her brothers. Her mother only moaned a tiny bit about their father leading them into his troublesome Radical ways.

McGilroy was strolling on easily, still holding Joan's arm, for all she didn't need it. "I mind you climbing those trees, you and your friend here. You were the only wenches who'd go as high as the lads."

Joan remembered how she'd torn her skirts often enough when about it, and been made to sew them back up, along with her brothers' mending.

Timothy Yorke was walking at her other side, saying nothing and looking glum. She saw how little he liked Marcie and herself joining in the marching. She was glad about that: it might put him off dangling after her.

Now he spoke up. "Do you recall too, Joan, that time you fell from high up in a tree, and near broke your neck, only I caught you?"

Joan didn't. In fact, she had a notion that he was making it up, and it riled her to be made out so foolish and helpless between the pair of them. Well, McGilroy in guiding her wasn't being quite so annoying; he was only acting the gentleman. Timothy Yorke laughed, and McGilroy raised his eyebrows at him. Like Marcie, he was a great one for eyebrow rising. Joan remembered that now from before.

She rapped out, "If I was up that high, 'twas a mercy you weren't squashed flat."

Now McGilroy laughed at Yorke. "That's one for you, eh?"

Timothy Yorke's face froze in the dim light. Though not one for cut and thrust in talk, he came back with a quick answer: "And McGilroy here used to play kiss-chase with the lasses, and troth plighted to both Ridley girls at once."

"Must have been a Mohammedan, then," McGilroy said easily, "And not had the sense to look above my head, eh?" He smiled on Joan some more. In fact, he looked set to do that for the whole of their walk.

She hardly heeded his words, being so taken up by those teeth of his, flashing in the gloom. They were all perfect, in a line, not one missing. Joan wondered how he kept them so dazzling. Did he have tooth polish, as grand folks did? Maybe they looked extra white because his skin was so olive, and his hair so dark. Those waves of his were near as flashy. If a lass had them, Joan would suspect she did them up in curling rags each night.

Timothy Yorke always had a high colour, his cheeks as rosy as those of a teething baby. How he kept them, when everyone else's were getting pale and hollow, showed how well the Yorkes were doing.

A mad picture came to Joan—she tended to get these notions, and sometimes wondered if it meant she was crazy, though Marcie always laughed fit to burst at them—of McGilroy winding his hair in strips of rags, and of Timothy Yorke painting rouge on his face, like some grand ladies. She had to smile at that.

McGilroy clearly thought she smiled at his words about lacking the sense to look above his head, which she only now took in. Joan reddened as she saw what he meant, but she wasn't going to act coy and avoid his glance by looking down. She left tricks like that to the Ridley girls.

Timothy Yorke scowled. He was on his mettle tonight, and found a new reply. "Lucky I did have the sense to look upwards myself, Joan, or else I'd have missed you, and you'd have broken your neck."

He was 'Joan-ing' her like anything, as if showing how he could do that, while McGilroy couldn't and keep his manners, not knowing her well; not now that she was a grown woman.

Joan refused to answer. McGilroy looked at him coolly and then told her, "And here's another rut on the track." He tightened his hold on her arm.

"It's clear enough in the moonlight," said Joan lightly.

You are both being a nuisance, now. Go away so I can think over my plans.

Marcie called out to her, "So, Joan, I'll see you tomorrow."

With a start, Joan saw that they were already up to the lights of the cottage windows in the lane where Marcie lived, across from the patch of land kindly given by the squire for use as allotments. They were coming up to the Wrights' own turning, and Joan hadn't even taken it in, what with all the cut-and-thrust between the men.

McGilroy still had hold of Joan's arm, and she guessed what it might look like to Marcie. It looked as though she was acting helpless and unable to make her way over rough ground, like to some flirty wench, so as to make free with this man.

Quickly, she pulled at McGilroy's hold. He let go of her arm, and bid Marcie and Mr. Royce goodnight.

Joan could tell by Tom's air that, as usual, he'd got nowhere with Marcie. He looked nearly as fed up as Timothy Yorke. Even as his sister, Joan thought him a lot more easy on the eye, with his sunny hair silver in the moonlight, and his square face, not highly coloured like Timothy's, not swarthy like McGilroy's, but with a light tan from all the hours he put in at the vegetable patch in the time he had off from the loom.

Joan felt sorry over his plight, as so often. She was the more sorry because it was due to her and Marcie's plans that he was always put down when he tried to act the lover to Marcie.

To bring a smile to his face, she said, "These lads have such faith in us, Marcie, that they soon have us leading the files. Yon Timothy Yorke's sworn to have his mother along, and McGilroy his Aunt Ridley."

McGilroy gave his hearty laugh. "You lasses will do a deal better at that than us, I'm thinking. Well, goodnight, misses and masters."

Joan and her father turned off, leaving Timothy Yorke and McGilroy to themselves.

Mr. Wright looked uneasy, even forgetting to swagger for a few paces. He cleared his throat. "No worrying thy mother with these notions about wenches marching for now, any of ye. I must find the right time to break it to her, tomorrow."

• • •

In their cluttered kitchen and living room, Mrs. Wright sat on another of the battered stools, doing some of the endless patching by the light of a rush candle. Joan's younger sister Hannah was at her side, the candle lighting up the gold of her hair. She was sewing, being the good girl that Joan wasn't.

As he set down the stool he'd used as a platform, Joan's father greeted his wife as warmly as if coming on her sour look was the very thing that he wanted. He rubbed his hands heartily, as if he thought to do away with all friction that way.

"Missus, we're all belated, that's a fact. I hope you haven't been fretting over our lass. A while since, myself and Royce saw how she and Marcie Royce roved so far afield picking these herbs, they'd nigh come on us at our drilling. With it coming on to dark, we said they might as well wait on us, and we came home together. Well, Joan, I've never known that Timothy Yorke say so many words at one time as he did to thee on our way home."

That was clever of him. Joan saw her mother's face change under the mob cap that covered her hair, once as fair as Joan's own.

"If yon Timothy is marching along of ye, then it just goes to show," she said, though she didn't say what it went to show. Joan knew that her mother thought that the Yorkes made anything they took part in proper.

Joan knew how her mother would be proud for Joan to take up with Timothy, but was torn, seeing she didn't want Joan to go on strong with any lad for a couple of years yet.

For her own part, Joan would rather get a great scolding than have people think that she was happy to draw him in.

Mr. Wright made things worse by giving his wife a meaningful wink. Hannah saw it and giggled. The boys would have jeered at hints about courtship, if they hadn't been too busy shoving into their mouths the slices of bread that had been left out for them. Tom ate his, brooding.

"And did thou not stop to think that I would fret over a pair of silly lasses rambling about so late? Any road, if those herbs are become so scarce you've got to be out till dusk in search of them, then we must do without them, that's all, my lass."

"Nay, Mam, we've found a new lot, hidden away behind that old ruined cottage. We were right close to Father and t'other men there. Besides, Marcie's as good a guard as any man."

Mrs. Wright shook her head. "Word will get round and they'll be grubbed up soon enough. No more of this staying out so late you come home with your father and the men, my girl. I'll not have light talk of my lass as some flighty wench let to run wild outdoors at night."

That made Joan sound like their cat, poor beast, who in these lean times had to get his own living, save for the scraps which Joan and Hannah sneaked to him.

These hard times seemed to be going on forever, though Joan's mother never stopped saying that they would get better. Then, last Wednesday—the worst day yet—when there'd been nothing on the table for tea but dry bread, and Hannah fighting back tears, Joan couldn't stand it. She went to the hiding place where she kept her savings, and took two shillings to her mother.

"Where did you get that?" Mrs. Wright had looked at Joan as if scared she'd stolen it or sold herself for it out on the king's highway.

"I had it saved for when things got really bad."

"That must be your life's savings. It is good in thee. I promise I'll pay you back, my lass. I don't know when, though." She shook her head sadly.

Joan took her hand. "When the good times come back, Mother."

For once her mother had forgotten to say that must be soon. "Aye, and they are as long in coming as the end to poor old King Georges'[12] earthly torment."

Now, to the sound of some more grumbling from Mrs. Wright, they got ready for bed. As they went up the ladder-like stairs by the light of the rush candle, Mr. Wright, Tom, Ben and Nat clumped into one room with their father, while Joan went with Hannah and her mother into the other.

When Joan had been small, she slept in a cot-like bed at the foot of her parents'. The world was safe, with two big brothers sleeping in

---

[12] In later life, King George suffered from periodic fits of apparent madness; these led to the Prince of Wales becoming Regent in 1810.

the room next door. Joan had been blissfully ignorant, then, how her great strong oldest brother Will would be dead of a fever so soon. Then Hannah had come along, bawling through the night, and after her, Nat and then Ben. Then the children had all slept together in the back room with her parents together in the front.

But when Joan had started to bud into a woman's shape - and she'd been late enough about it, two years behind the Ridley girls, with even Hannah not far behind her—then her mother would have it that she and the girls must sleep in one room, and father and the boys in the other.

"It's not decent else, mixing the sexes after a certain age," was all she would say.

Most other parents weren't so particular. She had heard that some went in for what Nancy Ridley called 'marital relations' in the hearing of their children. That was the coarser ones. The more respectable folk, if they still cared for such goings on, sent the children out somewhere.

On the whole, Joan had rather not to think about that, though it was how too many babies came into the world.

For herself, she had yet to meet the lad who could make her want to do something so rude and daft. The idea that the local lads who stared hungrily at her and Marcie wanted to do such things with them—which Mrs. Wright said was a man's nature—was bad enough, but that Timothy Yorke wanted to do it to Joan, as it seemed he did—was downright nasty.

The Ridley girls had known all about these feelings, and men's parts, and how they stood up and all the rest of it, early. They said how you could tell if a lad was right for you by whether or not you wanted him to do that to you.

As for Joan, she couldn't see herself ever liking the thought of a lad making free with her bits.

3.

Recruiting

Hannah was skilled at not waking up in the morning, even worse than the boys, who snored so loud Joan could hear them over the way. She was never awake enough to take her turn to get water at the pump. Joan did it, and mostly because she wanted a cup of tea before starting work.

Besides, Joan didn't like being cooped up in a crowded space too long. It was nearly a fear. However hot the weather, her mother shut the windows tight against the night air, and so Joan sometimes sneaked up in the night to open the door and let some freshness into the room.

Anyway, in the summer, it was a fine thing to get out early with the wood pigeons warbling on high and all the little birds chirruping. Then, Joan didn't mind at all. It was a different matter going out in the January sleet. Sometimes, Joan would go up to put icy hands on Hannah's back; only then she screeched out so loud at Joan that she wakened everyone, and they all shouted at the pair of them.

This morning, the cloudless sky had that look which showed that it was going to be another scorching day, like many of late. Joan could even see the air pulsing higher up. This wasn't what you'd expect round here, where the wet climate helped with the making of the cotton.

Joan had no idea how Marcie did it, but there she was at the pump already, as fresh as the morning breeze, and tackling the terrible Widow Hobson about the wenches marching. Joan admired her all over again.

Even the cockiest men tiptoed round Widow Hobson. If Joan and Marcie could only get her on their side, they'd be on their way to winning.

She even had a smile on her face—and that was as rare as the miller giving away flour—although she was talking about the Whore of Babylon, which generally boded ill. Joan smiled herself, remembering that when she had been little, she hadn't understood that the Whore of Babylon was a term for corruption and thought her a real woman who had somehow got round the Pope.

"It's as you say, Mistress. Customs may have been about a long time, and still be plain wrong." Joan would have thought Marcie was enjoying the talk, if she hadn't known her.

Widow Hobson held up one finger, and started on about the Curse of Eve, and Joan feared the worst. When Widow Hobson spoke of that, then there was nothing to be said or done for any woman under fire. But Marcie had her answer ready, in pride being part of the curse of Adam.

Mr. Royce, whose family had come down in the world to take up weaving, had taught his son and daughter a lot, though, unlike Joan's father, he had no interest in teaching anyone else. A while since, besides, Marcie had gone in for some high falutin' talks with the curate, on Genesis and such. Now she was saying, 'As you know better than me, the curate says'.

Joan thought she ought to come in on Marcie's side, save she had nothing to add. Besides, Marcie might be as fresh as could be, but Joan never felt ready to face the world on equal terms until she had swallowed her morning tea. It was Joan's dread that their stock would run dry, though they made it last as long as they could, eking it out with brews made from nettle and mint.

Sally Ridley came sauntering up with her tight lipped smile, swinging her pail as if it was an ornament. Her eyes were narrowed against the morning sunshine breaking through the mist, and still a bit puffy from sleep, but she'd tied a bright red ribbon in her hair. She was a sturdy wench, with a great belief that she must have what she wanted. That Joan knew well from many queues for treats when they were little.

Sally said at once, "You'd never guess what yon wicked Cousin Seán has been on about."

"What?" Joan was still trying to follow Marcie's debate with Widow Hobson. Now they were quoting Genesis back and forth, like a game with a ball, yet somehow, Marcie kept that amiable tone.

"He was on at me special to join in the drilling. What does thou make of that?"

Joan nodded sagely. "I think he's right: the lasses should, and the dames, too."

Sally, like Marcie and McGilroy, was another great raiser of eyebrows, only hers were more of a brown bow than sweeping dark ones. "You never do! He said we'd draw in loads more of t'lads, but Mam said it was unwomanly."

Mrs. Ridley wasn't exactly a model of respectability herself, taking a drop too much whenever she could. She was said besides to have done bad things with her last lodger, who'd gone off to sea—some said, to escape from her clutches. Still, she gave herself airs as a careful mother.

It seemed to Joan that anything interesting was seen as 'unwomanly'. That went for the wrestling and racing and jumping that Joan and Marcie had loved as girls, and smoking pipes, and drinking strong drinks, and making jokes if they weren't seemly, and laughing at coarse jokes if you thought they were funny—which usually, they weren't—and shouting, and answering men sharply, and going bareheaded, and getting out into the fresh air of an evening, let alone travelling alone.

"A lot deem it unwomanly," Joan pulled a sage face as she answered Sally. "There's things to be said either way. But maybe it's the best thing that we can do, to show we're on the men's side. There's lasses and women going from all the Towns hereabouts, after all…"

Before she knew it, Joan was in a debate herself, and before that cup of tea, though she made sure to copy Marcie and keep her tone friendly. Besides, it was clear that McGilroy had already mostly won the Ridley girls over. Joan could picture him doing it between homecoming and bedtime, urging them on with that flashy smile and eyes a-sparkle.

Suddenly, she thought of something. "Sal, guess what I've heard yon Samuel Bamford has planned for Middleton. They'll be led by a score of the finest maidens from the town, in their best dresses, under the first banner. They should look fine."

That did it. Sally saw herself as the belle of the village, even though almost everyone else said that was Marcie, with that light foot and mane of black hair and slanting dark eyes like a stage gypsy, and that waist a man could span with two hands, were he out for a clout round the head.

Tom had tried it at the last dance they'd had on the common, and she'd said, "Take your hands off before I lam you one." Joan suddenly remembered dancing once with McGilroy. He'd been the liveliest dancer on the green.

"I'll think about it." Sally's eyes sparkled, and Joan knew that she wouldn't be thinking of much else but herself prancing along under the banner in a light dress, drawing the eyes of the lads. "Cousin Seán will work on Mam for me."

Joan was pleased with herself, even if she had only finished the work that McGilroy had started. That was anyway half a person she'd won over, and Sally would drag Kitty and Nancy along with her.

Meanwhile, Widow Hobson and Marcie set down their pails to work their way through Genesis, with Marcie smiling as if she could think of no better start to the day. Joan filled her own bucket and stood by.

Still, she couldn't think of anything to add to the to-ing and fro-ing than, "True enough, Marcie; I've often thought so myself," though Widow Hobson took no more heed of her than if she hadn't spoken.

She was now on to a man being a woman's 'head', and Marcie was holding out that this could mean that he was the 'source' of a woman in place of being set up over her.

Joan thought that it was a poor look out for women, if they weren't even allowed to have their own heads, and supposed that Marcie must have got all this from the curate. Who'd have thought such ideas had gone on in his own mild-looking head, or that he'd be happy to talk them over with mere lass?

Other women and children came up, among them the youngest Thribble lad, carrying a pail that looked near on half his size. He said in awe: "Them's fair lamming each other with that scripture."

Sally Ridley, having taken her turn at the pump, set down her pail and wound a strand of hair around her finger as she turned a sudden smile on Marcie. "So, thy father goes into town today?"

A group of men were going into Manchester. Mr. Wright had hopes of working out some deal for supplying a man, who, from the sound of his talk, knew half the traders in Lancashire. Timothy Yorke had some errand of his own, and Jimmy Thribble would be walking with his shoes falling off his feet, his were so in need of repair. The local cobbler had been taken to coughing and his bed since his son died.

"Cousin Seán's going along and all, and with any luck he'll look out for a gee-gaw for me, to sweeten me into going out marching about with the men like to some hussy."

Joan forced a smile again. She thought it was typical of Sally Ridley to think of nothing but getting some fine trifle from her cousin for herself, with poverty all about, and her younger brother's trousers so patched. Still, it wasn't Joan's affair. If McGilroy had no better sense than to like such lasses as his second cousins, then they were welcome to him. Sally went off, still managing a flaunting walk, for all she was lugging a load of water.

There was a lot more on what was meant by words, and Widow Hobson tried to knock Marcie down with the apostles all being men. Marcie had some answer for that Joan missed, for now Ann Wilson, the blacksmith's pretty blonde wife, joined the queue.

She'd been the fairest village maid before Marcie grew up, with more admirers among the swains than she knew what to do with. She had settled on Adam Wilson the blacksmith, who'd once fought two men from the next village one after the other for her.

"Hark at this," Joan urged her. "It's about t'women marching along of t'men. We're trying to get yon Widow Hobson on our side."

Ann seemed interested, but soon shifted uneasily. "I cannot stop. He wants his tea and t'babby howls with t'teething." It seemed to Joan that she always spoke of Adam Wilson as 'He' with a capital 'H' these days.

Joan helped her draw up a pail of water and shook her head as Ann hurried away. "Not that life for me," Joan muttered. "Never."

Meanwhile, the debate between Marcie and Widow Hobson all took a weary long time. Joan would catch it for being so long away. They'd need the water for breakfast, and Joan's father would want his to start off for the walk to Manchester.

Then something amazing happened. Widow Hobson did what was unheard of in her, and called a truce. "Thou'rt an opinionated lass, Marcie Royce, and too fond of disputing with thy elders and betters, in place of listening quiet, as befits thy years. And I mind that if yon curate has said half o' this, then he's nigh on ready to give his breeches to the women, and take up the distaff himself."

She stood frowning, then suddenly went on, "But for all that, thou is in the right of it. Things are come to a pretty pass, when a man strives his best for long hours every day, and can't keep his family from want. There's summat wrong with how things is shared out when that happens, and we're all on us caught up in it.

"And that's why I agree we must set aside what is fitting for a female in the normal way, and go and show them as would keep us down while living in idle luxury, that we're all of a mind on this. I'd come too, only my limbs are too old."

Joan wanted to cheer. Widow Hobson's backing them up made all the difference. Now she wouldn't speak out against females drilling. She wouldn't go scaring them away with her tongue, even if flighty ones like the Ridley girls did see the march as a chance to be free among the lads, like the dances they used to have on the village green before folks got too short of the verve to prance about.

Joan hissed to Marcie, "Well done."

Marcie made out she was wiping sweat from her brow, and mouthed, "Whew." Joan picked up Widow Dobson's pail to carry it home for her, and the Thribble lad turned from staggering off with his bucket to say, "I'm coming and all!"

By the time Joan got back home, everyone was waiting for the water to make breakfast, even Hannah, and cross with Joan for taking so long.

Joan saw her chance. "There was a queue, and I had to carry Widow Dobson's water home for her, and she kept me talking."

Mrs. Wright huffed. "About what? She's never heard already, that you out so late last night? She's got no call to scold you for it, though, that's your mothers' part."

Joan cut in, "No, she's for women joining in the drilling so as to go with the men to yon big meeting. She says this isn't normal times, and we must all stand together."

Mrs. Wright stared. Ben and Nat, released from their vow of keeping mum on drilling wenches, began to speak against it at once. Joan quickly shoved a piece of bread in young Ben's mouth, and trod on Nat's toe, while winking at her father over their heads.

"Hush thee!" Mrs. Wright held up her hands for silence. "Widow Hobson said as much? Then she must be doting, and turned Jacobin. That harridan will scold the whole village till they turn again' loyalty and the King, and take to waving caps of liberty and singing that nasty French anthem and go setting up a guillotine in place of the stocks on t' auld common."

Hannah cried out against such horrors. Joan was awestruck at her mother's unknown gift for making word pictures. The boys said that it mightn't be so bad there being Jacobin goings on, if only Old Nadin had his head chopped off, and they could raid the bakers'.

Tom laughed aloud. So did Mr. Wright. "It won't come to that yet. But this about the womenfolk joining in is only what I've been saying, Martha, these last months, and yon widow's taken note of it, that's plain. I'm thinking I must take our own wenches along, by way of example."

Hannah moaned, "Not me, Father: I hurt my foot yesterday."

"Wench, then," said Mr. Wright. "Now where's the tea, lass?"

"I'll force myself to go, as she's in the right o' it," said Joan. Her mother gave her a shrewd look. Still, there was no holding out against it now.

4.

Hats Off

Now Mr. Wright made ready for his trip to Manchester. This meant brushing his hair—once fair, now silver—so that no shred of the cotton waste that got everywhere, could be found in it. Then he buffed up his shoes with a rag, though the leather was as parched as the ground was getting in this drought, with the toes curling up as if they were near ready to give up the ghost. Then he put on his best coat, which was only patched at the elbows.

Last of all he tried on his worn hat half a dozen ways, using the shady window as a mirror. This hat was too big, but Mr. Wright was a small man, and Joan wondered if he wore it to look bigger. At last, he nodded, satisfied at the image of himself with it at a jaunty angle at the back of his head, liable to be blown off by the slightest breeze. Then he threw back his shoulders and marched out, ready to take on the world.

Joan minded the days when she was little, and he would bring back sweetmeats or a toy from town. Hannah must too; the boys far less. Nearly all of the toys they ever had were made at home. Times had been getting bad for as long as Joan could recall, and her mother's chant was, 'Things must get better.'

One thing Mr. Wright always did, though, was to bring back a bunch of wild flowers for his wife.

Timothy Yorke came knocking at the door, sighting about for Joan when Hannah answered it, and then looking away quickly again. Joan thought that if some lad must have the bad taste to have a fancy for her, then she would have felt more kindly to him, had he been bolder, a bit more like—well, she didn't know who—but not like himself, any road. She knew this to be thankless, and most likely vain too, and that made her cross with herself as well as him.

Mr. Wright strode out in his hat to pick up Mr. Royce and Seán McGilroy. Tom and the rest of the family set to work in the hot, damp workroom at the jennies and the looms.[13]

Once more, the air was filled with cotton waste, tightening their chests. The flies buzzed under the ceiling, and the machinery whirred and clanked, and they sweated. But for all that, Tom, Nat and Ben sang some funny songs that made them all laugh.

Joan, looking at the birds in the bright blue sky at the top of the windows, envied them, free in the open air, able to feast on all the midges they could find, and a song for joy at the start and close of each day.

Mr. Wright wasn't back for their noonday meal. He always lingered in Manchester, being a sight more willing to walk the seven miles into town than he was to walk them back. Then he would call in for a jug of boy's beer from the nearest pub, bringing most home to share.

Joan was about to go to the vegetable patch to see if there were any potatoes left to grub up, with her mother saying, "No staying out till dark, my lass," when Mr. Wright walked in.

As ever, he carried the flowers and the jug of ale, but his hat dangled sadly from his hand, nearly torn in two. Joan could see from his look how his meeting with the man had come to nothing.

"Why, Nathaniel!" Mrs. Wright was shocked into calling him by his first name before the family. "What's to do with thy hat?"

He gave a bitter laugh. "Yon Church and King lot is to do, wife. I had a wasted journey besides. It's a long story. Here's some flowers as I found by the way."

As she took them, as ever, Mrs. Wright said, "Thank ye, Master." She handed them to Joan to find the ale pot to put them in, with the chipped side decently to the wall. If she thought about the 'long story', 'Isn't it always', seeing how Mr. Wright liked to hear nothing better than the sound of his own voice, she didn't say so.

---

[13] Jennies and looms were machines for spinning and weaving cotton. Traditionally, a whole family tended to be involved in a home workshop, putting in time in it amongst other activities such as agriculture.

Joan knew that was why she'd never make a wife herself. She couldn't hold her tongue when needful.

Meanwhile, Tom's eyes glinted as he looked over the hat. "If they messed you about, I wish I'd been there."

Mr. Wright sat down and Mrs. Wright poured out his beer, and some for the rest of them, with Joan and Hannah sharing a pot and Nat and Ben another.

"When we got to town, young McGilroy went off to carry out his orders from those Ridley girls," Mr. Wright's good humour returned along with the beer, "And young Timothy Yorke went about his, and I'm thinking, my lass, that if he bought you a present, you might look on him more kindly. That McGilroy has the way of it."

Hannah sniggered. The boys groaned and rolled their eyes. Joan scowled. "Even if I wanted a sweetheart, it could never be he."

"Hush, lass. Don't interrupt thy father," said Mrs. Wright. Joan scowled, not only over the quips about Timothy Yorke, but about her father being let down over the work. Now they must keep scraping along to get by. More selfishly, she fretted that it was most likely more of her savings from what she and Marcie called their 'Escape Fund' would melt away.

Mr. Wright began. "So Royce and I went to see yon fat fellow,"—Joan remembered that last week he had been 'that fine stout chap'—"And he said he was main and sorry, but he'd found another man who was cheaper, and close by. And there was me, knowing I couldn't price the work lower without undercutting t'others, but this miserable tyke had done it. It's as I always say: we'll never have fair rates without a union."

"And unions being against the law," said Mrs. Wright, "There'll always be folks around willing to price lower."

"They're digging a hole for themselves worse than those cursed cellars in those shacks put up for cotton workers of late," said Mr. Wright. "Any road, I was put about, and told him, 'You've wasted time I could've spent better and cost me a long tramp, all for nowt.' Then he made out he gave no promises, which was a lie, only I didn't want to tell you so and raise your hopes before, Missus, in case of disappointment, and as well I kept mum. And so me and Royce walked out, being too riled to speak more.

"We were coming up to t' Red Lion, when these fellows—who I could tell by looking at them were all thriving merchants' sons in one of those Loyalist clubs[14] and most likely MYC men to boot,[15] staggered out half fuddled. We tried to get round them, seeing they were ripe for trouble, but we couldn't move, for a group of women were going by.

"I knew a couple of the roistering fellows by sight from before, and one of 'em pointed me out, and plain they knew me at once: 'That little one strutting along in the big hat is a damned Radical agitator.'"

"Go and see if there's aught to be found in the plot," said Mrs. Wright to the boys.

They got up slowly, grumbling that they weren't a pair of babbies to be kept from rough talk. Mr. Wright cut in, "No sense in hiding this sort of thing from them, Martha. They're old enough to hear of it."

He went on with his story. "Another young fellow drawled out, 'One of those Radical scum, is he now? Then let's see how bold he is without that hat to hide under,' and knocked it from my head under the wheels of a cart passing by."

Tom swore under his breath, fists clenched.

"Then I saw my hat was torn near clean in half, and was of a mind to strike him down. Still, I knew that it'd be me had up for affray at the Petty Sessions, never those so-called gentlemen. So I went to pick up my hat, while the women took themselves away fast.

"As I bent to pick it up, the fellow darted over and stamped on it, laughing like an idiot. And I'd have laughed myself at the state he was in, with his eyes popping out with drink, if he hadn't ruined my hat.

"So then, I had no choice but to tell him to stand up like a man instead of an idle boy. Royce was trying to drag me off, when one of

---

[14] Loyalist: i.e., a supporter of the status quo in government.

[15] The Manchester Yeomanry Cavalry was set up in 1818 as a volunteer corps to keep order in times of civil unrest. The cost of the equipment, which included a horse, was expensive, and could only be afforded by the sons of the well-to-do.

them hit me from behind, taking me to my knees and saying, 'Mind your manners, you damned ragamuffin, that's no tone to take with your betters.'"

Tom swore again, louder this time, and for once his mother didn't rebuke him.

"From down on t'ground I could see t'others had got hold of Royce. They held him up by the elbows, saying, 'These damned rascals think to be our equals; lets raise this one above us.'

"Then, the next thing I knew, a fellow who must be the one who'd hit me from behind came sprawling down besides me, bleeding from his nose. There was young McGilroy standing over us, and all of a fury, asking the first if he wanted a scrap, here was a someone his own age."

Tom muttered, "That's McGilroy all over, right enough."

His father went on, "I was on my feet quick enough, and told him, 'I thank you, my lad, but I'm not in my dotage yet. You've done away with one of 'em, and I'll take on this one in a fair fight if he gives me time to get my senses back.'

"Then they hesitated. Likely enough, as they'd heard of me, then they'd heard tell that though I may be a little fellow, I'm handy with my fists, though never one to go looking for trouble. Meantime, the fellow McGilroy knocked down took his time about getting up from the cobbles, with his own hat in the dirt. Then his friends dropped Royce to move in on McGilroy, but seeing us both so fierce, they set up an outcry for a constable to take us in charge.

"Then, some respectable-looking type in middle years stepped out from t'snuff and baccy shop over the way, with young Timothy Yorke following behind. Well, the fellow calmly asked what's to do, reasonably enough, while young Yorke spoke fair to the others, calling them 'Gentlemen'. That would have stuck in my throat to use to such as they.

"But we heard no more of it, as young McGilroy gave us all the wink, and we took off fast, leaving the second fellow staring at us from t'ground and the others all grouped about him, too befuddled to take in that we were away, save Timothy Yorke, who stayed talking."

Coming to the end of his story, Mr. Wright looked as if he wished he could have cut a finer figure in it by knocking down at least three of his tormentors. Still, though he might add colour to his stories, he never lied outright.

The boys broke into talk of how they wished they had been there to join in with McGilroy. Tom didn't need to say that for himself; his look spoke for him. Joan approved of McGilroy's actions too, though she knew she shouldn't.

Mrs. Wright clicked her tongue. "Such idle types as those men must be! You shouldn't let them rile you. You never left young Yorke to smooth matters over?"

"It weren't like that, Martha. He saw McGilroy tip us the wink, but looked blank and didn't seem to want to come along of us, you might say. That man who came out from the shop, I'm thinking, was a special constable."

Mrs. Wright clicked her tongue, but Joan knew she never spoke out against the 'Master of the house' before the family. "The youth took a sensible view of it. That hot-headed young McGilroy will get himself locked up or worse in no time, I see. With any luck, things won't go any further, seeing they were so drunk and foolish themselves."

Hannah looked anxious, but Mr. Wright pinched her cheek. "Don't fret, my wench, they can't keep us locked up without charge any more."

That, Joan knew, was about this *Habeas Corpus*[16] thing that meant the authorities couldn't keep the Radicals in gaol without charge, as they'd done when it had been suspended—whatever that meant—a year since. Then, folks the authorities thought were causing too much trouble had gone missing for months. Now her father and the others were right glad that it was back in force and putting a stop to such goings on.

She felt torn and ruffled about McGilroy. She'd taken against him because of all the talk about his trifling with lasses. True, she didn't set

---

[16] Habeas Corpus was suspended in 1817, when persons suspected of 'sedition' were held for months in prison without trial.

store by gossip, but so much of that had followed him here from Jimmy Thribble, who'd been away working with him a couple of times, and his Ridley cousins besides, that she thought there must be something in it all.

Joan always sided with the women, seeing that nobody else did. For all that, she felt she had to speak up for him now. "I think McGilroy was in the right of it in coming in on Father's side and Mr. Royce's."

"By knocking one of them down? Fie, lass. Using force is always wrong." Joan wondered how her mother could say that, when she'd been all for fighting Boney. Still, Mrs. Wright smoothed the hat as if it was a living thing as she spoke. "We might cobble it together well enough."

"And you can use that ribbon of mine to hide the stitches," Hannah added.

That made Joan stare. Hannah had held onto that ribbon through their books being packed up and sold, and the clock from Mrs. Wright's grandfather, and most of their better clothes, and all but the most worthless of the ornaments.

Joan told her, "You're not cutting up that: it'd be a waste. I've that torn one we can use."

5.

POTATOES

Joan let out a cry of delight. She'd found a load of potatoes. Not six, nor a baker's dozen, but easily three dozen of them were hiding here in the corner of the vegetable patch.

But she'd looked yesterday, and found no sign of these.

She felt eyes on her, and turned about. She'd caught glimpses of someone digging on the Ridley's patch nearby, but most of it was hidden from her by the currant bushes. Then, Seán McGilroy came out from behind one, carrying a spade and smiling, as swarthy and vigorous as ever. Each time she saw him, his darkness and energy somehow caught her by surprise.

"I'm glad to find some taters," she explained.

He smiled some more at that, and nodded.

She had been meaning to thank him for taking up for her father, all the more as her mother had been acting so thankless, going round saying that he was a troublemaker. Joan could understand why he was, being one herself, just like her father.

Now, facing this McGilroy—with him looking a bit teasing and a bit admiring, the way he must with all the lasses - all of a sudden it was hard to get the words out. To make matters worse, her face went red. She supposed it was because she hardly knew the lad that she suddenly felt shy. She must look like her Uncle Wright in his fields in a raw eastern wind, with his beetroot face clashing with his yellow hair.

And thinking of Uncle Wright's yellow hair put Joan in mind of words said years since, talk she once heard between Sally Ridley and this McGilroy about her. She wished she hadn't recalled it, as it made her riled with Sally Ridley all over again.

Seán McGilroy had been on one of his visits to his aunt and uncle. As always, Joan hardly spoke to him. He had a sort of following of lads and lasses hanging about with him, drawn by anything new in the village, and this bold lad in particular. If Joan thought about him at all, it was to think how alien his 'Black Irish' looks made him.

Out early one morning looking for mushrooms, she walked round the fringe of trees to come on Sally Ridley and Seán McGilroy. She was hanging on his arm and chattering. Neither of them saw Joan.

"Well, Marcie Royce is a bonny lass, I'll grant you, though she's too tall already," Sally was saying, "While that Joan Wright's not even pretty."

"Which one's Joan?" he asked on a yawn.

"You know, the wench who always goes about with Marcie. That's smart of her, really; she'll get a chance to make up to the lads Marcie doesn't want. She's the scrawny one with wild hair like tow."

"You mean Joan Wright. I mind the wench. She needs to fill out: but I'd say come two years she'll be lovely."

Sally had tittered at that, buffeting him on the shoulder. "They must have made thee cross eyed in that prize fighting booth, I'm thinking."

"You must make sure you tell her so from me, and all," he insisted. "I want to be the one who said first what she'll hear soon enough from all the lads hereabouts."

Sally had only tittered some more, while Joan did what one of Nancy Ridley's stories would call 'withdrawing in high dudgeon'.

She had to agree with Sally about her own absurdly light-coloured hair—in some lights, it was near cream coloured—and back then she was bone thin; there was no denying that. Still—and this was one of the funny ideas she and Marcie shared—she didn't see why a lass was always judged on her looks. A lad might be a bit, but nothing like so much. A low and mean part of her said it didn't see why Sally thought she was so fine and bonny herself, if it came to that. When she laughed, her eyes near vanished in those plump red cheeks which the lads pinched.

Joan combed her long wavy hair a bit more after that, as she saw that Sally was right, in that it did look as wild as a hermit's at times.

After that, Joan started filling out; then the lads began to act silly when she was by.

Still, you could have beaten her down with a feather when her father said one day to her mother, 'Folks are talking of our Joan and Marcie Royce as the belles hereabouts.'

Mrs. Wright only clicked her tongue. "Don't set the lass up with fancy ideas of herself. There was none who could outshine her aunt when she was a lass."

Soon after that, McGilroy went off again, and Joan forgot about overhearing that talk until now. As like as not, McGilroy, should he remember what he'd said of Joan at all, could only feel let down on seeing her again.

Remembering it now, it came to Joan in a flash that Sally had never liked her much after hearing this precious second cousin of hers saying Joan would grow to be a beauty. That was foolish, when as like as not he was just teasing. Now she recalled too, that Sally had never told Joan what McGilroy had asked her to.

"I owe you thanks for taking up for my father and Mr. Royce t'other day, when those stupid boobies set on them," Joan spoke all in a rush. It came out sounding like a gabble to her ears, like one of those turkeys of the squire's holding forth.

"That was nothing. It riled me to see those strutting loobies setting on a couple of older men. Besides, I've respect for your father; he knows a lot. If he takes up teaching again at yon Hampden Clubs[17], I'll be along. " He laughed. "You don't need to thank me for weighing in that day. I'm grand at getting myself into trouble, anyway."

Joan smiled, proud of how well-read her father was. As far as she could see, he knew more than the curate and the village schoolmaster put together, save for their Latin, and he even knew a bit of that.

He turned his smile on her, eyes twinkling. "And that smile's reward enough. That's the first time you ever smiled at me so."

---

[17] Started in 1812, these clubs were educational, debating and political clubs for working men, with a penny subscription for membership. Permeated by spies and targeted by the Seditious Meetings Act of 1817, they were largely disbanded before 1819.

She stiffened. "We don't know each other anymore. And my brothers will smile at you in the same way."

"Wouldn't have the same effect on me." He pulled a face.

"Anyway, I'm glad you didn't get locked up, or Sally would never have got her beads." Sally had been flaunting those beads at the pump this morning. They were nice enough beads, made out of nuts, painted and strung on thread.

"Or Nancy, or Kitty, and all. I promised 'em that if I came out in one piece from some trouble I was in, I'd buy 'em all a gee-gaw."

"Summat more dangerous than the wars?"

He nodded solemnly. "No danger there. You mind I said how I ran off whenever I saw a Frenchman."

She knew that he was lying, from the twinkle in his eyes. She laughed. "Yes, I believe you. Not every lad who goes for a soldier can be a hero like Ned Pritchard, any road."

He winked. "Not enough medals to go round. So you'll be at the drilling tonight, Miss Joan, and I'll be glad enough to show you how we do it. You and Marcie Royce are in the right of it. If we all march into town, females and males together, those in charge has got to sit up and take notice. If that don't make 'em, then nothing will, when striking didn't help the weavers, back last year.[18]"

Joan nodded. "It seems to me we've never got the better o' that. Folks say there's too many working in cotton. There's many still flooding in, for all times are so bad, and it drives what we can charge down. But from all we hear, things have been bad all round since the wars, and folks have to work at summat. Well, things must get better."

She said the words that all folk came out with, like a sort of magic chant. She shifted, her thoughts on those potatoes, but his next words kept her feet rooted to the spot like a potato herself.

"Seems to me we'd have been better off not fighting the French at all."

"What, and let Boney take over?" Joan was shocked. Even her father didn't go so far: this was heresy.

---

[18] First the spinners and then the weavers went on strike unsuccessfully in 1818

"I mean before that dandyprat[19] came to power, and got himself made Emperor. They had some fine ideas when it all started out."

Joan stared even more. If he wanted her to do some sitting up and taking notice, he'd done it; she couldn't stop herself. "You're joking! Not with the guillotine and all."

It seemed to Joan that before being sent off to that island after the Battle of Waterloo, Boney had been in charge over in France for all her life. Still, the old folks in the village remembered before that, with the Terror, and things called 'tumbrels'—that Joan's father said were merely farm carts—rumbling through the streets, with the aristocrats in them. Those that hadn't been strung up from lampposts, that was.

McGilroy gave her a smile, not like Marcie putting on a brave face with Widow Hobson, but one that set his eyes twinkling yet more. They were amazingly blue, which along of his black hair might be typical Irish colouring for all Joan knew, though it was rare enough in these parts.

He said, "That's what folks think on whenever you say, 'French Revolution'. They went wrong there: they should only have packed them off abroad if you ask me. But I mean doing away with hereditary titles and great estates, and giving a say for the people in running things, and all the rest of it. None of it's so different from what many Radicals want over here."

Joan went along with that. Still, coming after the things he'd said, his talk made her uneasy. You didn't know where you were with someone who said things that no-one else did. Then it came to her that was how he must feel about her, as a wench who spoke her mind instead of listening demurely. Still, it didn't seem to make him want to go off. He stood there smiling at her as if he was happy to stay there all day.

Suddenly shy of looking into those teasing blue eyes, she poked at the earth with the toe of her shoe, which now struck her as clumsy, solid as it was. Well, that was daft, when all the females here wore such shoes. She looked back up again. "Does that mean that you thought the war was for nothing?"

---

[19] A trifling, insignificant fellow.

The idea that twenty-five years of slaughter had been about something that wasn't worth fighting for was terrible. Joan didn't know how many people from Britain had been killed in the wars, let alone all the other countries. It might even be thousands of thousands, which she knew made millions. That was an unthinkable number of lives wasted.

And then there were all those maimed. She'd seen enough of them in the streets when she went to Manchester, though there were those, like Neddy Pritchard, who said that half of them came by their lost limbs in other ways.

He nodded. "That's about it. I'd be fooling myself to say else." That look was back, the one on his face when her brothers were teasing him to talk about his doings in the fighting. It went in a moment, and he was saying, "You want to drill, Miss Joan, but I'm main and glad you won't be going off to fight in any wars."

His look was admiring, and she didn't trust it; by all accounts it had worked already on too many silly girls who made that mistake. To cover her real thoughts, she came out with something off the top of her head. "Seems to me, we who have to work for a living are always in a war without knowing it and with no blows struck."

His eyes dilated, exactly as when she'd first talked of drilling. "You're right, my lass. Of late, there's been real fighting, but in the general way, a different kind of war is going on." He looked wholly taken up with the notion. "It's been going on since Wat Tyler—you know, the fellow who led the peasants back in the time of the robber barons—thy father was talking on him t'other day—and before him, back to Saxon times as like as not—maybe even before that, to the time of the Romans."

Joan's father was always holding up the laws of Saxon times as a fine thing, and now the fellow was having a go at that. You never know where you are with this one. He was smiling at her as if she'd done him a favour. That was well enough, really, when he'd done her father one, but she had to draw back from that smile: it was too familiar.

Besides, she was hungry, and the taters drew her. The dirt under her nails was itchy. Sally and the other lasses were welcome to him and his curling black hair and his lively way of going on, as if he drew in energy from the air, a bit like a windmill or these new machines running on power taken from running water. She wanted her potatoes, and he could have her idea.

He saw her move reastlessly and went to dig up some more of the patch, unearthing yet more tubers. She knew that people had raided this plot often enough. Yet, somehow they'd missed this corner, by a gooseberry bush where once she and Marcie had gone looking for babies.

Anyway, now her family could have a feast.

"You must have some of these," she said.

He shook his head. "No need. I've still got some savings to the fore, or I couldn't have treated my cousins. " McGilroy put a stress on those words for her to pick up on, seeming to make out that they were family and nothing else. Joan might have taken notice if she'd been a silly wench enough.

They set off for the cottages, with him carrying the potatoes, his spade held over his shoulder.

He began singing a song:

> 'Owd Jeremy Gigg, a miller was he,
> In Lancashire born and bred;
> The mill was all he depended on,
> To earn him his daily bread.
> Owd Jeremy he was growing owd,
> His latter end it was near;
> He had three sons, and it puzzled him sore
> Which of 'em should be his heir. [20]

She had to laugh, as she liked this song. Then, McGilroy winked at her, as he shouldn't. Even as she began to frown, two of the boldest little village children saw them, and giggled.

One yelled, "Look: they're sweethearts! They're getting all excited: they're going to buss, and make smacking sound with their mouths. They're going to start with their-" she broke off, giggling too hard to speak.

---

[20] 'The Lancashire Miller' a traditional Lancashire song of uncertain age.

Joan felt herself doing an imitation of a beetroot again. Before she could think of an answer, McGilroy turned about and called out, as amiable as anything, "Hold your noise, wee wench, or I might start talking to thy mam about thee snaffling a tart from t'shop, when thou didn't think any kenned what thee were about."

Meanwhile, Joan was cursing herself for colouring up so, which might give him the wrong idea. The fellow was vain enough already. Those brats had shouted after her and Timothy Yorke, when he'd insisted on walking with her the other day. She'd been as cool as a lettuce, while his cheeks looked as if they'd caught fire.

The little girls jeered at the threat, but took themselves off. McGilroy waited until Joan stopped blushing before looking at her. "Any road, those youngsters still have enough life about 'em to be a pest, eh?"

Joan was wrinkling her nose at the thought of kissing, and other worse stuff with a lad, even with a fine looking one like this fellow. Anyway, he was a male slut, that's what he was, and Joan didn't care how much folks said there was one rule for males and another for females.

He was 'used goods'; that's what, even if he did have flashing teeth and a fine mop of curls. That's what they said of a wench who'd let suchlike fellows as him tumble her, and she didn't see why it shouldn't be said of the fellows themselves and all, though it never was. This was another of her funny ideas.

McGilroy went on. "Those wee wenches give me too much credit, worse luck. I reckon it'd be a brave lad who made free with you, for all they all gawp after you, now you've grown up so lovely. I told my Cousin Sal I knew you would, and to pass it on to you."

Now he was giving her a sly look. She could see why he could draw in gullible girls. She was glad that she wasn't one.

As she said nothing, he went on—with male foolishness—"What, did she never tell you as I bid her?"

"I think she forgot." Joan forced herself to be charitable about Sally's motives, adding, "And it'd be a fellow without sense who thought he'd get away with making free with me, that's certain."

She acted as unmoved as if her looks were praised like that every day. Her heart was beating fast—it must be distaste at thinking about kissing and worse—and this was another nuisance, when she didn't want to sound breathless and flirty.

"I wouldn't call Timothy Yorke a bold fellow," he went on, looking at her, eyebrows raised. "But he's got his eye on you, that's plain. He's a lucky fellow, if he's in with a chance."

Two years since, Joan would have been riled and rapped out that she couldn't abide Timothy Yorke. Now, being all grown up, she said, all dignified, "If he is so minded about me, I fear he has no chance at all. We'd never be suited, even if I was of mind to think on suchlike things."

He looked so pleased that she added with all speed, "Which I'm not."

He wasn't riled; he went on looking pleased. "Now, if any of t' other lasses I knew said they didn't like a lad, I'd take it things were the other way round with 'em, but you're a lass who says things as they are, and I do like that. There's two reasons why I'm glad you don't like him in that way. But I'll say no more of the first as it's too soon, and nowt o' t'other as I could be wrong and I don't want to act as one of those tattlers myself and repeat things I'm not sure of."

You could have knocked Joan down with a dandelion stalk. The rascal was up to his tricks, that was plain, with his hints about the first of his two reasons why he was glad she hadn't taken to Timothy Yorke. Obviously he was making out he had an eye for Joan himself and didn't want rivals. Most likely this was the way he went on with girls who had to be drawn in slowly. But what was his second reason?

For, if he'd looked warmly on her a moment when he came out with the first piece of nonsense, his face hardened when he spoke of the second.

She said bluntly, "You're beating about the bush, after saying you liked things said straight out."

He nodded solemnly, but with those blue eyes still twinkling, which was a nerve. "I do. I'm just going to say, Miss Joan, that I know some folks hereabouts likes to talk, and then their tales get ever more fancy as they go from mouth to ear. So, if there's wild tales told of me—

and there's a deal more interesting things to talk on than me—then it is likely enough true of others."

Joan stared. Was McGilroy saying that some gossip was going about on Timothy Yorke getting up to something improper? That tickled her so much, she hardly spared a thought to what he'd said of himself. She had to laugh, and that set him to smiling again.

She said, "Humph! Well, that's hard on yon lads so miscalled. Maybe they should ask some of their family members how all this talk came about."

He laughed, and had his mouth open to reply, when they came on Tom.

Now, Joan realised that McGilroy had taken her the long way round from the vegetable patches, and she hadn't noticed, being so gleeful over their find of the potatoes.

Tom shot McGilroy a look that was a question, getting back one that looked like an 'I'm sorry,' and she wondered what it was all about as he said, "Tom, lad, I'll get round to it soon, my word on it."

Tom looked cast down.

Joan, gloating over her treasure trove, said, "Seán McGilroy, won't you take some of these, seeing you dug up so many?"

He smiled. "Well enough; I'll take one for each of my uncle's family, and one for me." That made eight, and she had dozens left.

Now they came up to the cottages, where Mr. Wright was taking a stroll along the lane with Mr. Royce, and doing well at strutting without his hat.

Joan thought her father looked like a squire ready to sit down to a dinner of soup, roast goose with side dishes, with tipsy cake to follow, just like the damsels in Nancy's novels. Usually those damsels could only pick at a morsel, having hearts too full from their romantic misfortunes, so that they went near as short of food as Joan herself.

"Where did you dig up this young fellow, my wench?" said Mr. Wright.

"Along of some slugs and worms," said Joan, and the lads guffawed. "But look what a fine number of taters McGilroy has unearthed: you must take some, Mr. Royce."

Now McGilroy handed the potatoes over to Mr. Wright and took Tom's arm. "Me and Tom's got things to talk over before supper, if you don't want him straight away, so good even to you all." He flashed a last smile on Joan. If it carried some hidden meaning, she ignored it.

He added under his breath, "I'll say more of those reasons another time, Miss Joan." He looked serious for a minute, but Joan was too busy hoping that none of the potatoes was black inside to think more about it.

6.

DRILLING HOYDENS

As Joan left the cottage for the meeting, along with her father and the lads, Mrs. Wright shook her head. "I never thought the day would come when I'd see my lass being so bold and unwomanly. There's only this little lass acting with any sense among the lot of yo'."

She smiled on Hannah, who was sitting on a stool catching up stitches with what Joan thought of as her 'Goody Two Shoes' look.

Joan didn't believe her mother really thought that about Joan herself, unless she'd suddenly lost her memory. What with the tree climbing and all the rest of it, being a rumpskuttle[21] was a thing that came naturally to Joan the minute she was old enough to go out alone.

They set out for the meadow, with folks coming out of houses to join them.

Mrs. Wright made Joan wear the oldest of her three dresses. It might sound grand to have three, but one was kept packed away for great occasions, and this one was so ragged, Joan thought she looked like a much less bonny Cinderella. Perhaps her mother feared she was about to start turning cartwheels again.

Despite Mr. Royce and Mr. Wright, Tom and Seán McGilroy, going about telling the other men that lasses would be coming along, most of them still stared. Many made jokes, with Jimmy Thribble and his friend Jack Hooper loud among them. Joan and Marcie and the other women took it in good part, so there was laughing and joking all the way.

Ben and Nat were still vexed with Joan and Marcie for bringing all these lasses along—even if Widow Hobson had given her orders, as

---

[21] A tomboy.

Joan made out. Timothy Yorke came to walk alongside Joan, clearly no happier with her.

"So you lasses are dead set on drilling." He frowned over to where the young Widow Smith walked on one side of Ann Wilson the blacksmith's young wife, both having left their babies with their mothers. Joan felt proud that Ann Wilson had heeded her and Marcie's urging enough to insist on drilling along with her husband.

The pair of them were all smiles at getting out of their dreary cottages into the sweet air for some hours to try out something new. The blacksmith was sullen as he strode along close by, his muscles bulging through his shirt, so possessive that hardly any young man dare look in his wife's direction.

"As you see," said Joan, smiling as Marcie fell in with them. "Marcie Royce, thou'rt done bravely: you've got nigh on thirty woman come along, and only six down to me."

Tmothy Yorke shook his head. "You'd have best stayed at home, working on those foolish banners. There's been trouble before, after all. That is, if this meeting is allowed to go ahead. Most likely it won't be, if it's found to be against the law."

"Why is a banner saying 'No Taxation without Representation' foolish?" Joan heard her voice sharpen.

"You don't change things by biding at home," said Marcie.

"I don't hold with the wild things that are being said." Tmothy's colour was higher than ever, though maybe part of that was the red colour in the sky, boding another hot day tomorrow. It lit them all in a fiery glow.

Now, Tom greeted Marcie, looking so fine with the reddish light on him, turning his hair dark gold, that Joan admired Marcie's strength of mind in keeping him at arm's length. As he said something to Marcie in an undertone, Timothy Yorke took the chance to say low to Joan, "You're getting led away, Joan, by others."

"Who by—my father?" she asked scornfully.

"I'm not speaking against your father."

"Stop being such a wet blanket." Joan was annoyed enough with him to turn away rudely, and say to the others, "You know that Danny is such a dab hand at the pipe? I've asked him to play it, joining with the rest of the band, and then it won't matter so much if he's out of step."

"It's a fine idea; he plays a good tune, and it can't make him worse, anyhow," said Tom.

Timothy Yorke said, "He might as well be that Pied Piper from yon chap book[22] I mind reading, for all the sense you've all got, with him leading you off like those boys and girls in that tale."

Tom looked as vexed with him as Joan. "You reckon? I mind there were rats in that tale and I was thinking that we could do with him here, to magic all those rats of paid informers into yon rindle[23] for a ducking."

Timothy Yorke said seriously, "No chance of that, with it so low in this heat."

It was indeed, one of the hottest spells that in a long time, here in their usually damp part of the world. Each eventide, the sky was pink, and the heat haze hung over the day like a low cloud. The grass was drying up underfoot, and so were any wild herbs left unpicked.

What Joan's family would do when her find of potatoes ran out, she daren't think. She could only hope that something would come up. It always had, so far. Though they had lived hand to mouth these last few months, they hadn't starved yet.

"Shame the water's too low—a ducking would be just the thing for suchlike sneaks, eh, lasses?" Tom gave Timothy Yorke his amiable smile, but his eyes were hard. Feeling rose ever higher against these tale bearers, who got paid for every wild story they ran to Deputy Constable Nadin, and higher up, the magistrates. Was Tom making out that Timothy knew a thing or two about them?

Now Seán McGilroy and all of the Ridley lasses joined the group. He went to talk to Mr. Wright, and the girls fell to giggling at Jimmy Thribble's quips and silly noises on his bugle, and Jack Hooper's clowning with his dog.

Mrs. Wright was still striving to mend the gashes those loyalist fellows had made on Mr. Wright's hat, so he came without it, and

---

[22] A small pamphlet containing ballads etc., and sold by pedlars.
[23] Dialect for 'stream'.

made up by putting on twice as much of a swagger. Nat and Ben strutted by his side, undersized young lads as they were from too little to eat. They may have thought they looked tough and fierce, but they seemed weedy little fellows to Joan, too slight to deal with the blows the world might rain down on them.

In the meadow, Mr. Royce, Mr. Wright, Tom and Seán McGilroy divided the numbers of women up and took them in their own columns. Jimmy Thribble, who'd spoken out loud against having any wenches in his, looked put out, and said they were keeping all the fun for themselves. Laughing, Mr. Wright sent the young Widow Smith and a couple of others to him.

The blacksmith Adam Wilson and his wife were together in Mr. Royce's. Timothy Yorke was still in that group, looking as sour as a crab apple.

Tom made sure that he got Marcie. He was stuck with Daffy Danny, who was as devoted to him as Jack Hooper's dog, which followed Jack everywhere, and came along to the drilling, too. At first, those in charge were against it being there, but it followed at his heel, marching better than many.

So far, it kept better time than Daffy Danny. Now though, once Danny had his pipe, things changed. Warbling away upon it, he forgot about his feet, and they started keeping time by themselves.

Joan nodded, pleased with herself. Mr. Wright said, "There now; what did I say? The lad does well enough, with his pipe between his lips."

At that, Jimmy Thribble, who played the bugle, said something coarse to the lads next to him, which Joan half overheard. After all, her mother said that men talked so when they were by themselves, so Joan supposed that you had to put up with that, if you started doing male things.

McGilroy took his Ridley cousins as part of his file. Sally giggled and squealed to the point where Joan hoped that she would wet herself.

Meanwhile Kitty called out every few minutes, "Like this, d'ye mean, Seán lad?" She joined Sally in shouting over at Tom and Jimmy Thribble as they led the other groups. They joked back.

Nancy, meanwhile, was as solemn as she was when reading aloud tales of brigands, kidnapped maidens and haunted castles.

McGilroy also took Joan in his group, giving her a smile that could have melted ice.

She was a hard frost, as far as lads who trifled with lasses feelings went. She only gave him back the sort of twitch of the lips she forced herself to make at the curate's sorry tries at a joke.

McGilroy was a good drill sergeant, anyway. Joan found learning drilling easy.

Sally Ridley, who was close by, tripped on something exactly as Jimmy Thribble said all the women would, letting out her loudest squeal yet.

Danny said, "Yon is a noisy lass."

Sally called to Seán McGilroy, "I've turned my ankle."

They all stopped marching. Leaning on McGilroy's arm, Sally hobbled to the edge of the field, where she raised her skirts to her ankles. Some of the fellows whistled and cheered, urging McGilroy to take a good look at it. Paying no heed to them, he said, "You must sit out a bit."

Sally moaned, "Nay, but feel it swell already."

Joan was encouraging Danny to wipe his pipe on the grass, but she caught herself looking over, thinking it was a wonder that Sally had turned such a hefty ankle. Then she was annoyed with herself for thinking the sort of spiteful thing that Sally herself would have said. Joan didn't like this McGilroy fellow, so why was she riled about him paying attention to Sally?

Then McGilroy called Joan over, as one who knew about herbal cures and poultices, and even drawing teeth, some said better than Dr. Healey[24] from Oldham. From habit, she hadn't liked to put herself forward when Marcie was about, for time was when Marcie had known more. Somehow, though, her heart wasn't in it in the same way as Joan's was, and in the last year, Joan had learnt more of herbal cures and healing than she.

---

[24] Dr Joseph Healey of Oldham was a 'quack doctor' and one of the Radicals charged with treason after the Peterloo Massacre.

Joan felt the ankle, while Sally pouted. It didn't feel hot to Joan, nor look any more swollen than the other one. Still, she mustn't give in to suspicions about how the tiresome wench staged that accident for attention.

So she said instead, "Nowt broken, and it doesn't seem swollen, but rest it as much as you can. Wrap it about with a damp cloth. That does wonders."

"Take my kerchief to dip in yon rindle," McGilroy told her, bossily enough, but after, all, he was acting as corporal or drill sergeant. "We'll be finishing soon enough, and I'll help my cousin back home. Sit out for now."

Joan was annoyed at missing some of the drilling as she set off for the stream with the kerchief in her hand. The cloth was crimson, and she thought that well suited for the flashy McGilroy.

When she returned, she wrapped the damp cloth about Sally's ankle, which still felt no hotter to her. She muttered, "Maybe we could use some of that wet blanket yon Timothy Yorke takes about with him."[25]

He gave off such a dismal air that Joan had to snipe at him. As ever, she felt guilty, and added, "I should give him credit for coming at all, seeing he finds it such a chore."

Sally tittered. "That's a fine thing to say about your swain. I thought it was all along of you he came at all, what with your Radical talk. But it may be he found it worth his while to keep up with what's going on." She nodded sagely.

"Swain?" Joan was so riled that her breath came fast, but she tried to speak calmly. "There's nowt between us." It took all her willpower to put Sally's ankle down gently, as befitted a proper healer.

Sally flexed it, gingerly. "Tell that to the birds, lass. It wouldn't stagger me to learn, your father hasn't been taken up only on account of Timothy Yorke being sweet on you, and putting in a word with some as he knows."

---

[25] A person who discourages fun, from the practice of smothering a fire with a blanket.

Joan's heart beat fast. "Father hasn't broken any laws that I've heard of. Any road, why him any more than McGilroy, who's Radical enough himself?"

"Cousin Seán's too smart for them to hold him for long. He can talk like a lawyer." Sally tossed her head. Joan was about to answer that jibe that her father knew less than the Ridleys' precious cousin—or second cousin—but then, she saw it was more important to find out what Sally meant by these hints about Timothy Yorke having some weight with high up people. She remembered how Seán McGilroy had said something about suspecting him of something, only he didn't want to speak out before he was sure of his facts.

She asked, blunt as ever, "Are you saying Timothy Yorke's an informer?"

Sally gave a laugh with no humour in it. She was usually ready for a spat with Joan, and more than ever these last few weeks. In fact, Joan now saw that Sally was downright hostile since McGilroy's return.

Sally sneered. "Don't take on about your swain, lass. If you can turn a blind eye to his telling tales on others, you'll be well set up and all thy people."

"You dafty, a group of those MYC set on Father t'other day! Didn't you hear of it, seeing your cousin was there?" Joan was furious. "They all took off fast before that special constable fellow could take them in charge."

"Seán said your beau stayed talking."

"He's not my beau. But if folks are saying he's an informer, I've a mind to ask him what he makes of it."

Sally tittered some more. Joan stalked away from her to re-join the drilling.

After a short while, Joan could see there was a drawback to this exercise. It was giving her an appetite, with little enough food in the house. But wasn't that why they were marching in the first place?

For the rest of the drilling, Sally sat on the stool with her skirts pulled up and rubbing her ankle, while the lads saluted her now and then as they went by. When they were dismissed, the men clapped so loud Joan wondered they didn't hurt their hands. This made a couple of the sillier girls shriek, so the men did it even louder and Jimmy Thribble ran up to clap his hands right under Joan's nose.

As they broke up, Tom escaped Kitty Ridley to go over to Marcie, while three more lads moved in on her from other directions. Joan didn't blame them, though she would have preferred a private talk with her. With her mane of long black hair loose, her fine features and her nearly black eyes, her cheeks glowing from the exercise, Marcie looked ridiculously pretty.

Meanwhile, Seán McGilroy was approaching Joan from one way, while Timothy Yorke hurried over from the other.

McGilroy said, "I must help yon Cousin Sally home, seeing how my uncle and her brothers aren't here tonight. On those things I spoke on before on your vegetable patch, will you be there about the same time as before, tomorrow?"

Joan felt a stir of excitement bubbling up in her, like the ginger beer she'd had a few times. This must be about whatever he wanted to say about Timothy Yorke, surely.

Again, she told herself off. She was being a mean minded thing if she was looking forward to hearing ill of Timothy Yorke, pest though he made of himself to her, and ruffled as she was at how Sally Ridley had made out that there was something between them.

"Well, I might be, it depends on what Mam permits." Joan tried to keep her voice level.

McGilroy pulled a face. "I was saying earlier to thy father, make sure and thank her for allowing her lass to show us all how to march. Any road, I'll be about there, and I hope to see you soon." He took her hand, squeezed it with one of those 'meaningful looks' and then went over to Sally, who was shouting out for him.

Jimmy Thribble offered her a ride on his back.

"Away with ye, now, lad, yon cousin's taking me." Sally limped along, leaning heavily on McGilroy's arm. Now and then she gave a shriek, loud enough for Joan to feel for McGilroy's ears, yet still managing to sound coy.

Joan was of no mind to get stuck with Timothy Yorke after what Sally said. She would ask him about it after hearing what McGilroy told her. She dodged round to the other side of Marcie, out of Timothy's way.

Marcie muttered to Joan, "I'm riled with Sally for acting so foolishly tonight, giving the men a chance to say that all females are ill cut-out for drilling. Mind you, she was doing it to draw in that McGilroy cousin of hers. It's plain he has his eye on you, and she thinks of him as a likely sweetheart for herself, and she won't let any likely fellow get away easily. She wants to pick and choose among them."

Despite herself, Joan's spirits surged. She couldn't have felt more pleased, if Marcie had said that she was due to be paid a hundred pounds a year from now on. It must be vanity, and she'd never thought of herself as vain before, except that she didn't like being called 'The scrawny one with wild hair like tow.' She'd never been one to get lads to dangle after her, unlike many other lasses.

Timothy Yorke, now talking to Tom, would be a downright pest even if he wasn't a suspected informer, so why lasses like Sally and Kitty Ridley wanted a whole crew of admirers after them was beyond Joan. Still, he wasn't lively and teasing, like Seán McGilroy. That did make all the difference. It was rather a fine thing, after all, to have a lad like that after you.

It was finding this vanity in herself that made Joan blush; that and the way Marcie's mocking dark eyes were turned on her. They never missed a thing.

Marcie went on, "I don't hold with gossip, but even by Sally's own words, that fellow seems to be a trifler. If you credited the rumours, though, he'd have a list of females he's drawn in as long as that man in the opera—what's he called—Don Giovanni."

Joan snorted. She was glad that she wasn't silly enough to be drawn in by some fickle fellow herself. Back in the vegetable patch, McGilroy had made out how he didn't deserve all the talk about him. Yet, even if three quarters of it was fanciful, that still left enough reason to think that he'd trifled with a few lasses. That wasn't good enough.

It was always the lasses who were blamed, and if some man played false by some wenches and then went on to court another seriously, she always made out that it made her special that he chose her above the ones before her. That was true for the women round here and if Nancy's books were anything to go by, it held with the grand folks as well.

But Joan didn't see it that way, herself. So, it was a bad sign that she was so pleased how that others saw how McGilroy admired her above his cousins, and that Sally Ridley was jealous. The idea of being drawn in by that fellow made Joan so cross that she snorted again.

Timothy Yorke was staring over as if he wanted to join in their talk. Though they spoke quietly, he might still have heard, sharp as his hearing was.

"Tell me about this Don Giovanni you talked on," Joan urged Marcie. It was a marvel, the stuff that lass knew. Joan's own father might be a knowledgeable self-educated man, but Marcie's information was a sight more interesting.

Jack Hooper's dog let out a bark, and streaked over to the fringe of shrubs and trees at the end of the field.

"Get 'em, boy!" urged Jack. There was more barking and crashing in the gloom among the trees. That might be nothing more than hedgehog or two taking off, being such noisy creatures. Still, you'd expect them to roll into a spiky ball the dog would know better than to stick its nose into. Now the dog rushed back, wagging its tail as at a job well done.

"That could even have been Nat Pritchard again; Joan and I came on him watching the drilling before," said Marcie. "Maybe he's just nosing: I hope he'd not tell tales."

"We're not important enough for spying on." Timothy Yorke spoke firmly, as if that was the end of the matter.

Tom and others took him up on that. No doubt they were roused by that tone of his—as if he was talking down to infants—quite as much as Joan was. "You think Nardy Joe don't pay narks?" he said. "Don't talk through your bloody hat, York. How about that letter from yon tinker that Jimmy found, eh?"

"I didn't say he never did it, but he's more interested in Bamford and Healey and those in touch with people like Hunt and the reformers from the gentry."

Joan thought again how terrible it was that you couldn't trust your neighbours. She wondered where all these letters which folks said were written to Nadin and the Magistrates by the police spies ended up. Were they ever delivered?

Weeks since, Jimmy Thribble came by one of these scrawls through getting in a scrap with a mean little fellow, a tinker. It had fallen from his coat during the fight. Jimmy had got Marcie to read it out, being only able to spell out the words himself. She said it was all worded wrong and full of wild talk about marching on Parliament, like those Blanketeers[26] a couple of years back.

Did these spies' letters go to Westminster Palace, carried solemnly along great corridors?

Maybe, they were full of details of Joan's father, and his walk, and his hat, and his talk of Wat Tyler and the Saxon laws, and of dark and solemn Mr. Royce, and Tom, and now the wickedly grinning Seán McGilroy. Maybe they even had tales about the tow-headed lass and her bonny friend, all written down for those rich folks like the Home Secretary - whatever that meant - Lord Sidmouth was what her father said he was called— to turn his nose up at.

That was worse than being unknown—which was all common folk like them could expect. In better times their weekly dance on the village green wasn't exactly reported in *The Times* and *The Gentleman's Magazine*, like those balls at Carlton House.

Did men plan to march on Parliament? At times, Joan felt herself ready to do as much herself, when she saw the youngsters going short of food. Some of the drillers—the young lads particularly, who Mr. Royce said hadn't learnt patience—did talk of 'showing them we mean it'.

Still, that didn't mean that they were set on a fight, so much as showing that there were masses of them, all feeling as one, and that things mustn't go on as they were. While they could riot and use force,

---

[26] The young Radical working men John Baggtuely and John Johnston organised a protest march to London in March 1817 to present a petition to the Prince Regent. The Riot Act was read, and it was broken up by yeomanry forces and dragoons with dozens arrested and many injured.

like the Luddites[27] had on machinery not so long since, that wasn't what they aimed for now.

What they wanted was to show how they were set on change, disciplined, and must be taken note of at last.

They had been left to starve for too long.

---

[27] The Luddite movement among textile workers involved the breaking of the machinery which put traditional artisans out of work. It was demolished in a series of trials in 1813, with harsh sentences including hanging and transportation meted out to the leaders.

7.

Words

For breakfast, there was oatmeal porridge as ever of late, and not a lot of that. Joan couldn't stand to see her family scraping along, when she still had her savings. When that went, there would be an end to getting ready to escape. Yet, holding on to it was more than she could do. And how could she explain keeping so quiet about the rest of those savings for so long?

"If you have yon grand meeting in town, will there be more to eat soon after?" Ben wanted to know.

"Things will get better, lad," said Mrs. Wright.

"They're taking their time," said Nat. "That petition to the Prince of Wales got us nowhere." Being eighteen months older, he could understand more of what their father, Tom, McGilroy and the others said about the reasons behind the low wages and lack of food.

"We'll make them better, one way or the other." Mr. Wright spoke as if he really believed that.

"Mam, when I -" Joan began, but her mother spoke at the same time.

"You're lucky with the vegetable patch, my wench. You go out later and see if you can find any onions or carrots for a stew."

Joan thought that things must be bad, when her mother who scorned superstitions, said things like that.

The thought of McGilroy and her strange excitement made her want to keep away from those allotments. Still, it was another hot day and as the hours crept by in tending to the machines in the damp heat that made them sweat, strands of hair clinging to their foreheads, in that haze of cotton waste, Joan slowly changed her mind.

They had bread, and half of the cheese that they got from a nearby farm, in return for a little weaving. At last it was time for Joan to pick up the spade and go off to the vegetable patch.

If she found nothing there, she hoped that included McGilroy. It was earlier than last time, and with any luck she would miss him, should he turn up. She'd much rather meet with a rabbit than McGilroy. You could eat a rabbit.

But it was taking a risk to kill it, when it belonged by law to the squire. They were only allowed to have this remaining bit of common land for allotments through his grace and favour. Well, she felt that she'd risk it for something to eat.

She'd always pitied rabbits, twitchy nosed, soft, furry creatures as they were, but now she felt if she caught one eating the vegetables her family might have had, she'd break its neck without a thought. It could serve for a tasty couple of meat dishes, too. They'd had little enough of those lately.

It was daft, getting all coy about meeting McGilroy the way she was. Joan cursed herself. Silly, flighty wenches acted like this. Still, she urged Hannah to come along. That would show the man she didn't welcome his coming after her. Hannah was willing. They put on their bonnets, and went out.

They hadn't got far before they ran into Widow Hobson. She waved her stick at them. "I have summat needs taking somewhere for me. Yon wee wench must come along to mine."

Hannah knew that the fearsome widow wouldn't let a youngster leave her house without eating, so she said in her sweetest tone, "I'll come, Mrs Hobson."

Joan had to go to the vegetable patch alone. She found neither onions, nor left over potatoes. There were some withered carrots. Somebody had been digging there since McGilroy, and she had to poke about fruitlessly with her broken spade for some time.

Then, hearing footfalls—a man's, too—she started. Her face burned. She turned.

Timothy Yorke was coming up behind her.

"Joan, I'm glad to see thee." He looked it.

She couldn't say the same. She was too busy cursing herself for wishing it was the other fellow.

For the first time, she began to fear for herself over the good-for-nothing trifler. The idea that she might have no more sense than others who'd been ready to listen to that lad's false talk, so goaded Joan that she could hardly speak.

Timothy was flushed, his dark eyes bright. He looked at his best, with his thick dark hair combed to look disordered, as was the fashion among those who copied those grand society folk, and he had knotted a fine yellow kerchief about his throat, an odd way to dress for grubbing up things from the plots.

He wasn't a bad looking fellow. Sally and the other wenches would have been happy enough to have him for an admirer, for all he so rarely made merry. He was the sort of fellow who would get ahead, too, you could see. But there was something about him Joan couldn't take to, and somehow it was all to do with him being so respectable.

He began, suddenly, as she crouched there with her wobbly spade, "Joan, I've wanted to speak my mind to you this while, but you are never alone. You and Marcie Royce getting all the other wenches mixed up in this marching can lead to no good. I've said as much to your father, but he wouldn't hear me, being an enthusiast for radical notions."

Joan stood up to be on a level with him. "Good. I think you had a nerve to speak to him over my head like that."

He shook his head. "There'll be trouble over this drilling. It's too military, and all the more when the men clap their hands, copying gunfire. I know most of them don't mean anything by it, being as good patriots as anyone. Now this Henry Hunt and his agitator friends are calling for a great meeting to elect a member to go to parliament, by those who have no vote. Things are getting out of hand; yon magistrates will never stand for that. It's only a matter of time before they act against the drilling. I wouldn't want you to be dragged off to gaol along with that no good McGilroy and his like."

"And my father?" Joan's cheeks flamed. "If there's arrests made, they can take me along of the men. You can sneak away from it, if you please."

He wasn't provoked by that. She supposed that was because he saw her as only an emotional female. "Joan, there's bad ideas going about, and all this stir will do no good. Things will get better by themselves; they always do. Then people will forget all about these wild ideas troublemakers have been putting into their heads."

"Father's no outsider; and I hope folks have more sense than giving up on such fine ideas, which have been going since Wat Tyler and before. You won't sway me, so you may as well stop talking."

Now his eyes did spark a little. "That McGilroy's turned up like a bad penny, stirring up bad feeling all round. He's dangling after you too, and with such a name as he's got with the girls. They say he's even seen the inside of a gaol once—and that's only what's said by his own family, mark you, Joan. You must take care not to be drawn in."

"I suppose you told my father that and all?"

He nodded. "I did, and more, but this is no time to say it."

There was a jeering laugh from behind them. Seán McGilroy, himself stood at the edge of the plot, glowering at Timothy. His blue eyes were flashing, and with his arrogant stance, and his black ringlets, Joan thought he looked like as fierce as a picture of a pirate she had seen in a chap book, minus the cutlass, of course.

"I heard that, Yorke. It seems to me, you and I need a little talk. Doesn't do to dispute before t'lasses, and all that, so if you'd care to come along." He nodded to the lane by the distant plots abutting the meadow. Then he turned a warm smile on Joan. "I hope you'll wait on me, Miss Joan."

Timothy looked ready to explode. "They say eavesdroppers never hear good of themselves, and least of all a ne'er do well. You're for a mill[28], McGilroy, but I don't hold with such loutish ways."

"I'm only for a brawl if you're up for it." McGilroy looked so fierce Joan skipped in between them.

"Don't go into it now. Do as folks say, and wait on it for a day. You're both acting daft, and like to harm each other. That's no good now, when we must all stand together."

---

[28] A fight.

McGilroy said, "What I've got to say can't be heard by any but Yorke himself till I find out the truth of it."

Timothy's face was too highly coloured for his face to redden, but he scowled and breathed hard. "You've heard some mean gossip from those who hold it against our family that we're not in rags and starving, and who make up wild stories out of envy. And I'll say outright in front of Joan: I see you've an eye for her, among others. A girl like Joan is too good for a roving good-for-nothing, who's got a name as a light o' love besides, to come trifling with. How your Ridley cousins behave is their parents' affair."

Now McGilroy's dark face was flushed with anger and it showed as it didn't on Timothy's. "Some of the tattle you've been hearkening to is in the right of it. I have lived wild and reckless, and got myself into a deal of trouble and all, and never could settle since coming back from the wars. Maybe I could change if I found something to keep me rooted, but I'm not talking on that before you, or aught else that matters."

An aloof bit of Joan's mind noted his use of 'rooted' as wholly fitting, when they were standing in a vegetable patch, and she had earth on her hands and teasing grit under her nails.

"You're an insolent ruffian." On the other side of Joan, Timothy Yorke drew back from McGilroy as from a filthy dog ready to spring on him.

Joan broke in. "I don't like lads scrapping over who is to talk to me like dogs over a bone, just as if I've no ideas of my own."

She put on a haughty air, and again this was like one of Nancy's books, though those heroines did it in grand drawing rooms. "If either of you has owt to say to me, you can say it another time."

McGilroy smiled at her, as if delighted. "You're in the right of it, Miss Joan. Let me do the digging for you." He took the wobbly spade from her grasp with a gentle twitch.

Timothy looked ready to burst with fury. "Yes, you're in the right there, Joan, and if this fellow leaves quietly, so shall I."

McGilroy didn't take kindly to being called, 'that fellow'. He clenched his fists, his eyes glinting. Joan saw no way of stopping a fight, and from what she'd heard of McGilroy going in for fighting at fairs and so, Timothy must certainly lose. She didn't want him hurt, trying though he was.

Suddenly, Tmothy's younger brother, Jem was with them. A weedy youth of maybe sixteen, he seemed as ill at ease in the world as Timothy was sure of his rights in it. His nervous look scanned Timothy to Seán McGilroy, to Joan and back again. "You're wanted at home."

Something about his nervous look seemed to decide Timothy at once. "I'm coming." Ignoring McGilroy, he turned to Joan. "If you're done here, walk along of us."

"I've found nothing yet," Joan said indignantly. What did he think she wanted in the vegetable plot—him?

Timothy stood staring. Then his young brother jerked out, more insistently, "Mam needs you." Timothy had no choice but to go with the boy. Then, as they turned onto the footpath, he said loudly, "It's fitting that Irish fellow is set to scrabble after potatoes as eager as a terrier after rats. That's all they live on, after all, and they bed down with their pigs."

McGilroy shouted after him, "Rats, eh? I could talk about rats, I'm thinking, such as your tale bearing friends."

Timothy jerked, as if hit by a pebble, but he walked on with his brother. Joan heard them muttering to each other as they moved off, and now she thought she caught distant sounds of raised voices. Some dispute was going on nearby, with a number of people at it.

She frowned, remembering what Sally had hinted about Timothy being in league with those informers, if not one himself.

McGilroy stood, glaring after the Yorkes, looking as if he was only just stopping himself from chasing after Timothy and knocking him down. Joan hoped that he wouldn't. To stop him, she put a hand on his arm.

And she shouldn't have done that, as touching him made her feel funny, and made him look at her in an odd way too. It brought them together in a way she didn't want. She took away her hand. "Damn his eyes for a hypocrite," he said.

Joan knew that fine word from Marcie. She was a walking dictionary, that lass. "Take no heed of him. Yon's a hypocrite right enough, and he doesn't even know he is one."

That made him smile. He still stood looking at her with those hot and sparkling blue eyes, and seemed about to say something. He even moved his lips, but then shut them. She saw what well shaped lips they were, full and a bit too wide, but not loose, and fitting in well with the rest of his face, with his short nose and high cheekbones, which she'd heard was a typical Irish face. He swore, which wasn't good manners before her, and not something he'd done before, for all he was a bad lot, having a smooth sort of way with him that was part of his being that bad lot.

Then he shook his head, and said, "Sorry for that. I suppose we might as well see if there are any more taters. Might be an onion or two left over, at that."

He turned away, and his walk was less jaunty than usual as he went over to pick up the spade.

He set about digging with a vigour she yearned for. "I thought as much." He began unearthing another fine crop of potatoes from an unlikely corner of the plot over by the gooseberry bushes, with almost no leaf above ground. Joan could have sworn that she dug over that part yesterday, finding nothing.

Suddenly, the wild idea came to her that he had put them there, though she had no notion when. He winked as he looked up at her. Then stood up, dropping his joking air along with the spade.

Joan still heard the distant hubbub, but took little notice, for now McGilroy said, "What that Yorke says of me has a lot of truth in it, though. I am a roving good-for-nothing." He looked downright dismal when he said that.

She supposed that he was suffering from a bad conscience about the way he'd gone on with too many lasses and other things. She thought it served him right. Still, he looked so cast down that she felt for him despite herself. Then he shot her an intent look, as if all this was to do with her.

She wondered what she was supposed to say to him about it all, when she hardly knew him. Was she supposed to deny what he owned about himself?

She sought for some bland way of heartening him that he didn't have to stay as a 'good-for-nothing', while at the same time making him keep those unlucky wenches he'd trifled with in mind, "I suppose people can change, if they truly want to."

She meant generally. He gave her another look with a lot of meaning in it she couldn't understand. "Maybe not enough to deserve something special, eh?"

He gazed at her a moment, his eyes all glowing. "Now I'm going to say something that isn't manners. I can't blame yon Timothy Yorke for coming after you, though I can't abide him. You're enough to turn any man's head—even a cold fish like him—when you've grown up to be so lovely, just as I always said."

Joan was uneasy as he went on giving her that look. She came out with the first thought that came into her head. "Never mind about Timothy Yorke's plans. We've ones of our own, me and Marcie, that don't include any lads at all, least of all him. We mean to use our healing to earn a living, and go out into the world and see things."

Somehow, said out loud, it sounded foolish, like an infant talking about growing up to fight giants.

That certainly made him stop giving her that intense look. He started and stared, eyebrows up in the curls that spilled over his forehead. He looked wrong footed, but then he smiled. "I never met a wench with such ideas. Still, I always knew you were different. It's a brave plan for a couple of lasses, but it won't do, Miss Joan. It's too risky for any lass, leave alone a couple of beauties like you and Marcie Royce. You'd get too much trouble from men with low notions over the pair of you on your own."

Joan had sometimes wondered about that herself. She and Marcie might well be mistaken for harlots, or those women who preferred women to men and got put in the pillory for it.

Having him say what she'd feared made her riled at him for trampling on her dreams of escape. "We will find a way." She spoke grandly and vaguely, hoping he wouldn't press for details, seeing she hadn't any.

Instead he said, "So this scheme of yours is why yon friend of yours is so frosty to poor Tom, whose fair spooning for her? For I think she likes him well, for all that."

Joan nodded. "Once a wench takes up with a lad, that's the end to her freedom."

He shook his head, smiling. Joan thought he had the look of one humouring a child's fairy story. "I'm thinking this is a long term plan. You'd not leave your parents when times are so hard."

Joan had to agree over that. "We must save up a lot more, any road." She thought gloomily over her savings melting away. How awful if they were all used up, and she had to start at the beginning again. Nobody could afford to pay her or Marcie for their herbal cures these last few months. They had treated their neighbours for free.

He smiled. "I'd be sorry to see you move away, when I've only just come back myself."

She was too wrought up fretting over her plans to take much heed of those words, which most likely was what he said to all sorts of lasses, along with giving them that warm smile. With those flashing white teeth and sparkling blue eyes, it was no wonder too many foolish girls had allowed themselves to be drawn in by his ways.

Then he added, musingly again, "A lass who wants to move about needs a man along of her to watch out for her."

Joan tossed her head. "Marcie and me will look out for each other and no need of men."

"You'd not be able to safeguard each other enough." Now that shadow passed across McGilroy's face, the same as when Nat and Ben pestered him about his adventures in the late wars. "You'd do better, Miss Joan, to see what you can make out of your doctoring here at home and then see."

This humdrum future seemed all too likely. It made Joan feel cast down: more likely than not, she and Marcie would be stuck at home for ever, or at least until they were over twenty and getting long in the tooth.

"So we are trying to make something out of our doctoring, and unpaid, when we're allowed time off from housework and the workroom," she snapped. She saw that this was turning into a dispute, and she didn't see why she should explain all this to him. It was her own fault for speaking of her dreams to him. She wondered whatever had made her do that.

She said sullenly, "But we do want to see other places and do things. Why aren't females supposed to want that? Anyway, you must have been younger than us when you left home."

"I was, and ran off to join t'wars. But it's different for a lad."

Joan thought he said that smugly. "Humph," was all she could think of to say. She had a let down feeling about their talk, and she didn't know why. "You spoke when last we met of having two things to tell me."

Now he looked caught out, but spoke lightly, "I was talking too soon, about what I thought I knew for sure."

Before Joan could make anything of that, he broke off at a sudden outburst of shouting from down the lane.

They had both been so wrapped up in this talk, they'd had no ears for what was happening in the world outside. Now, the distant noises surged up, too loud to ignore.

Voices shouted; one shrieked; thuds sounded. Among them came the jolly notes of piped music.

"Stay here!" Seán McGilroy thrust the sack of potatoes at her.

Unthinking, she took them, and he was off like a shot, rushing down the lane.

"Is that likely?" Joan put them down and hid the spade among the bushes, not wanting to tempt anyone into taking it. Then, snatching up the skirts of her raggedy brown Cinderella dress, she took off after him.

8.

BREAD

As Joan followed McGilroy out of the lane, they saw a crowd round the Yorke's bakery. This was one of the older buildings, standing by itself at the end of the lane, so that the space in front formed a small yard.

Now it was full of shouting people. The shutters were up on the window to the downstairs room which served as a shop. Mrs. Yorke leaned out of the one upstairs, screaming at them.

She looked as Joan had never seen her before. Her cap was off, and her grey-streaked hair streamed about her shoulders, her face twisted with rage as she shook her fist. "Be off with you, dirty rabble as you are. We pay yon miller dear for the wheat, you bloody fools: go and yell at those who keep up the Corn Laws!"[29]

Jimmy Thribble, crimson in the face, roared back: "Damn your eyes for a miserly harridan, them prices is down to you lot. There was no call to raise them again. Some neighbour you are, fattening off hard times."

Jack Hooper smashed a stick on the shutters. "Bloody open up!"

Mr. Yorke appeared at the window. "Stop that, ye ruffians!"

Joan's father was at the front with Mr. Royce, trying to quieten things down. He seized Jack's shoulder. "Nay, lad, that's not the way…" The rest of his words were drowned in more yelling from the back of the crowd.

---

[29] The Corn Laws imposed taxes on imported grain and in forcing up the price of bread, causing much suffering.

"Break 'em down!" a woman's voice screamed. "I cannot stand seeing my bairns clemming at home. Break 'em down and be damned to the bloody hoarders!"

The worst thing to Joan was the background music. Daffy Danny, standing aside from the crowd, played on his pipe for all he was worth, fingers moving in a blur, a jolly light in his eyes. The notes flowed in a festive tune. Perhaps the crowd put him in mind of dances on the remains of the village green in happier days.

"Stay back, Joan!" McGilroy thrust into the crowd, forcing his way through and yelling for calm.

Joan, lacking his strength, had to worm her way through. Someone caught hold of her skirts, pulling her up. It was Nat. "Sis, keep out of it."

"For heaven's sake, you lads are full of that today." She wrenched her skirts away, tearing them and struggled forward.

Of course, these people were her neighbours: now, wild as they were with despair, faces strained, yelling, eyes staring, hollow cheeks flushed, she would hardly know them. There was Widow Smith, bonnet awry, bawling baby under her arm, shaking her fist. There were the two little brats who had shouted after Seán McGilroy and Joan the other day and in their dimpled hands they held stones.

"You dare." She wagged a finger at them. Now she was near the front of the crowd. Her father and Mr. Royce were still keeping back Jimmy Thribble and Jack Hooper from battering in the shutters. Tom shouldered his way through the crowd, coming to their aid.

McGilroy got there first. He jumped on the broken bench, where a few years back, Joan and Marcie had sat munching pastries and starting to make their plans. It made a type of platform, battered as it was. "Hush ye!" he roared. "Eh now, lads and lasses, this won't do. Calm down: we can sort out matters and get you bread without a riot."

"Hold your own noise, you dirty Mick[30] wencher—this rabble won't heed you." Mrs. Yorke's shriek sounded nearly gleeful.

Hoots answered her. Joan had never heard an angry gathering of giant birds, yet thought now they might sound like that.

---

[30] A slighting name for an Irishman.

THE PETERLOO AFFAIR

"Will you lower your prices, and calm things down, Mistress?" McGilroy turned to her. "We can stop this getting ugly. Keep on as you are, and you'll end up with your shop pillaged."

Mrs. Yorke shook her head: "I'll not barter with rioting, looting rabble."

Suddenly, Marcie was up on the bench besides him. She stumbled as an arm reached out and tried to pull her from her perch, but skipped back, regaining her balance by a piece of footwork which Joan thought fitting for the best dancer on the village green.

She shouted, "Please think back! There've been so-called bread riots before, only they weren't. They were actions done nice and orderly:[31] They set a price and left the money. That's what we must do now."

A male voice bid her hold her tongue for a scolding slut. Tom, busy as he was in keeping back the leaders, found time to glare.

McGilroy shouted, "She's right, you bloody fool. Listen, you've got to keep calm. Can't you see Nadin's lot are on the lookout for trouble all round? There's nought they'd like better than a riot, so as to lock half of us up and keep us from yon march and maybe shoot a few of us at that."

"They're narks, they are—the whole bloody lot of 'em!" another voice rasped. Rage had changed their voices so that Joan couldn't tell who shouted. She at last made the front of the crowd.

McGilroy yelled back, "There'll be time to talk over that later…" He had to break off to regain his balance as Joan made the bench wobble by jumping up next to them. Marcie did some more fancy footwork, and cursed.

Joan didn't see another way, though, that she could have made herself heard, little body that she was. She turned to yell up to Mrs. Yorke, "You'll be paid; I'll take the money."

---

[31] The organized (and often nonviolent) nature of these actions - which have gone down in official history as 'riots'are recounted in EP Thompson'in his 1963 classic, 'The Making of the English Working Class'.

Mrs. Yorke opened her mouth to reply, but suddenly, fell back from the window. Timothy Yorke was there instead, leaning out to yell, "Quarter price for half a loaf."

"Hear that? That's a fair offer," called McGilroy. "Make a line!" He might have been drilling them.

"About wheel!" Mr. Wright quipped, trying to turn the mood of the crowd. Jimmy Thribble, good humour restored, added, "Left, Right: Arses Tight!"

"Everyone, give your coin to me!" Joan held out her apron.

"Eh, hoos[32] taking coin for showing her legs. I can see her calves," called Jack Hooper, and the youths guffawed. Joan saw McGilroy scowl, his own eyes flicking to her legs.

Somehow, it was all sorted out. The crowd formed itself into a line. Joan and the others jumped down from the bench as, with a weary creaking, it sagged in on itself.

People threw money into Joan's apron. The men got the group into a line. Timothy Yorke threw open the shutters, while his father, a much smaller man, now moving as quick and fearfully as a vole, brought out and cut up the loaves.

Many of the crowd had no money, and wanted credit. Others sent their wide-eyed children home for coins. Marcie called to Mrs. Yorke to mark so-and-so up for credit on the slate. This happened so often it became silly, and Joan had to fight down laughter.

Tom and Seán McGilroy were beside her and Marcie, making sure they didn't get crushed, and as Joan struggled not to laugh, his eyes met hers.

The next moment Joan felt his arm slip about her. "Just to keep you safe from getting squashed," he said. "There's not much of thee for so much spirit."

Far worse, she almost dropped the coins she held in her skirt, not just out of shock, but because it felt right—dangerously right—that he should hold her so.

"Stop that!" She tried to wriggle out of his hold.

---

[32] 'hoo' was dialect for 'her'.

"Can't have you trampled, can I?" he pretended to sway as one of the little girls thrust by him.

And now Marcie saw them, those black eyebrows of hers going up like glossy caterpillars wriggling in her quick glance at Joan, who felt herself turn bright red. She slapped McGilroy's hand, and reluctantly, he let go.

Sally Ridley saw, and said, "You've given the lads the wrong idea, showing all thy legs like a wanton."

"I had other things on my mind than suchlike rubbish," snapped Joan.

"We all know she's not such a lass," said Seán McGilroy, and had to turn away to deal with a man who was trying to get past without paying, while Sally tossed her head.

But now, Jimmy Thribble was pretending to take two half loaves—though he was only larking about—while Sally Ridley jumped up on the bench and began to sing. Kitty Ridley joined in.

Joan thought they did it badly enough, and saw how, for all her taunts, Sally was now showing far more leg than Joan had as she drew up her skirts and danced.

Still, it lightened the mood. Some of the lads began clapping. The crowd started to break up, going off holding their loaves, and, Joan thought, looking half ashamed.

Daffy Danny came up and began to play his pipe again, picking up their tune. He could play anything, that lad, by ear.

Mrs. Yorke took the money from Marcie and Joan with an air as if she was doing them a good turn. "Put it down over there. If you think I'll thank you for egging on that mob to loot my shop, you'd better think twice, you bold creatures."

"But Mistress, you haven't gone hungry, and worse, seen your young ones crying for want," Marcie urged. "It makes people wild, when nobody will hear them or aid them. These are your neighbours, after all. In normal times, they'd no more think to loot your shop than walk on the moon. I'm guessing that come good times again, they'll pay you the money owing."

There came a long, shrill note from Daft Danny's pipe. Different as it was from his tunes before, they turned without thinking.

There, at the other side of the field across from the village green, trotted three horsemen, with Timothy Yorke's younger brother Jem running behind them.

Two of them wore the flashy blue livery of the Manchester Yeomanry Cavalry. The third Joan recognised as Mr. Harrison, a wealthy retired tailor who'd acted as special constable so often people thought of him as being as much of a fixture as Joseph Nadin—only less hated.

"Soldiers!" she shouted.

9.

Justice

Joan's words ran through the thinning crowd, and it melted away like ice in a pan on the fire.

Sally Ridley and her sister jumped down from the bench, calling, "Come on, Seán!" Jimmy Thribble and Jack Hooper were gone in a trice. The little girls made off, still pulling pieces from their bread as they scampered away like mice.

"Now, Mrs. Yorke, we've got you some coin, so don't get those boobies of Yeomanry mixed up in this," McGilroy urged.

She opened a mouth as tight as a trap, to snap, "I shall say that my neighbours raided this shop, urged on by the lot of ye."

Mr. Yorke startled Joan by speaking up. "Without them keeping back the crowd, we'd have been looted outright."

"You would," said Tom. "McGilroy and my father, Royce and me have stopped a few fists to keep the lads back. The least thing you can do is to keep silence."

Mr Wright, Royce and Seán McGilroy meanwhile, had turned to Joan and Marcie. "Be off with you, lasses," said Mr. Royce.

"Go and tell they mother that all's well," Mr. Wright ordered Joan.

McGilroy smiled on them both, his eyes fixing on Joan. "You're as wild as hares, my lasses. There's no keeping you in check, but you don't want to talk to those MYC loobies[33]."

Joan crossed her arms over her chest, making no reply, and Tom rolled his eyes. "You'll get nowhere with those two."

---

[33] ie fools.

The riders were coming towards them at a fast trot. That gave Joan a sinking feeling, somehow worse than fearing that they'd all be blamed for the disorder and dragged off to the local lock up and then gaol.

The Yeomanry men were stout, though young, wearing their grand livery proudly. Joan wondered if they'd been about their own drilling today, amateur soldiers that they were. Their fine tall mounts seemed only half in control as the riders came up close, the horses' steaming flanks on a level with the group's heads.

While the other males eased in front of the women, Timothy Yorke came out of the house, with Mr. Yorke behind him, looking as guilty as if he had stolen his own bread. Mrs. Yorke brought up the rear, and curtsied to Mr. Harrison. The male Yorkes, being hatless, touched their foreheads. Young Jem ran to take refuge beside them, twitching.

Mr. Harrison, as a wealthy former tradesman who'd bought a fine house nearby, was second only in status to the squire. He gave a lot to the poor, so Joan heard often enough. Her father said that, as a good Anglican, he'd see that as his duty, but he liked the working people to be docile and grateful.

Now Mr. Harrison, wiry and alert, dapper in his gentleman's dress, and the two MYC men glanced round at the rest of the group. They clearly expected some forelock tugging, as they were hatless, too. Getting none and no curtseys from the girls, they scowled.

Mr. Harrison barked, "Yorke, this lad of yours comes to me with a garbled tale of the villagers looting. I heard shouting and saw a mob around your shop, though most of the wretches made off when they saw us. Are these the ringleaders? I must take you all in custody: riot is a serious matter. You must come up before the next assizes."

Joan's heart lurched, as much as at the unfairness of it all as with fear of gaol.

McGilroy spoke up, sounding easy. "No, there was bad feeling about the price o' t'bread, but no more done than shouting and fists waved. Mr. Yorke put down his prices for the day, and we kept order."

The taller MYC man, who would have been thought handsome, had he been thinner, gave a jeering laugh. "Order?"

Mr. Wright nodded. "That's so, eh, Yorke?"

"Not with our say so: you forced us to hand it over," Mrs. Yorke got in quickly.

Joan turned on her furiously, but Marcie squeezed her arm. She said nothing, but glowered at Mts. Yorke, who shut her lips primly. Joan saw that they would be seen as the leaders of a bread riot, when they had been doing their best to stop outright looting.

Marcie said almost amiably, "But Mrs. Yorke, Mr. Yorke agreed to it, and you took the payment; and many who had no coin put their names down for credit to show goodwill. Yon Danny even played his pipe and some of the lasses danced. That was no riot."

"That sounds unlikely enough," said Mr. Harrison. "Are you asking me to believe that, after all the Radical agitation some of you have been about these last few months? Wright, do not believe that the authorities are ignorant how you and one Mc-Something have been stirring up trouble these last weeks. This young fellow here fits his description. Now you claim you did all you could to calm your neighbours. More likely you set them up to it. We've never had riots here before, but neither did we have these nonsensical Radical notions being stirred up by half-educated men who ought to know better. "

Mistress Yorke nodded. If looks could slay, she'd have tumbled down on the spot under Joan's glare.

Timothy York stood silent, one hand on young Jem's shoulder, avoiding Joan's eyes.

"True, we have had some talks about conditions," said Mr. Wright easily. "Me and this young fellow are by way of being looked up to hereabouts: that's why the folks heeded us when we held there should be some agreement with the Yorkes' over the price of bread. Compromise, that's it. Meeting on the middle ground."

For all he only came up to the chest of one of the great horses, he spoke proudly, his own chest thrown out.

The nearest horse made a rude snorting noise, tossing its head just like Sally Ridley. Its dandified rider took a closer look at Seán McGilroy, and drawled out, "Damme, I think this to be the same fellow who caused trouble in town a couple of weeks since, and attacked a fellow member. A hulking Irishman—wild Black Irish,

I heard, like this fellow, with the gift of the gab, and with him a little man like this orator here, only hiding beneath a big hat."

He was dark himself, with hair that looked carefully curled. Joan thought he might half envy Seán McGilroy those 'Black Irish' looks.

Tom said casually, "There's lots of Irish in these parts of late, and many a weaver who's a little fellow; it pairs with the going hungry." His eyes ran over those well-fed MYC men.

"You are in the right of it, Mangnall, it must be the pair of them," the shorter MYC man spoke briskly. "Best take them all in, Mr. Harrison, before they get up to more mischief."

"Master Yorke, you know the truth of the matter." Joan appealed to him. "Do speak out."

Timothy Yorke turned an odd look—maybe one of warning—on his father.

"Why, Timothy!" Joan was shocked.

Mr. Yorke said, "They speak true. There was some shouting and hard words, but our neighbours here quietened things down, and that's the truth of it. My wife was against our selling cheap, true. Yet, times being so hard, the sight of t'bairns hungry and their mothers not knowing how to put bread on the table was more than I could rightly endure."

"He's just making that up, to get them off being charged," sneered Mangnall. "Damme, they've got those allotments, courtesy of their squire, to grow their potatoes and suchlike fodder, and still they go poaching on his land."

Mr. Yorke suddenly took heart. "No, it's true. The lad panicked. My wife's just mithered[34] at the money we've lost by it, but there's times when you shouldn't trouble over that. Eh, Timothy, lad?"

Mrs. Yorke's lips thinned into a tight purse, as if she'd like to thrust all that lost money into it. Timothy, glowering from Joan to McGilroy, spoke flatly after fully a minute, "That's so." He made it plain the words were dragged out of him.

Mr. Harrison scowled still more. "So when this lad of yours came crying out that he's been sent to say your house will be torn apart,

---

[34] Dialect for angry.

there was nothing behind it? Come, now: I don't take kindly to my time being wasted."

McGilroy said, "The lad feared for his parents. It's natural enough."

"Nobody asked you to speak out, Mick," said the dark MYC man Mangnall. His friend laughed as at a sharp witticism. If earlier they were practicing manoeuvres, Joan thought that they must have taken a fair bit of wine or something stronger since.

"We've got a right to speak out against unfair charges." Marcie's eyes flashed. Even she was riled now.

The dandified Mangnall turned clumsily on his horse to get a look at the girls standing side by side, screwing up his eyes to focus on them. "The saucebox! But she's a bonny one, too." His friend sniggered some more.

Mr. Royce, calm as ever, moved in front of Marcie. "That's no way to speak to a proper lass." Tom and McGilroy stirred, scowling.

Mr. Harrison said loudly, "You be warned, Wright, and you, too, the Irishman, whatever you're called. It so happens the lock up is full today with a group of vagabonds, so I'm letting you off for now."

He stared solemnly round at them all. Joan kept her face as blank as the others. "But hark ye, if there's any more trouble then I'm taking you all in, yes, and the girls too. They should be at home, behaving decently and helping their mothers, rather than traipsing about and answering their betters. You will be hanged or transported for starting a riot, you know. There had better be no more trouble."

"Then, Mr. Harrison, yon magistrates would do best to change the constable from Joseph Nadin." Joan knew she should have kept her mouth shut, what with them escaping with a warning; the words were through her lips before she could stop herself.

Mr. Harrison took no more note than if one of the horses had snorted. The dandified MYC man, though, leered down.

"Taken against Master Nadin, has she?" his voice came thick. "Hold thy tongue, my pretty hoyden, or he'll put you over his knee and smack your plump -"

Mr Royce caught hold of Mr. Wright, just as he seized Tom's shoulder and Tom caught hold of McGilroy, gagging him with his forearm.

79

The sight of that chain nearly set Joan giggling even in her wrath.

Mr. Wright spoke through his teeth. "Don't speak to my wench so."

Mr. Royce urged, "Master, your companions are the worse for drink, and fair riotous themselves."

The short MYC man broke in, "Damme, leave these paupers be to give the magistrates enough rope to hang 'em. Some of them have got above themselves, but they'll swing for it soon enough, with all these insane notions of equality. Gad, they ought to mind what happened to that ranting upstart lackey Bagguley and his wild march on the Prince Regent."[35] He looked hard at McGilroy, who stood gagged and pinioned by Tom and Mr. Wright. "Eh, Mick?"

McGilroy could give no answer, as Tom still had his arm over his mouth. Joan and the others stood looking their scorn.

Mr. Harrison raised his eyebrows in some sort of signal to the Yorke family, though Joan thought he didn't use his eyebrows as well as Marcie or Seán McGilroy. "You, the Irishman, McKilroy or whoever you are, you'd better mend your ways from here on, whatever they do in Ireland. You're headed for the gallows. If you come to my attention again it'll be the worse for you. Come gentlemen. We have better things to do with our time."

"Such as to drink," muttered Marcie.

Mrs. Yorke, her face sour enough to curdle her dough, made her curtsey to the gentlemen. Joan and Marcie did not. Again, the male Yorkes made the gestures of respect the others overlooked.

Abruptly, the gentlemen wheeled their horses about, knocking down the bench, and set off at a brisk trot over the dry meadow cropped clear of any edible weed.

---

[35] John Bagguley led the ill-fated 1817 'blanketeers' march to petition the Prince Regent., for which act of subversion he was kept in solitary confinement for many months.

10.

Weakness

The first to speak was neither McGilroy nor Joan's father, fond of the sound of their own voices though they were, but Timothy Yorke.

He fixed a bitter glare on McGilroy. "There's been too much talk of informers. We held our peace when we could have complained of looting."

"And we stopped any looting." Tom spoke between his teeth. Seán McGilroy regarded the Yorkes inscrutably.

Mr. Wright said. "Thank ye, Yorke. I hope that's so about the talk, young Timothy. For sure it makes sense to keep in with yon Nadin and his cronies rather than fall out with him outright, though a civil word to suchlike would stick in my throat."

Mistress Yorke made a noise like a kettle about to boil over and flung away inside.

"Hold." Mr. Yorke turned away, and came back with some half loaves, which he handed to Joan, Marcie, and McGilroy. "It's only fair you should have bread at the same rate as t'others."

Mr. Wright turned to Joan. "Thy mother will be beside herself. Run and tell her all's well, and take this loaf. Master Yorke, do put us down as owing, though we'll pay this very day. Meanwhile, we men must talk these latest developments over." He liked the sound of that, and nodded sagely.

Timothy Yorke stalked off into the house with Jem following him.

Joan said, "Well, I will do as you say, Father. But you must have marked how without Marcie and me playing our parts along of you men, there'd have been a riot."

"These lasses." Mr. Wright shook his head.

"Aye, go on, there's good wenches," urged Mr. Royce. "Hark at them, Wright. These women folk are taking over t'world, what with auld Widow Hobson egging them on, and yon Samuel Bamford giving females their say in meetings over in Middleton, and this Henry Hunt saying, as I hear tell, that they must have the vote along o' us. On top of all, there's these women's groups and all. It's a poor lookout, I say." He shook his head solemnly.

Joan's lips twitched. Oddly enough, Marcie humoured him. "We'll be away, Father, so you can talk over such things our ears mustn't hear, and there's things Joan and I must talk over between ourselves."

As Marcie took her arm, Joan could sense how some of the normal friendliness was lacking in her fingers. As she led Joan off, so that Joan felt almost felt like a suspect being taken in charge. She knew what was coming.

They went along the narrow lane back home from the Yorkes' house, the earthen path warm under their feet and the heat of the late afternoon beating down on them.

Marcie was straight to the point, as ever. "Anyone can see that McGilroy has his eye on tjeee. Small wonder for that; so do many of the other lads, but I fear thee likes him too well thyself."

"But I don't!" Joan spoke too heatedly, and for some reason her face got hot too. She went on more calmly, "As thou said yourself, if only a quarter of what is said of him is true, then he's played false by a lot of lasses. I couldn't like him over that."

She looked straight into Marcie's too knowing gaze, vexed at its mockery. "But thou likest him for all that," said Marcie.

Denials rushed to Joan's lips, but she couldn't say them. She went a shade redder and her heart raced. She saw that Marcie had taken note of what Joan herself couldn't credit. Something about McGilroy drew Joan to him despite herself, rascal though he was. That was why she'd always been so set against him.

That was what her let down feeling back in the allotment was all about—she'd wanted him to pay court to her. She'd been half expecting that, without admitting it to herself; and all he'd done was talk on Timothy Yorke and pull down her plans.

Joan winced and swallowed. This was—what was that grand word that Marcie had used about something else—'humiliating', that was it. She was another of those foolish lasses who fell for his lively ways and dark good looks.

Marcie's hawk eyes softened as she saw it. "We can't always help our feelings. It's what we do about them that counts."

"Maybe," muttered Joan miserably, dropping her gaze to her toes. "I know thou likes our Tom, for all thou'rt so cold to him."

Marcie looked none too pleased with that. Joan didn't see why; it wasn't as if Tom was a fickle type like McGilroy. He wanted Marcie and no-one else. "It's a sad thing to have a weakness for a roving fellow like McGilroy," she fretted. "I don't know how it crept up on me. It must have been like the two of us with Neddy Pritchard t'other day." She laughed feebly at her own joke.

"I can see he's got a real eye for thee," said Marcie, just as she had back at the meadow, and her words were like balm to Joan's wounded pride. "Maybe even a roving type like him might be thinking of going on strong with thee. And it might come harder to hold out against him than thee reckons upon."

Joan drew herself up. "No. We can only work on those plans of ours, if we keep free of getting tangled up with any lads." She didn't think that good-for-nothing fellow would be paying any serious court to her, anyway. The awful thing was that she wanted him to, even though she'd have to turn him down. Why did she want that? It could only be pride. No, it was more; she wanted him to want her the way she saw she wanted him. She'd never thought she'd be weak enough to long for him like this.

She went on, as calmly as she could, "A trifler who's let down a string of lasses is no prize, even if he did come on strong to me. The Ridley girls are welcome to him, if they can draw him in, which won't be any easier than one of those foxes yon squire rides after."

"I'm happy to hear thee say so, Joan, but I wanted to give thee the chance to decide if thou wants to go on with our plans..." Marcie broke off as they rounded the bend and they saw her mother standing at the garden gate.

She was talking with a couple of neighbours, but on seeing them, she broke out with a "Thank the Lord, here they are!"

Even as Mrs. Royce spoke, Joan's insides lurched as she realised she'd done something terrible. "Marcie, you talk to your mother. I've gone and left some taters in t'allotment." So saying, and with a quick nod to Mrs. Royce and the others, she picked up her skirts and rushed back there.

Back at the vegetable plots there was no sign of that sack of potatoes. Joan scampered about looking for them like a mouse desperate for seeds, but they had gone. Someone must have taken them. The scraggy carrots were in with them, too.

Now there would only be the bread that she still held, some dried herbs and that last little piece of cheese for supper today and dinner tomorrow.

Coming along with the shock of learning of her hopeless feelings for that fickle McGilroy, it was all too much. Joan sat down on the bench which Mr Wright had fashioned from a plank and two pieces of wood, and burying her face in her hands, sobbed aloud. She'd caught a glimpse of the spade she'd left hidden among the bushes, but that was cold comfort.

Now she heard someone coming towards her, but she didn't care. Then someone was kneeling in front of her, and she'd know that body scent anywhere. His arms were stealing about her.

"What ails thee, Joan?"

"Those potatoes are gone," she wailed, and was disgusted at how weak her voice sounded, all chocked up with tears.

"I've got 'em hidden on our patch." He held her close against his chest, his grip gentle but strong enough to astonish her. She could even hear his heart beating, and quite fast, too. "For a wild brave lass like you to take on over a score of taters shows how hard things are for your people. It makes me want to take care of you, Joan, so you never have to worry over where you're next meal comes from again."

"Let go: I'll not have one who trifles with lasses' feelings holding me."

He tightened his arms about her. "No, I won't let you go: I've been wanting to hold you for too long. As for my bad name with lasses—what if I say you've made me want to change?"

She was so stunned at his words that all she could do was mutter, "I want my handkerchief."

Still holding her close with one arm, he gave her his own with the other. She blew her nose, glad that her hair was all down about her face and hiding it, disgusting as it must look.

Now he took her chin between long finger and thumb, and gazed at that tear stained face again as if looking at something wonderful.

"When I saw your mettle during that trouble at t'Yorkes', I knew I had to tell you that you were the one for me. I was going to ask you to be my sweetheart before. Then that bloody Yorke brought up my bad name. He may be a stuffed shirt who opens his mouth too freely, but he was in the right of it about that. So then I had second thoughts that maybe I shouldn't ask so fine lass to take a risk in trusting me. But now I see I'd curse myself forever if I didn't try for you. " The tender look in his eyes was real, anyway.

Marcie; our plans…

He went on, "With t'other wenches, I never meant to ill use any of them, but I wasn't content with any. I never knew what it was to have one light up my day till I came across you grown up so fine. Only you can do that for me. I reckon that if I lit up the day for any of those lasses, then she must have wanted sense and a pair of spectacles. Still for all that, I know let down a few of them, and I'm sorry for it now."

"Humph." Joan seemed to have been saying that a lot today. "Even if I was of a mind for courtship, how could I trust you, if just a bit of the tattle is true? What of those girl cousins of yours?"

He looked so surprised, she supposed it couldn't be put on. "They're fine lasses, but they like a laugh and a joke and sometimes they let the lads make a bit too free with 'em."

Joan thought that was putting it politely as he went on, "Even if they weren't family to me, I'd be a simpleton to carry on strong with any of them and lay up trouble for myself, living at my uncle's house as I am."

Reaching out as warily as if he was drawing in a wild creature, he made to draw her to him again.

She stiffened. "I cannot let Marcie down."

"We'll work something out, " he said in that way of his, as if he could sort out half the world's problems before breakfast, leaving the other half until after dinner, "Don't worry: my word on it, you'll go on your adventures yet, Miss Joan, and all above board."

Earlier, realizing that she wanted him hopelessly, Joan had felt a pang that made her writhe. Now it seemed that she might be able to have him after all. Yet, how could she let go of that freedom she'd dreamed of with Marcie?

He smiled, shaking his head as if in disbelief. "I never thought to fall for a lass with such wild notions as you. Still, that is part of what makes you special. I'm a sight too wild myself to be happy with any tame creature, and I don't want to make a trap for you. But it sends a chill through me to think of the pair of you walking blithely into danger, my pretty. You've never seen what brutes men can be: I have."

"Marcie's as good as any man for looking out," began Joan. But he laughed.

"I do believe I love thee true, Joan, and I never knew what it was before. That was what ailed me. Thou forgets Tom: Marcie will come round, and be the happier for it, and all above board when we take you to see a few things, and your doctoring is a fine idea."

"Taking us along' sounds like some baggage you're carting about," Joan began again. McGilroy cut in, "No more on that now. Baggage you're not, in any sense. I must kiss you."

She wanted to say no, and talk about how sorry she was for those other wenches he'd let down, but she wanted him to kiss her more. He drew him to her, slowly and gently, and brought his lips down on hers, gently too but firmly.

Her insides melted and she parted her lips under that kiss. Now she saw why women wanted to do those rude and unaccountable things that made babies. Her lips kissed him back without her willing it.

The warmth, the life and strength of him in her arms made her body throb and her head spin. She wanted this man—rascal though he was—and she couldn't send him on his way keeping her heart shut. Yet, neither could she let go of her dreams of escape into adventure beyond the horizon.

She wanted everything at the same time, and didn't wish to let go of any of it, that's what it was. Joan saw that she was like one of those spoilt brats her mother talked of, who lived in the fine house where she was once nursery maid.

But for now, all she wanted was to kiss Seán McGilroy and never stop.

• • •

McGilroy said, "I want to get you a present as soon as may be. When I was choosing those beads for my cousins, I kept on looking at a string of 'em dyed blue, and thinking of how they'd go with your eyes."

"I don't know if I should let you," said Joan.

"Of course you should, as my sweetheart."

They were walking along, he with one arm round her, while the other carried the spade, while she had the potatoes, carrots and bread, happy and relaxed now after all that kissing. She said, "Well, you haven't asked me."

"Haven't asked you? Didn't I tell you I was falling for you as I never thought I could? You're going to be mine, and I won't let you go."

"I see. And my say so counts for nowt?"

He even looked a bit anxious when she said that. "Will you have me for your lover[36], Miss Joan?"

"I think I might have to put up with you."

His eyes lit. He looked ready to dance a jig. "I'll talk to your father fast enough to ask him if I can come courting you. I think I can get him round, but your mother's a different story." He grimaced. He may have acted as if he hadn't seen those cold looks Mrs. Wright turned on him, but Joan had the idea now that there wasn't much that this McGilroy missed.

She nodded. "I fear so. She doesn't like the talk about thee and thy cousins, leave alone all the rest from Jimmy Thribble and t'others. I still don't like it myself."

---

[36] 'Lover' then meant a suitor or sweetheart, not a sexual partner.

"Don't start on that again, my lass. I'm another man with thee." He sighed, and then brightened. "As to thy mother, well, thy father's word is what counts, after all."

He shook his head. "I feared for thee before, Joan, with Yorke's wife out to have us marched away. That Harrison only let us off with a warning because Yorke's word would count for more in a court than those of his missus."

"Then we must hope she doesn't get on to him too much o'er it, mean spirited creature as she is," said Joan. "I almost wish we'd left them to be looted."

"Not you," he said, laughing. "And after Timothy Yorke's fine talk about being miscalled, we must hope he and his mother don't go to tell another tale that gets to Nardy Joe, eh?"

He squeezed her waist, drawing her to him again, urging her towards the lane to the copse and the meadow beyond where they did their drilling practice.

Joan was so stunned by it all, that she didn't for a moment see what it was that made McGilroy break off his brisk walk and the tune he was humming to her, while the sunshine fled from his face.

He swore, putting down the spade. "Wait there."

Then she took in what looked like a bundle of rags lying by the side of the road, with the flies making a humming blanket over it.

The sweet smell that came from dead animals was in Joan's nostrils. McGilroy went to lean over the body. She could make out the hands like bones, clenched among the stalks of grass, and she feared that he would turn it over it with his foot. That was the way that her father had said he saw officers do with the dead bodies of the Luddites in those times he remembered so well.

Instead, McGilroy squatted by it—all among the stench—to turn it over.

And because he did that, she felt a surge of love for him then and there. It swept over her, for all her disgust at those flies about the body. It was just the way it had been with Marcie, years since when they'd been brats running about together, and she'd stopped a group of boys tormenting a frog, rushing in to snatch it away from them.

This wasn't a part of the urge from before, that had all to do with his bright eyes and thick wavy hair and spare body and fine walk. This was something deep and different. However, Joan had no leisure to think of that now, as they stared at the corpse.

The woman's body was like a skeleton, the sunken dead eyes staring out of a skull face, the gaping toothless mouth sagging open. Some flies buzzed out of it. Joan's stomach heaved. As she was still fighting back the urge to spew, he spoke.

"Starved to death," he said hoarsely. Indeed, the old woman's corpse was a dried husk of a thing, as light to lift as a dead branch of leaves.

Joan had seen dead bodies before—her eldest brother for one, when she was little—but those were decently laid out. She forced herself to go over to stand beside McGilroy.

His face had lost colour, but his look was masked. That was always so with these manly sorts of men: so often, they couldn't show what they felt, unless their passions ran away with them, as his just had with Joan.

His voice was flat as he said, "Starved to death, at the edge of our village. Unless summat's done, there'll be others soon enough."

11.

CHOICES

McGilroy spoke to Joan, after he and Jack Hooper, who was the first lad he came across, carried the old woman's body on a piece of board to the storeroom next to the makeshift chapel. Jack's dog frisked merrily behind. Ann Wilson, the blacksmith's wife, covered the dead face with a sheet too torn and thin to be further mended. The parish would do the burial, grudging the expense.

"I'll see thee tomorrow," he said, "when I come round to talk to thy father. And don't you go fretting about that dead woman—that won't help her now. Think on light things, like the beads I mean to get you the next time I'm in town."

McGilroy carried the spade for Joan up to her lane, and said goodbye with a snatched kiss. She went home, feeling as near to what fine ladies called 'vapourish' as she'd been in her life.

Her excitement and misgivings over McGilroy and what her family and Marcie would say over it all, were nearly numbed by the horror of finding that starved dead woman who must be buried as a vagabond.

Joan stepped through the front door that led straight into the main room of their poky cottage for which they paid so much rent, and did what heroines in novels did. She 'tried to compose herself' before her family saw her. Meanwhile her mother's voice sounded fretfully in her ears.

"Nat's been gone this half hour after our lass, and no doubt in mischief too. More looting might break out at any time."

"There was no looting," Mr Wright said calmly. "Haven't I told thee, wife, how I put paid to that, with a little aid from Tom and young McGilroy? Ah, here's the lass now. Joan, whatever dost thee mean by gallivanting about outside like this? Thy mother has been fretting this half hour, and sent thy brother after thee."

Joan set down the sack of vegetables on the floor, with the bread on top. Her guilty conscience made her feel as she had as a child, when she was sure that her mother could see straight into her head to her misdeeds.

"I found a dead woman. Jack Hooper and—and some others carried the body to yon chapel."

Hannah squealed. Ben nodded as if it was only to be expected. He had a theory that Deputy Constable Nadin went round murdering people whenever the whim came on him. He knew at once that this was one of that man's victims.

"Hannah, run and get thy sister a cup of the last of that elderberry wine," said Mr. Wright, while Joan's mother hurried to take her in her arms. "That's what comes of lingering out at all hours. I hope thou did not breathe in the air about it or lay hands on it? It was touching Grandmother Wilson's rotting feet that did for yon cobbler."

"No, there isn't much sense in doctoring the dead, Mother. She must have starved to death. Only the lads touched her." Now Joan felt with a quick stab of alarm that there might be something in her mother's ideas, and McGilroy would be struck down. Well, Jack Hooper and the others too, but above all, McGilroy.

Joan's legs felt weak, and she was glad to sit down. As she sipped her wine, it was all she could do not to gabble before her younger siblings about the dead body and how the flies had risen from its mouth.

Tom and Nat came in together, having run into Jack Hooper, who told them of the corpse, and how they'd chosen Mr. Ridley as a quiet, orderly man who hadn't been involved in the trouble earlier to go and see the squire's steward about the burial.

Joan was allowed to sit and sip wine like a grand lady while her mother and sister boiled some of the potatoes on the fire.

For all the dead woman and the coming trouble, the memory of McGilroy's hot words made Joan shiver, while a flush rose to her cheeks. That made Mrs. Wright so anxious that she nearly forgot to scold her about acting the hussy in standing up and talking out to the neighbours as if she thought she was a man. Marcie Royce may have done the same, but there was nothing better to be expected of such a spoilt hoyden as that.

At last, Joan lay in the close, hot darkness with her mother with her long grey plaits on one side and Hannah with her grass sweet breath on the other. Gloating over McGilroy some more set her off sighing, and then Hannah cried out in alarm that now Joan was wriggling her toes besides.

Mother and sister both felt her forehead, sure she had a fever setting in. They begged her to light the rush candle and take some of her own herbs. But Joan knew well how useless they would be against this particular sickness.

...

Joan crept out early into the morning sunshine to fetch the water. She tried to look casual as Marcie came up to the pump with one of her many admirers tagging along behind, eager to carry the pail back from the pump for her.

Joan decided to be cowardly and put off telling Marcie about Seán McGilroy until he had spoken to her father. She told herself that after all, he did change his mind about paying serious court to her before. She would look silly if she spoke out, only for him to do it again.

At the same time, though, she knew how that was only an excuse to put off admitting to Marcie how she had given in to her weakness for McGilroy. She had no real fear that he would really change his mind after the way he looked at her last evening.

It seemed Joan wasn't much of an actress. Marcie raised her sweeping eyebrows at her. "What's to do, Joan? You've got on your Keeping a Secret Face."

As Joan muttered something, Nancy Ridley came up to tell them all about how the squire's steward had acted when her father saw him about the beggar woman. She called the woman that, and so did everyone. Joan didn't see how they could tell that she was a beggar, when she didn't look so different from the worst off in this village. Perhaps they had to believe that she was one, to keep from thinking how the same thing could happen to them.

Nancy told Joan how the squire's steward had seen her father after so long a wait he feared he had been forgotten. The steward already knew of the trouble earlier.

On Mr. Ridley's coming into his office, he began at once: 'What? More trouble? That's it. I'm sending word for Joseph Nadin: he and the Devil can take the lot of ye.'

On hearing it was a dead body Mr. Ridley came to see him about, and not people driven to riot to keep the soul in live ones, he was scarcely less angry.

"One of those bloody vagabonds, I'll be bound." He'd been indignant. "Why couldn't the wretch die over the boundary? More expense for the parish. Well, get that carpenter to make up a pauper's coffin, cheap as you like, thin pinewood, for it doesn't have to hold together. We don't want to go having burials in sacks as they do in some places. We'll have the bell tolled, too. That's only right, even for a vagrant. We'll cart the body for burial as soon as may be."

"I'll walk behind the coffin," said Joan as she worked the pump.

"It annoys me that we females aren't allowed in the burial ground until we're dead," said Marcie, "But I will too."

Joan hurried back to the cottage to put the water on to boil, wondering when McGilroy would turn up.

He came as they were finishing their meagre breakfast of oatmeal.

"Well, my lad," said Mr Wright, as Hannah let McGilroy in. He looked even more vigorous, swarthy and handsome than Joan remembered as he sneaked her a wink.

"Master, there's a private matter I'd like to talk over with you," he said after polite greetings. Tom couldn't hide his smile, while Joan blushed like a coy maiden. That wouldn't do for a wench who meant to go out and deal with the world on its own terms. Hannah giggled while the boys looked puzzled.

Mrs. Wright was dumbstruck as Mr Wright, still clutching his chipped dish of tea, went outside with McGilroy. She found words soon enough.

"Surely, my wench, thou cannot have let that good-for-nothing fellow come about thee, with such a name as he has, after all thy great show of keeping aloof from lads?"

Joan couldn't stop herself going a shade redder. The boys hooted their dismay. Seán McGilroy was their hero before as a likely fellow who'd been at Waterloo, and marched smartly, and had a name for being handy with his fists, and could drain a pot of beer without pause. Still, if he was soft in the head enough to go dangling after their Joan, then he must be wanting good sense after all.

Mrs. Wright sent them to the workroom, still groaning and rolling their eyes, and set Hannah to clearing the table. Only then did she turn a look of vinegar on Joan. "So, now we know what ailed thee last night. When I thought thee digging for taters, thou was grubbing up ne'er do well rovers. Is that what thou was about, and that talk of dead bodies in the woods was by-the-by?"

"The dead woman wasn't in the woods. She was by the allotments," Joan said absurdly, as if that made any difference.

Tom said, "Mother, Seán McGilroy's a good enough lad. He been wild enough, but I think he's set to leave his roving ways behind and settle with our Joan."

"Isn't that rascal meant to be plighted to one, or as like as not all of yon Ridley girls?"

"You know you never take heed of gossip, Mother," Joan urged straight faced, "That was when McGilroy was about twelve."

"It's true I'm never one for giving an ear to tattle," Mrs. Wright said solemnly, "But I heard thee say thyself that if only one bit of that talk about that lad is true, then it's bad enough. He's got a way with him, I see, and been about filling thy head with all sorts of empty promises, my wench, to make thee join t'other foolish lasses he's talked into believing in him before thee. If thou'rt not wholly daft, thou wilt think twice about yon wild fellow."

Mrs. Wright scolded on—with Hannah all ears across the room. In a few minutes, Mr. Wright was back, smiling broadly. "Young McGilroy's just been asking me if he can come courting our Joan. There's for you, Missus!"

On his noting that his wife looked as if she'd just taken a swig of vinegar, he went on, "Well, what with her being so young, I said he must bide his time before rushing her into anything. But he's a likely man, and full of spirit, and I'm thinking our lass likes him well enough, and it's for her to say yea or nay at last." He smiled at Joan.

Before she could answer, Mrs. Wright spoke. ""You are the master of this house, and if you see fit to allow a roving lad we scarcely know to pay court to our daughter, then it is not my place to dispute, and if you take no heed of that fellow's bad name you must have good enough reasons for it."

Mr. Wright shifted uncomfortably. "Any lad of spirit has to sow his wild oats, and that's a fact."

"Well, he's working for his uncle, and they're doing poorly enough, so he'll be in no position to support a wife in a long while." Mrs. Wright's tone was one of grim satisfaction. Joan kept silent about her secret plans to support herself.

No doubt McGilroy had enlisted Tom's support, as he cut in, "He's got some money put by, for all his roving ways, and is due to come into his uncle's farm—that one in Northampton who has no sons."

"He did speak of that. What does thou say, my lass?" asked Mr. Wright.

"I say I'll see." Joan couldn't help smiling her joy. Mrs. Wright shook her head. "They say he went in for prize fighting, and shame that didn't spoil his pretty face, and then thou might not be so keen to have him come about thee. At your age, all that lasses see is a lad's fine looks and bold ways."

"Truly, Mother, it's not the only thing I think counts in a lad." Joan managed to get a word in. "There's if he wants to act rightly by his own people. T'other day, Timothy Yorke sidled up to me and I sent him on his way. Even if I had been looking for a suitor and could like him as a man, I don't like his way of keeping in with those who would keep us down."

Mr. Wright nodded. "Thou speaks true, Joan, of these seemingly upright types like the Yorkes who think themselves above us. T'Yorke lad hinted he wanted to court thee, but never spoke outright. I like a man who comes straight to the point, like yon McGilroy. Thou'rt too hard on him, wife. He's only twenty-one and has time enough to turn steady and settle down."

Mrs Wright muttered her disagreement. Still, Joan knew she never went openly against her husband's decisions: only scolds ripe for a ducking tried to rule over their husbands. No doubt she hoped that a lot might happen in a year or so, such as that fickle Seán McGilroy going roving again.

Joan wondered what they would think if they knew how eager to go roving she was herself. It was only that suddenly, she wanted McGilroy to be part of her adventures.

• • •

Joan was allowed out to see McGilroy for an hour by way of a treat, there being little enough work to do. She could gather some herbs while she was about it. Her mother said sourly, "And I know I can count upon you, my wench, to allow no forwardness from yon rascal."

Joan threw up her nose. "Indeed I will not." That was an odd way round to speak, and she saw it came from McGilroy, and no doubt his part Irish background. This was alarming; if she was starting to talk like him already, how else was he changing her?

But when she saw him patrolling in the lane outside, looking nervous as she never thought he could—even in battle—her glowing insides melted.

"Thy father talked round thy mother?"

She was tempted to tease, but she didn't. "Oh, aye. She makes a song and dance of being a docile wife, and so had to go along with his word, though she scolded."

He threw his arms about her and kissed her, out there in the lane. Luckily, everyone was at work, save for poor old Mr. Scott sitting on the makeshift bench warming up like a lizard in the sun, and he couldn't see two yards from his nose.

"Let's take a walk," Joan, struggled halfway out of his hold. "I'm allowed this hour off, but half of it I'll spend telling Marcie."

He pulled a face. "Another admirer of mine, that lass. Thou sees how all these women love me. But if thou can try a little, ne'er mind. I'll win thy mother over by making a long upper lip like yon Yorke and we'll win Marcie round through her liking for Tom. She'll come to see the best way for the pair of ye to go on adventures is with two guards."

"That sounds more like an arrest than an adventure," said Joan. "Thou said that would be 'above board' but our parents would never stand for it."

He gave her an assessing look. "It could be by way of a honeymoon."

Joan ignored her face going hot. "I'm none too sure about that; it's too far off in the future. We must see how things turn out. But I'll not let Marcie down."

"Enough on that Marcie, troublesome wench as she is."

"Spoken by one who never causes trouble," retorted Joan.

McGilroy squeezed her waist and they walked to to where the rindle[37] made a sluggish trickle through the high banks, with him talking softly to her all the way. He talked a bit about his uncle's farm, too, in the lush country of Northamptonshire.

Then they kissed. Once again Joan's insides did strange things. Again, she saw too well how girls could let one thing lead to another and end up with child out of wedlock. She pulled away, and then they saw Daffy Danny ambling towards them.

Maybe he had been sent out to gather plants. He was made to turn the old fashioned wheel in his parents' workshop, but he often got fed up and shouted out, and was put outside for a run, much like a big dog.

McGilroy greeted him in that amiable way he had. "Danny my lad, you can be the first to hear of our being troth plighted."

Danny nodded solemnly and thought a minute. "You need a sixpenny bit to cut in half, and there's none too many of those to be had these days."

"I've got one here I'll cut in half to thread with a ribbon to go about thy pretty neck, Joan," McGilroy drew one from his pocket. "For some reason, I have a blue ribbon that will go exactly with thy eyes. A funny thing, my buying it like that." He winked.

"That's moving too fast for me," Joan objected. "After that promise to Father thou'd court me slow."

"And so I will, when thee wears it to keep off other lads."

---

[37] Rindle: Lancashire dialect for stream.

Danny looked thoughtful. "A while back, sometimes we had music and dancing with a troth plighting," he said. "We don't have such fun anymore. Father says it is down to hard times."

McGilroy slapped his thigh. "By God, we will as soon as that poor woman is buried. We'll cut short the drilling, and kick up our heels instead, eh, Joan? I mind thee as a fine dancer from when I danced with thee, that harvest home years since."

Joan remembered he was the liveliest dancer about—naturally. "Mother makes me wear my raggedy dress for drilling," she fretted. Still, her eyes glowed.

"You'll still be as lovely as Cinderella in it," he picked up a lock of her hair and let it flow through his fingers.

• • •

Marcie said, "I see." People always said that when they didn't, or didn't want to.

For all Marcie's eyes like hot pitch, her breath coming fast as she stood, arms akimbo, Joan trusted that she could be brought round in time.

First, though, Marcie must wear out some of her anger with berating Joan for a weakling who didn't know her own mind. Joan saw this. St, Marcie's scornful look and tone still made her flinch.

"We've always told each other the truth, and I won't spare you, Joan Wright. You've sneaked out of your word to me through vanity and feebleness. I thought so much better of you. This is the same fickle fellow you spoke so strong against before, only now somehow it's different, because you're the one he favours for now. Do you truly believe he'll keep true to you? What of all that fine talk of caring for t'other wenches he's trifled with?"

"I do care about them." Joan got a word in. Was Marcie right? Was she flattering herself that McGilroy had changed now he knew what it really was to fall in love? Yet, somehow she knew that his feelings for her had changed him. Yet she had no proof she could pull out of her pocket.

"I don't believe he knew before what a hurt he'd done to some of yon lasses," she muttered.

Marcie snorted. Joan had done some of that to McGilroy of late, and now she saw how annoying it was. Marcie went on, not in a rush, but in what one of those novels about grand folks would call 'in measured tones', as if she'd thought it all out beforehand.

"That he is the no good fellow he is makes it worse, when you know well I held out against your Tom, worth three of him, who I could like well. But the same is true of any man. You know that we agreed that we must keep aloof from all courting until we had worked out our escape plan and were far along with it. Yet all that McGilroy had to do is give you some soft talk and you lie down and roll over before we've even begun."

Joan flinched as Marcie held her eyes mercilessly. "I saw you were weakening, and gave you the chance to draw out, and you wouldn't have it. You said no, you'd hold firm against him."

Joan mumbled, "What thou says is true, save McGilroy's worth more than thee makes out. I feel worse about it that thee can ken, and am mightily sorry for it. But thou spoke now of liking our Tom. It can't have been easy, giving him the cold shoulder. Thou hast shown the strength I haven't. But heed, Marcie: it is so hazardous for females trying to make their way in the world—for those without any money behind them, anyway. That poor dead woman lying in yon chapel made me think of that."

Joan blundered on under Marcie's scornful gaze, the words coming out all wrong. "It's safer with a man looking out for ye a bit—I don't mean, coming the lord and master over ye, but being by your side. Thou and I have got two likely ones to the fore, and…"

Her words trailed off under Marcie's look. Joan hadn't thought that it would be possible for her to look more disgusted; now she did.

"Seán McGilroy told you this. There can be no adventure for any female who is with any man, only cooking and cleaning and having babies."

Joan thought that the latter bit wasn't quite true, anyway. They both knew from crude talk from the more forward women that there was a way of putting off making babies which relied on the man's careful timing. Still, now was not the time to point that out.

"Maybe there might be a way of living differently, what with the healing taking up much of our time. Maybe the men could shift for themselves a bit, as those two did as soldiers."

Marcie snorted again. "Is that what McGilroy told you? The tups[38] will live side by side in mating season, before men will change their ways when a female's about, thou sorry thing, thee."

There was no friendliness in Marcie's using the familiar form of address, as that 'thou sorry thing, thee' was what she said to any fool who particularly riled her—tedious elders who had to be treated with respect excepted.

"Marcie, I am so sorry about going back on my word, but -"

"I'm sure you are." Marcie took herself off at speed, leaving Joan staring after her. There was no point in going after her and trying to reason with her. Joan's heart yearned as she gazed after her beloved friend, stalking away from her with that light-footed gait.

Marcie had always had the best shape in the village. Even the famine of late hadn't made her look scrawny, as Joan thought it was starting to do for herself. Somehow, she seemed unaware of her beauty.

She never went in for fluttering her lashes, and pouting and strutting about and wriggling her hips, like Sally and Kitty Ridley, and others in the village who couldn't hold a candle to her. She walked as if she had a right to a place in the world. She talked straight to everyone, too, though she had a pair of slanting black eyes that could slay a man, and a mane of jetty hair down to her waist.

For years, they had been nearly as close as twins. They were always so close, and so cold to the lads, that some girls had tattled that they might prefer each other to any lad, even though none of the men would believe it.

And Joan had let her down over that rascal with the flashing smile, wicked blue eyes, and black ringlets. Marcie's equal in looks and charm he might be; but her equal in honour, never: not towards lasses, anyway.

The thing about Seán McGilroy was he had a way with him when he talked to you that made you feel as if it was you and him against

---

[38] Rams used for mating.

the world. That was so with the men, when he was giving his speeches. Those mightn't grip the heart so much, without his being the way he was, and giving off that warmth. And Joan knew too well from herself how it was with the lasses.

Though she bit her trembling lip, the tears would come anyway. She was getting to be like one of the heroines in Nancy's daft novels, who were always weeping when they weren't fainting away into the hero's arms—which were always ready.

"She'll come round," she sniffed.

But there was another thing that Joan knew. She saw that marching along with the men had taught her something. Now, she saw that escape from this want and struggle for just herself and her friend wasn't enough.

Nor—even if Marcie would agree to it—was escape for Joan and Marcie along with Tom and McGilroy enough now, no matter how many adventures they had on the way.

She wanted to help everyone to escape from this daily misery.

They had all the powers-that-be against them. The fight for a decent life for them all was very likely hopeless, but they had to do it anyway, or agree with those rich folk that all they deserved was to starve quietly.

Whatever happened to Joan now, this struggle had become part of her. She couldn't give it up. She saw the belief behind her father's strutting and ranting, because she shared it too. 'Committed':- that was the grand word for it. She and McGilroy and Tom and Marcie—they were all committed to this fight for their people.

12.

Closer

Nobody but Joan and Seán seemed happy about their getting troth plighted - as now they were - Seán having slipped over Joan's head the beautiful blue ribbon he'd bought, threaded through her half of the sixpence he'd divided between them.

Joan's mother said several times a day, "That feckless young McGilroy has got round my master with his smooth talk and his ready smile. It's not for me to question thy father's wisdom. Still, many things my change in above a year."

She seemed to think that was a gentle hint.

Mr. Wright was out a lot looking for the work which was not to be had, along with Tom. Hannah agreed with what their mother said as usual, and Nat and Ben made jeering noises whenever talk of Joan's troth plighting to McGilroy came up.

All that was as nothing to losing Marcie as a friend. Joan had never thought Marcie could be so wrathful with her. Still, nobody had ever let her down in the way Joan had. Joan saw that.

Joan acted the coward in trying to avoid the Ridley sisters at the pump the next morning by going out earlier. Naturally, she ran into Sally and Nancy anyway. They stared, and their looks were not friendly. Joan greeted them as usual.

Sally Ridley giggled. "Well, fancy a nice[39] prim lass like Joan Wright taking up with our Seán, roving rascal as he is! Thou'rt heading for a come down, I fear."

---

[39] 'Nice' used to mean fussy, prim or precise.

Joan said as calmly as she could, "I'm not setting myself up. But it doesn't seem right to talk lightly, with that poor dead woman lying starved to death in yon chapel."

The carpenter and his son were still knocking up a hasty coffin for the body, a cheap rushed job that wasn't expected to hold together. Still, that was better than some parishes, where they just threw the bodies of paupers naked into the ground.

Sally jeered, "Don't be such a preacher. It won't touch yon auld tramp woman now what we says."

"Maybe she was a respectable body, who lost her home," said Nancy.

Sally tossed her head. "That ribbon about your neck is t'same as McGilroy offered to me first, and with a token and all, but I told him he couldn't talk me round. But what does your keeper Marcie make of it?"

"You must ask Marcie about that. I wouldn't speak for her."

Sally giggled knowingly, while Nancy Ridley began to talk of 'Lotharios'. Joan wasn't sure what they might be. She was pretty sure that Sally didn't either, but she tittered anyway.

It came to Joan again, as it had on and off since finding the body, how her own adventures—if ever she had them—might end that way if things went wrong. McGilroy got all het up about the thought of men attacking her, and how he wanted to protect her from them. Maybe starving was near as likely. It had shaken her a bit, seeing the reality of the end of that poor woman's adventures in this world.

Yet, Joan still wanted those adventures; she was fast getting used to the idea of McGilroy being part of them. Those dreams of escape together she and Marcie used to talk over would be near impossible for lasses, however much they learnt about doctoring. They could only have done it by pretending to be lads, and even then they might not be safe.

Besides, their parents would forbid it outright. The only way to do it would be through running away together to be forever spoken of as being lovers, like those two women from the next village whom Kitty Ridley had seen kissing by a gooseberry bush, and said that if they hoped to come by a baby that way, they'd be waiting a bloody long time.

Joan thought it was wrong to laugh about how you were made, though she and Marcie weren't made that way, that was the problem. If only Marcie could be made to think of Tom, then they might be able to work something out together. Yet Marcie would have none of it. There was no talking to her.

Joan trailed after her—with people staring—trying to make up.

"Marcie, do hear me. I want to say about Tom -"

Marcie cut her off with, "Well, he's worth three of yon flashy McGilroy, any road, but that's not saying much of him." She stalked off, leaving Joan staring helplessly after her.

Tears stung behind Joan's eyelids, blurring her vision. Certainly, without Marcie's friendship, she felt as if she had lost the use of an eye or an ear.

Widow Hobson stood near, shaking her head. "'Tis t'way of the world. Two wenches is great friends, till a lad comes between them, and t'other casts off her friend at last."

It was amazing the way the old dame knew what was happening in the village almost the minute it happened. She'd known of the near riot by the Yorkes', and scolded all who didn't manage to avoid her about that. Joan had come in for her share before she could sneak away.

"I'd never cast off Marcie," snapped Joan, too fired up at to add 'Mistress'.

Widow Hobson took no notice of that. She shook her stick at Joan. "And no allowing yon rascal to leave you with a bastard, neither. None of that fornicating."

She didn't think to lower her voice. Neddy Pritchard, walking by, overheard and gave a nasty laugh. Widow Hobson saw and pointed her stick at him in turn. "Yon Pritchard was near enough born nameless, himself. His mother was brought to bed of him the day after her marriage."

Neddy Pritchard marched off, as stiff as if someone had shoved a poker up his behind.

Despite it all, this new feeling with Seán McGilroy added a glow to everything for Joan, even those sour faces at the water pump of a morning.

Yet, she didn't entirely trust McGilroy. She still felt bad about those other wenches he had trifled with. She even felt uneasy about the Ridley girls, and Sally Ridley in particular, for all that they were a lot of flirts. They seemed so put out about his choosing Joan, that although McGilroy swore that he had only treated them all as cousins he'd had a laugh and a joke with, Joan thought there might well be more to it than that—to their minds, if not to his.

Timothy Yorke behaved as if Joan had turned invisible, like that man in the story in the chap book that Ben and Nat loved so much. Sometimes, though, as in the field that time, she semsed an angry glare on her back, particularly when she was with McGilroy, and looking round, she'd see Timothy turning away.

Joan thought that now he could start paying court to some lass who was better suited to him, just as she, being a bit wild, was better suited to an unruly fellow. He didn't seem to see it that way.

Joan hoped that he hadn't really cared for her the way she could see that Tom did for Marcie. With such a cold fellow, though, she found it hard to believe.

Mrs. Yorke was as bitter against Joan's family, Marcie, Seán and the Royces as if she thought they'd done her a bad turn that day, not saved her business. She was more angry with them than she was with Jimmy Thribble or any of those who had been set to raid her shop. Joan wondered if she knew about her son's former interest in her. It did make it embarrassing buying bread. Mostly, Joan wriggled out of the chore, and got Ben or Nat or Hannah to go.

With all this, she still couldn't stop herself from going about singing. Their diet might be as poor as ever, but somehow she'd got a new spring in her toes. The most exciting man she had ever met was her true lover, and acted as if he mistook her for one of the wonders of the world.

• • •

They buried the pauper woman.

Before the burial, Tom came up to Joan, muttering and shuffling his feet, asking her to put in a word for him with Marcie, as he couldn't get her out of his mind. She'd said she would try, but what with Marcie being so riled at her over McGilroy, she wouldn't listen.

Tom said, "Go on, she'll come round; you've always been thick as thieves."

Joan and Hannah went to follow the coffin as McGilroy pushed it on a cart to the graveyard. Marcie did too, though still not speaking to Joan. Tom came with them, snatching secret looks at Marcie when he thought no-one was looking.

At this rate, Joan began to fear that he would pine away from what Nancy's books called 'unrequited love'.

Mr. Wright would have come, if he and Mr. Royce weren't off on another of those eager trips to Manchester to talk to some new fellow, full of promises. As it was, Daffy Danny was the only other mourner, playing a mournful tune on his pipe. Mr Royce said it wasn't seemly; Marcie, as usual, came back with a fast retort: "Nor was the poor body's end."

Everyone else had something to do, even if it wasn't work. Joan thought it was because they couldn't let themselves feel for this poor woman. She was an ugly reminder of how they might end up themselves, if things didn't get better.

Somebody tolled the bell, which was something, and the curate muttered a quick prayer over the mass grave set aside for paupers. In this way the unknown woman went to her final resting place.

It made Joan feel solemn, suddenly a lot older. She and Marcie didn't go into the graveyard. The Rector was one of those who wouldn't have 'Daughters of Eve' at a burial. So, for all his curate's shocking views on women, Joan and Marcie stood outside.

Joan hopes that Marcie might relent were dashed. She wouldn't look properly at her, and Joan's heart quailed.

Standing there together, watching the little group about the shallow grave, and the curate's voice intoning the burial prayer, Joan knew that trying to champion Tom would be a waste of time with Marcie in this mood, and it didn't seem right anyway. She was thankful to have to put it off.

This was hard on poor Tom, but there was nothing Joan could do about it. Still, she knew what love was herself now, and why it drove people to act foolishly: that was the problem.

Courtesy of the steward, the squire had laid on bread and cheese and ale in the local tavern for those who had helped at the funeral.

"You must go, lass, but I won't take anything from that Harrison." Seán McGilroy scowled.

Joan's mouth watered at the thought of the bread and cheese and ale, but she walked off with him, sending Hannah along with Daffy Danny to get a good meal. Neither Tom nor Marcie went either. She heard later that Ned Pritchard and some others dropped in and ate up the greater part of it.

•••

Joan and McGilroy took the chance to walk off together. Joan felt solemn at first, still thinking of that poor woman's end, and he was unusually quiet too. But happy at this rare chance of being alone with him as she was, her spirits soon roused even as his did.

They went looking for plants, both to pad out the dinner, and for her potions. He teased her about that. "I think you're a witch, and that's how you've made me fall for you so hard. You've done some magic on me, the same as I heard that Sam Bamford[40] tell he saw done with a special herb."

They sat by the stream, slowed to a muddy trickle with the hot summer. McGilroy's arm was about her, where it felt as if it belonged, and always had.

She tickled his nose with a blade of grass. "Thou'st found me out about what I want with herbs. I tiptoed up to thee, fast asleep in the sun some weeks since, and landed a kiss on thy face, like so, and stuffed the weeds down t'back of thy neck, like so." She walked her fingers down the back of his neck, so that laughing, he caught her hands. "I had my eye on thee from the start. 'Twas the only way to fix thy roving one."

He tickled her waist until all she could do was laugh. "No more roving for me," he sounded wholly sure of himself. "There's only one place I want to be, and that's where my lass is." They kissed.

---

[40] Samuel Bamford relates this anecdote in 'Passages in the Life of a Radical' 1840-44.

"Courting you slow isn't going to be easy," he said, when they came apart to draw breath.

"It's the only way Mother will stand for it at all." said Joan "She always says she never heeds a word of gossip, and yet she's taken in every tale going about on that rascal Seán McGilroy."

He pulled a face that set her laughing. "Never was a fellow so miscalled as me, save maybe Tom Paine[41] for his writings.

"And Boney," laughed Joan. "I mind thee'd sooner have him in charge than King George."

"I'd sooner have an annual parliament in charge, with our own member who's there to get things done for the working man."

"Will we get that, just by having so many going all orderly to yon Manchester meeting?"

He shook his head impatiently. "We're not that daft. It's a first step. There's many of us, few of them, yet they say the greater part of t'people must endure hard times, like cattle out in t'fields in winter. Sam Bamford and a deal of the leaders are too timid for my liking, with too much respect for the law as it is, which is made by rich men, any road.

"But while we set about changing it, we've got to judge the right time to go forward and the right time to use roundabout tactics. That young John Bagguley had some fine ideas, but he went after it too hasty. This isn't France. First, we must show 'em how many wants change, and get as many of the better off who want it too on our side. Then we must push a bit more, and still more, drawing in as much of the press as we can. And they won't give in easy, those lords in the government, but the time will come when we will win the vote, and can stand as a member of parliament and all, and then we'll have members in yon House of Commons who will get things done for the working man."

Joan shook her head. "Seems to me half of us will have starved by then." Harking to him, her mother's chant, 'Things will get better' rang hollow.

---

[41] Tom Paine was forced into exile to avoid arrest for publishing his 1791 radical classic ' The Rights of Man'.

"We'll get there," he sounded as sure of himself as he had over leaving behind his roving ways. "And thou won't starve, my pretty; not while I can snare a rabbit." He smiled on her, those deep blue eyes as warm looking as the summer sky.

And when he looked on her like that, as if she was the most wonderful thing about, she knew that Marcie and all the others were wrong about how he felt for her. No doubt he was mistaken in seeing her as so special; still, it wasn't just words with him.

Joan didn't say out loud—for the bushes might have ears - *So long as thou can snare a rabbit in yon squire's grounds.*

Her mother had taken that last one that Joan's father handed over and made it into a stew without a word, but her look spoke her disapproval.

She was nervous all the time the rabbit stew cooked and sent out a fine scent. She was worried that people nearby would talk. Still, as their next door neighbours were the Thribbles, with Jimmy, like his friend Jack Hooper in on any poaching expedition, Joan knew they at least would not. To ease her mind, Mr Wright took some fire and burnt some rubbish outside.

Joan's mother was as bad as Sam Bamford for upholding the law, just or not. But the sight of Hannah and Nat and Ben's hungry faces won her over. Joan, being full grown, could handle going hungry near as well as an adult.

"I've heard tell, this Orator Hunt says that women should have the vote too," Joan said now.

"You're all for that, I know." He grinned. "Both thou and Marcie— and she'll talk to thee again, lass, never fret—have done yourselves proud in getting so many women in it. You've learnt to drill as well as any of the men, Amazons as you are. The same is true of groups of women from all the places all about, who've been speaking out at meetings, too."

Joan sighed: she'd sometimes wanted to do as much herself, and never dared.

He went on, still gazing down at the sluggish stream beside them, "There's word that this great meeting coming up will be the biggest ever, with people from all the villages all over. We mun show our will by marching orderly. Yet, we'll make it sport and all, with the music playing, and be all decked out in the best we have, with t' lasses and women coming along too in their best dresses. Where they go, t'babbies in arms and bairns go with them. It will be a grand procession and gathering, and most look forward to it as a holiday outing."

Yet, he fell to frowning as he stared down at the trickle of water, all that was left of that once fast flow.

Joan said, "Are you thinking there'll be trouble, and t' little ones best away?"

He looked up. "I am, and maybe with no good reason. But I'd as lief none of the women or the bairns were coming, and I wish you weren't an' all, Joan."

As she fired up, he took her chin between his lean, strong finger and thumb. "Don't get in one of thy temper fits—I know I'll never stop thee. Well, you and my girl cousins will be in my group, and Marcie in Tom's. I want to take no chances with you. In these big crowds, sometimes folk get squashed when there's no harm meant. I must make sure I have you right behind me, when we come up to St Peter's Field."

Joan laughed at him. "I'll look after yo', never fear." She wasn't troubled herself. In a great crowd, a bit of trouble always broke out, if only between lads who said others had shoved them. As like as not, that would be away in the other side of the crowd, and she felt safe with him.

Then she told herself off for being a feeble wench in only thinking such a thing. There was all this weakness in her that she'd not unearthed before meeting him. She'd scorned it in lasses hanging on lads' arms, and wanting to be looked after like a bird opening its beak for its mate to feed it like a fledgling.

He was going on, "I reckon I get these feelings from my mother. Did I never tell thee, my lass, how my mother often had feelings about things that were never wrong?"

Joan put up her own hand to wind one of his ringlets round a finger. Such a fine looking fellow as he was; she'd always been forced to give him that, though refusing to say any other good of him.

"Do you ever go home?"

She was thinking on how little she knew of this man to whom she'd agreed to be troth plighted. He'd told her this and that about his wanderings. He'd said little enough of his family, though she knew he'd spent a lot of time staying with his childless uncle in Northamptonshire, who wanted to make over his farm to him in due time.

"Only for a day or so, once a year. They are better off without me. From the age of ten, I took to spending most of my time at my Uncle's. I kept out of the way of my step-father's fists that way. When first I left home, if ever I was in pocket, I'd send back some coins, but now that fellow is in steady work in saddling, and they do well enough. He doesn't beat my stepbrothers."

She thought on how she'd always seen him as being too full of himself, and in a way he was, but all the time he'd had this trouble with his stepfather. She looked her sympathy, but didn't speak it.

"Thou must have been younger than me when you went to t' French wars," she mused. "But thou never will talk of what theee id there. Was it so bad, how things were in Flanders? If so, I won't tease thee to tell of it. It's a funny thing, how lads will go and fight in any war they can. Our Nat wishes he had been old enough to."

"There's always a war somewhere in t'Empire," McGilroy said, "But I'd never give him tales of glory, as there is nowt fine about war, and that last one as we fought, wasn't even a just one."

Joan held her peace about how, for all he might say about their system being better, she didn't want to be ruled by the French. She saw that at last he was about to talk of his times in the late war with Boney.

He let go of her, and she stopped fondling his hair. He put his hands on his knees, his eyes on the rindle again, yet looking into the past, and when he spoke, it wasn't as he did when he was making his speeches about political matters.

13.

Waterloo

McGilroy's tone was flat and without any feeling. He didn't look at Joan, as if he couldn't bear to tell his tale to an audience and was lost in his own memories.

"I went for a soldier when I turned fourteen. I thought it would suit me, fighting in the wars. I was all fired up to be a hero, and win medals, and come home and tell fine tales. I'd envied men who'd been in the Peninsula, and t'other places, talking on it in taverns. I know now that the sort of fellows who talk most in taverns more than likely did the least in the army—but as a lad, I couldn't wait to do the same myself.

"So, when I went to help out with the harvest at my uncle's—the one with the farm near Northampton—I planned to take off after we'd got most of the harvest in. I told them I would, and my uncle laughed and said I'd no sense, and to wait a year or so, while my aunt threw up her hands and said I would be killed. The next day, I left word with their youngest lad, walked to near Daventry, found the recruiting office, and signed up for seven years or t'end of the wars, whichever came first."

He shook his head. "I had a sweetheart back home. I thought I cared for her, but that was before I found out what that really is, from a tow-headed lass who'd only have been a wee bit of a thing then. When I told yon wench I would go for a soldier, she said in that case, we mun forget about each other. So I said, 'As you like,' and went off footloose and fancy free an' a bit riled she'd valued me so little. I did want to have a sweetheart at home to shed a tear or two if I got killed, before seeing about finding a replacement.

"I wrote to my mother and my aunt and uncle, sorry how worried they'd be. I'd seen more of my aunt than my mother in recent years, but my mother meant well by us all; it wasn't her fault that miserable fellow she married turned against me.

"At the drafting centre in Northampton, the recruiting sergeant didn't seem impressed with the looks of me. I had a lot of growing to do yet, and I was a skinny fellow at that age. I filled out later on. He said I might do for the third battalion. Maybe I'd grow into a likely soldier before we'd done for Boney. The other men in the room, grown and hefty they looked to me then, set up a great laugh.

"So, I grinned too, for all it wasn't the best start to my new life as a hero, looked up to by all. I told myself how maybe my army career would glow more brightly for that bad beginning.

"I were peacock enough to reckon I'd cut a fine figure in that red coat. Sure enough when I tried it on, it were a well enough suit of clothes, though thinner than I'd looked for. The drilling and so on was no problem to me, and after my stepfather, I didn't even mind the discipline.

"So, I was put in the third battalion of the Fourteenth Foot, stationed at Weedon. It was full of youngsters like me, and some likely enough militia fellows and some other unfit soldiers, all being got into shape to fight overseas. There were lads who'd seen action, great objects of envy and respect to us. There were a lot of country fellows straight from the plough, lubbards who gawped when given orders.

"We were known locally as 'the Bucks,' being supposedly from Buckinghamshire, but there were recruits from Ireland and Tower Hamlets and all over. Some wags called us 'the peasants'.

"Then one of the bumpkins, Blundell by name, deserted. Strayed away would be more my way of putting it. They caught him, drinking in a nearby inn, without sense enough even to change out of his uniform. There was a wanted poster pinned up above his head, with his description on it, only he couldn't read. The inn keeper could: he claimed his reward.

"They sentenced the poor fellow to a hundred lashes for desertion, and he screamed like a trapped hare with every cut of the cat.[42] None of us liked seeing it, save a stout fellow called Taylor, who sniggered under his breath, as if it was the biggest joke he'd seen.

"After thirty strokes, they asked Blundell if he had learnt his lesson, which was good of the officer. He bleated out that he had. Then we were all marched by to look at the poor fellow hanging there like a dead man from his manacles, with the skin flayed from his back.

"I saw that wasn't right, when the rustic only needed someone to poke him back in the right direction with a stick, as with strayed cattle. I'd heard that in Boney's army they didn't use the lash, and thought that was one good thing to be said for them, anyway. And that made me think, over time; if they had the right idea about that, maybe they had the right ideas about other things. But meanwhile, I were just a silly lad, wild for glory.

"They were good enough fellows about me, so I thought. It were only with a couple of them, Taylor, and his fat lackey Smith were the only ones I had trouble. I had to fight 'em both, one after t'other, to get 'em to leave taunting me for having girlish ringlets. I had done some of the new style pugilism, using skill rather than toe-to-toe slugging, and that stood me in good stead. After that, I was treated well enough by t'others.

"Meanwhile, we'd all heard about the brave fighting of the other two battalions, in the Peninsula at Corunna and other places, and many of us were wild to go and prove ourselves too. We heard we were to go to the north west coast of Italy, wherever that was—I was none too sure. So off we were marched to the south coast.

"I was fit to be tied[43] when I heard of Napoleon's stepping down as Emperor, and the peace. While the civilians were celebrating—and the veterans—I was mourning. The more, as in the months since I'd joined up, I'd shot up and filled out and started thinking of myself as a man.

---

[42] The cat o' nine tails was the whip used in the military for floggings.

[43] Furious with anger or disappointment.

"We were to embark to America, only then a peace treaty was made there too. Now we heard that our battalion was to be disbanded, before we'd seen any action at all. Then, days before we were to be broken up, we heard how Boney was free. We were at war again, and our battalion was ordered to embark for Flanders. Me and my messmates did a jig.

"We groaned over a seasick passage across the channel to Ostend on the heaving March seas, and staggered ashore. It was a fine thing to be on dry land again. What came as a shock to me was, it didn't look so different from England. I felt let down on seeing this foreign land. It made sense it wouldn't be so different from England—after all, it's under twenty miles or so across the channel at t'nearest point—but this was country flat as a pancake, and poor from years o' war and looting. They were meant to be our allies, according to the officers, but many of them shrank from us. There'd been too much plunder.

"The daft thing was that I wanted to fight 'em at all, because I went along with much of what the French held out for, when I put my mind to it. More than all the stuff we get rammed down our throats from our leaders, any road. But t'other men never gave it a thought, and I wouldn't stand for the French invading and taking over as they did with those Normans thy father speaks on.

"A lot of t'others only used their heads for keeping their ears apart, and still believed all the talk about Frenchmen being hairy and half our size, like the Hartlepool spy[44] as I heard of, and ready to turn tail in a fight—never asking how they'd won so many battles, if that were true.

"Seeing how most people found our looking about twelve such a fine joke, it was fitting that our first loss was to a woman—some fellow I hardly knew was stabbed to death by his missus, one of the camp followers.

"When some old general named Mackenzie inspected us, he cried out: 'I never saw such a set of boys, both officers and men.' Our own officer, a war hero we all respected, named Lieutenant Colonel Tidy,

---

[44] According to folklore, the sole survivor from a French ship wrecked off the coast of Hartlepool, Co. Durham, a monkey dressed in military garb, was hanged as a spy at some time during the Napoleonic Wars.

said something, making out he'd hurt our feelings, I suppose. For then, the old fogey added, 'I called you boys, and so you are; but I should have added, I never saw so fine a set of boys, both officers and men.'

"For all that, he was going to send us to the garrison, but Tidy got us a reprieve from Wellington himself, and were marched off to join to join up in a battalion with the Welsh Fusiliers and the Light Infantry.

"We were stationed by the village called *Deux Acren*, and we spent a lot of time drilling and practising with the other battalions. We were put to work to help plant potatoes and weed the corn, and a lot of the lads looked far more at home doing that than drilling. With all my practice at farm work, I was at home at that too. It felt like the natural thing to be doing, if I'd stopped to think about it. But I was still all fired up about seeing action and rising in the ranks.

"We would go swimming in the river when it was hot enough and we had an hour to spare, and sometimes, a few of the local girls would come and laugh at us, in the buff as we were. Most of the lads, for all their big talk about having women, were as shy as could be.

"Not Taylor, though. He waved his tackle at them like a flag, and Smith joined in, giggling like they say hyenas do, and was all for chasing them and giving them what he said they were asking for, only we held him back.

"The officers had been living it up, dining with the local families, and dancing, and a race meeting too. There was a grand ball held by the Duchess of Richmond, I heard tell, only for some reason, I weren't invited. It was there that Wellington learnt that the French army had crossed into Flanders. In our quarters, we did a dance ourselves when we heard.

"We marched off in the midsummer heat, with a storm threatening, singing, *The Girl I Left Behind Me* and other songs. Then as we got closer to the fighting at *Quartre Bras,* we heard the thunder of the cannons, an' that sobered us up. We slept in the fields near some village called after a count's brain,[45] I heard tell, and then set off again. We were passed by wagons going the other way, full of wounded from the battle. A sobering sight they made for Johnny Raws like me.

---

[45] Braine-le-Compte

"Then the rain came down in torrents, and we marched in it to a ridge behind a chateau. *Goumuunt,* they said it was called. The rain stopped for a bit and we hoped for something to eat. But we lost touch with our supplies through some error—there's one mistake made after another in war, that's something they never tell you back home—and some had scraps of food, and some got nothing at all. I'd two biscuits given me by a wench in town, and I gave one to my Trusty Trojan[46] Wheeler and ate t'other.

"We all had ration of gin, and that had to serve many for dinner. Then that rain came on hard again. We got what sleep we could in the mud, hunched up with the coats over our heads. A filthy lot we were, by morning, plastered in mud and shivering from the night's drenching. We spent the first bit of that day cleaning our weapons, fingers numb. Then was breakfast, which for most of us was just a tot of rum. We were living like topers.

"Boney's army didn't turn up until about mid-morning, and from where we were in the ravine, we could hardly make out what was going on. There was thundering from cannon hissing from shells, shouts, and groups dashing about, with half of it hidden by smoke. Still, I'd heard that was typical. Mostly, the ordinary solder only knows what's going on in his bit of the battlefield and only then if he has the sense to work out what's to do there.

"Round the mid-afternoon, we had orders to advance. Now we were out in the smoke and hissing shells and gunfire. We were made to form a square. That drilling had some use, after all. The first two rows knelt down, bayonets fixed, to keep the French cavalry from charging, while behind, two rows of soldiers fired over their heads and reloaded as fast as they ever could, biting off the top of the cartridges, and spitting the ball into the barrel and hoping that bloody rain wouldn't stop the charges going off.

"After a bit of that, my throat was on fire. In the middle were the officers and the colours, and the wounded. We thrust out the dead in the front; no sense in protecting them any more. Their bodies could give us a bit of protection instead.

---

[46] Good friend.

"A bugler from another regiment ran up, saying he was safe, but a ball took off his head, spraying the nearest fellows with his brains. Then Ensign Fraser, a fellow laughed at for his girlish ways, said, in that right mincing voice of his, 'How extremely disgusting. Now I shall have to wash.'"

Joan stifled a smile, even though the horror of the battle had taken away all words. Seán McGilroy went on, speaking in all seriousness for once.

"I don't know if Fraser was having a grim joke, though even the dirtiest of us felt the need of a wash before that, caked in mud as we were. It drew wild laughs and relieved some of the fear. After that, one of the sergeants was hit in the chest, and his groans and cries made us all shudder. Then came orders to lie down.

"I heard that another ensign, a young fellow named Keppler, some earl's son, was holding Colonel Tidy's horse, patting its muzzle and sitting on a drum. A piece of shot went between his head and hand and killed the horse outright, leaving him unhurt. We were glad enough to get out of the way.

"We then got orders to move on to a place further forward, but safer, behind the brow of a hill. Our station was taken over by a battery of artillery, but a shell hit the ammunition wagon, tearing open a lot of horses. They galloped wildly about the field with their guts hanging out, falling down dead here and there.

"Then, as I looked on those poor creatures, I remembered how I'd asked for nothing better than to take part in a great battle, and here I was, and I couldn't see any glory, anywhere. Yet more than anything, I was sorry that I'd only just started with the girls. I'm willing to bet thou'll scowl darkly over this, Joan, but I swore than that if I came through this, then I'd take as much fun with t'wenches as they'd allow.

"We were now in a cornfield, all flattened and trampled into the mud. I could see crushed poppies and cornflowers all brown and torn. And do yo' know, at that time, I felt a greater pang about that ruin of that farmer's corn, than I did over shooting at t' nemy.

"Those French with their sabres on their great horses, all in metal armour, were a sight to strike terror in your hearts. *Cuirassiers* they were called. Now we saw them making ready to charge on us. It was just my luck to be in the front line of the square, and no easy thing to stand still. Still, we knew that if our squares broke up, then we would all be done for.

"They charged instead at the Brunswickers, who stood their ground, keeping them back with a volley of fire. Colonel Tidy shouted out to us to see how easy it was for infantry to scare cavalry off, so long as they stood firm, keeping to their lines. Then the *Cuirassiers* looked our way again, and we all stood as firm as we could—though I'll admit it—I had to tense myself rigid to keep from shaking.

"Perhaps, boys or not, standing there brandishing our bayonets as that looby Taylor had his male parts, we looked a bit more fearsome than we felt. Anyhow, they turned aside, and charged elsewhere.

"By now I was fired up with battle-lust as in a boxing bout, and ready to fight 'em all. Every time a sergeant shouted above the din for volunteers to go out on skirmishes, I was the first to offer. Now I'd say I must have been driven half out of my wits by the slaughter all about. My mate Wheeler seemed near as eager, but I think he didn't want to lose face before me, eager young fool that I was."

"A few of us the sergeant led took cover in the cornfield over the way, and when a group of Frenchies walked up to us unseeing, I shot one without a second thought. He went over without a sound. Likely enough, he wasn't the first man I'd done for, when I was firing in a fury into the smoke, though scarce able to see a thing.

"Then, when the sergeant shot one of t'others, as he went down, his eyes seemed to fix on mine, hidden by a fringe of standing corn though I was. He seemed to tell me with that look how he'd wanted to live. That brought me out of my battle frenzy. I hadn't killed him; but I felt far worse than I did about the one I had."

Now Joan dared to take his hand. She hadn't before, as it seemed what Marcie would call 'intrusive', but he seemed so caught up in his memories that he hardly noticed.

"After a long time, a brigade of troops in blue coats appeared at our right, cheering and singing. We formed up into a square again. We were about to fire on 'em, when an officer called out that those were Netherlands troops, and our allies.

"We were looking to withstand a cavalry charge from Boney's Imperial Guard. We saw 'em line up—masses of 'em in glinting armour, easy to see even in the battle haze—and the earth thundered again under the horses' hooves, with all of them yelling, *'Vive l'Empereur!'* and waving their sabres.

"But our side held firm in their squares, firing on them as they charged, knocking down great rows of these fearsome soldiers as if they were toys toppling over.

"We cheered to see that slaughter, again and again. This was Boney's last ditch attempt to break our lines, so the officers said. They must have had word from one of those messenger officers you see galloping all over the battlefield and having horses shot from under 'em.

"Our lot half hoped the Frenchies would come for us again, so battle maddened were we. Now I was caught up in the fighting again, and that clean chased away my odd sorrow over that Frenchman who'd looked my way as he went down dying. We wanted to show 'em all over what we were made of, but we were too far away from t'ridge.

"At last, they were beaten back into retreat. Now we joined in the general charge after Boney's retreating forces, yelling like barbarians. A horrible sight we must have made, plastered in mud, and I roared as loud as anyone, running past and leaping over all those dead and wounded and the torn horses still struggling to rise.

"Later, when the firing stopped, I wondered what that odd noise was; then I realised that was the quiet. That night, we lay like dead men in all our mud and dirt near the entrance to that chateau. The picture of the falling Frenchmen didn't come back to haunt me then, and Wheeler didn't groan in his sleep. That all came later.

When we woke up, it was light, and we remembered that we'd won the battle and we hadn't eaten since that biscuit the day before.

"The day dawned on such a sight as made me shut my eyes tight when we went down to look. It was a good way of keeping back the hunger pangs, that was for sure. All those dead—most of them should have been good for at least thirty more years living—all tangled up in mounds along with the wounded and dying. and dead horses, and blown off limbs and pieces of flesh, and pools of dried blood. There were thousands and thousands of 'em.. It was as if half the people in

Lancashire had been cut down. And already, the scavengers were busy among them, stealing anything worth taking, and pulling out their teeth.

"I stumbled over what I thought was a ball, only it was a head. I thought, though, that through the mud those bloody sunken eyes, seemed to look at me. It put me in mind of those two Frenchmen, t'day before. And then I could have sat down and wept like a babby, to see it all, and no way to undo any of it, but for saving a few by going out looking for wounded to bring back. I thought then, that nothing could be worth that: never our King and Country or their *Vive l'Empereur.*

"We found a few wounded to bring back, poor fellows. But before long, we were marched away, to a place called *Nivelles* to the sound of a jolly tune. One of the ensigns told me was a song from the other side called *Ca Ira* and that meant 'It'll be fine.'

"I was right glad to hear that.

"Afterwards, we marched on a fortress called *Cambrai,* and we in the Third Brigade earned more of a name for ourselves, storming the gate, in what was meant to be a feint, but it turned into a real battle. Everyone said that was glorious.

We marched in the victory parade along with the veterans, and for just a bit, I felt as I'd thought I would, when I joined up.

"That sergeant I went out skirmishing with had taken to me, not knowing what was going on in my head. He'd seen a couple of the things I had done, and was eager to get me promoted as soon as he could. Still as I was only sixteen, and some of t'others had more experience, I'd have to wait a bit.

"Meanwhile, we were at a place called St Denis over the winter. It was there that I remember a group of young wenches near the camp waving at us, and spotty-faced Taylor and his lackey, Smith- who always managed to stay fat, I never knew how, with the short rations we were on along of all that marching—sneaked out later. They came back with the same smiles on their faces as they had when that bumpkin who'd been flogged for deserting was howling with the skin off his back.

"So I chose the right time to pick a quarrel with Taylor, and gave him another thrashing, taking good care to knock out one of his front teeth. Fighting between ourselves was again' orders, as they wanted us to save our spite for the enemy, but those in charge turned a blind eye if you didn't do it right under their noses, and now it was peacetime. Anyhow, there was a dealt of talk about it, and t'sergeant had to put off talk of promotion for me for a bit.

"I still couldn't find any of the glory I'd come looking for in Flanders. Must have been in short supply, like our rum, I'm thinking, for I never found my share. And then we sailed back to Plymouth and our Waterloo medals.

"After that, they decided to disband our battalion, with those who'd signed up for life—and a fair amount of those bumpkins had done that—sent over to the second and first battalions, and chary fellows like me and Wheeler, who'd only signed up short term, discharged.

"I kept my promise to myself, about having fun with the wenches. First I went rioting about with Wheeler, but he soon found a lass he wanted to marry. As for me, I never could settle, and somehow, those dead eyes looking at me on the field at Waterloo was all bound up with that.

"But then, I met a lass with funny ideas called Joan."

Joan waited to see if he would say any more, but he had finished talking.

She put her hand on his shoulder, feeling the muscles tense, and drawing him back towards her, she massaged that taut back. She wondered what to say.

At last she said, "It must have been too terrible to talk on, with all those wounded piled up with the dead. Still, there's one thing; you will never have to see such horrors again."

"We can hope, lass," he said. For a moment, before they came back to her, his eyes were still distant.

14.

DANCING AND WENCHING

They were to have their dance after the marching practice this evening. As McGilroy planned it in honour of his and Joan's troth plighting, in a way, Joan was a guest of honour, as they said of those grand balls.

Joan was excited. They hadn't had any dancing in a long time. What with the poor diet these many months, nobody had the spirit and energy. She saw how much she'd missed those old dances on the green, with the lads gambolling and playing the fool. Besides, this was special. She'd be dancing with Seán McGilroy as her sweetheart.

Joan kept on her better dress instead of the raggedy Cinderella one she wore for marching. Her mother had forbidden her to wear the one she still had for best. Somehow, Mrs. Wright had kept onto a best set of clothes for them all when most of the fine furniture and ornaments had been sold for food. She stored them in that split, battered old chest that nobody had wanted.

Joan was humming as she combed out her pale hair using the broken comb they all shared. Her tresses waved, even when, as now, they fell down her back halfway to her waist. She wore the string of beads that McGilroy had given her, besides the ribbon with the divided coin.

Tom came up to comb his hair, and to take his best blue kerchief from the chest to knot about his neck.

With the lack of a decent mirror—that was one of the things that went first—Joan put on the finishing touches to the knot for him. "Thou must do thy best with Marcie this even, Tom lad," she urged him. "She won't heed me, being so riled at me for weakening about McGilroy. Then maybe if things get better, we can all go off bound enough for our elders not to forbid it, and have some adventures before we must settle down."

Tom showed no surprise at her words. Joan saw that Seán McGilroy had already told him about those schemes. "You and those adventures," he said.

Like McGilroy he smiled. Perhaps he was thinking of the late wars, too, that had made him set less store by adventures than herself and Marcie, who weren't allowed to have any.

Hannah sighed loudly at the foot of the stairs. Joan took pity on her and called down. "Mother, can't Hannah come along later, if she doesn't want to be part of the marching? One of t'lads can come back for her."

As Hannah shot Joan a grateful look, Mrs. Wright called back sourly, "If thou wishes to talk to me, thee can come and address me respectfully." Disliking the betrothal of Joan and Seán McGilroy as she did, she resented this celebration.

Joan pulled a face and was about to run down the stairs when Mr. Wright spoke up. "A fine idea, wife. Thou ought to come too. I'll warrant thee could yet dance near as lightly as in our courting days. Mind how we would dance everyone else off the village green?"

To Joan's surprise, though her mother jeered at such a notion, she smiled, said that Hannah might go and came puffing up the stairs to unfold her younger daughter's better dress from the chest.

...

"Thy mother will come round about yon lad," said Mr. Wright as they walked to drilling practice in the meadow. "I stand by what I've ever said: he's got heart, and I'm thinking him and thee is well suited."

They came on Marcie with her father. She was looking lovelier than ever, and had put a scarlet ribbon in her dusky hair in honour of the dance. There was the slightest chill about the way she greeted Joan, like the first hint of autumn in a warm late summer day.

Meanwhile, Mr. Royce was telling Mr. Wright, "Yon Ridley says he gave the steward his answer, though, up at his place, when the fellow minded him of t'order from yon magistrates banning drilling.

He says he came back with, 'Folks must do summat with their time, with work being so scarce, to keep their minds off their empty bellies.'

Joan hoped that Mr. Ridley truly did say as much to the squire's steward. If so, what with Mr. Yorke taking their part before, it was a day for meek men speaking out. The worms would be turning, next.

"Ridley said, though he might be no Radical in the general way himself, he was riled, when that fellow shook his finger at him and went on, 'Take my advice, my goodman. Find a better way to spend your time than playing soldiers.'"

Nat urged, "Maybe there's to be trouble, and t'lasses should go home to their pots and pans."

"Only to bring them out to use as helmets," snapped Joan. Marcie stifled a smile.

"No dissuading them, lad, no dissuading them," sighed Mr. Wright, showing off one of his fancy words. It was a shame how he'd had to give up teaching proper reading and writing, history, geography, maths and all sorts at those classes now things were desperate; folks could no longer spare pennies for them.

Joan's heart lurched at the sight of McGilroy standing on the meadow talking with a couple of the others, with the bright pink sky behind him, and his longish curling black hair tousled in the evening breeze. She had always thought that lasses who went in for such feelings about a lad were acting like simpletons. Now she was one herself.

"So Marcie is still not on terms with you." Kitty Ridley came up bright eyed to her.

Sally exchanged a meaningful look with her sister. "Folks always said you were too close and it's not natural in growing lasses to stay that way. You know, though, a serious lass like you's not suited to our Seán. You'll take it too hard when he sees amother lass he likes better. She don't want to end up going into a decline like Hannah Lee, does she, Kitty?"

They both sniggered.

"No, or ending up crazed like t'other lass I heard on he went on strong with. What was her name? Peggy, that was it."

They both looked at Joan. She saw they were waiting for her to ask for details. But she, already smouldering at Sally's gibe that Seán would 'find another lass he likes better', refused to give them that satisfaction.

"If he left those lasses sad then it's no jesting matter. I think it is a fine thing for female friends to be close as may be, and foolish of folks to go in for idle tattle over it, as if there's only one way to be close to another."

Sally drew back. "Hoighty-toighty. Thou'rt giving thyself fine airs, Joan Wright. Watch out thou dunnat get taken down a peg come a month or two, eh, Kitty?"

Without waiting for a reply, the two sisters turned their backs and strutted off arm in arm, leaving Joan fuming. She wasn't so vain that she didn't think that there was a good chance that they were right about McGilroy returning to his old roving ways when his current passion for her wore itself out. Then that pair would delight in crowing over her.

"Damned fools," she muttered, thinking how she would love to run after them and pull their bonnets down over their faces. Then she remembered how she and Kitty Ridley had once come to blows over a wooden doll, which had then meant far more to them than any lad.

Kitty Ridley was strapping and a dirty fighter, but Joan was quick and lithe. Kitty had grabbed her by the hair, and maddened by the pain of that, Joan caught hold of her nose and twisted, meanwhile kicking her hard on the knee. Letting go of Joan's hair, Kitty fell in a squalling heap. She hobbled about with a sore nose for a couple of days, while Joan got a smacking.

Joan had to smile, thinking of that. And now McGilroy was coming up to her, looking on her as if she was a living marvel, while Jimmy Thribble was teasing the pair of them. Joan thrust those hints from the Ridley sisters to the back of her mind.

Adam Wilson the blacksmith came up with his wife Ann, both smiling, with her in her best white dress, looking nearly as rosy as she'd been as a maiden.

"I'm glad that you could come," Joan said, and realised that she sounded like a society lady receiving guests in some grand ballroom.

She meant that she was glad that Adam had allowed Ann to come the dancing, jealous keeper that he was.

"He took some bringing round." Ann shot a humorous glance at Adam, who gave a wry smile. "But even mother said we all needed some fun for a change."

"We all do." McGilroy caressed Joan's arm.

They turned as Timothy Yorke came onto the field. Others watched. There was a sudden hush, though up above, the blackbirds and thrushes went on trilling.

"And now that Yorke's joined us," McGilroy said, in a casual sort of way, but looking hard at Timothy, and stressing the words, "We'd best start."

Timothy Yorke said nothing. He was careful not to look at Joan, then or later. Joan supposed her father would have said he looked defiant; anyway, he looked angry and hard done by and full of himself all at once.

The marching went well enough, though Jack Hooper's dog started barking. He sent it off into the shrubs that lined the meadow with a 'Get 'em boy!'

Joan thought that she made out a cry and running feet. The dog came back, wagging its tail as at a job well done, carrying a torn piece of cloth in its mouth.

Everyone was delighted. with Jimmy Thribble making some coarse jokes about what he hoped the dog had torn off from one of those blasted spies working for Nardy Joe Nadin.

As before, sometimes when they halted, the men all clapped their hands at once, and it sounded like gunshot. Perhaps it had started as a joke. It might be, besides, that at age forty as much as twelve, a man never quite got over playing at soldiers— unless he'd been one for real, like Seán and Tom.

Perhaps they did it to let off steam, for this marching raised a sense of power in them. For whatever reason they did it, now, as twilight fell, they clapped more than ever. There was a sort of wicked glee about them when they did it. It made these men feel strong, this marching; and for too long they'd been victims, going without, because of the say-so of those so-called betters.

For this little while, they felt like men again, and shouted and whistled in triumph, and the women laughed at their play. Still, there were those men who did not laugh, their faces hard and serious. Were they seeing a grim outcome to this sport?

Sunset was coming on when they fell out and made ready to dance, and Tom sent Nat off to fetch Hannah. McGilroy came up again to claim Joan, looking so fine in his crimson kerchief that she was foolishly proud, while admiration of her glowed in his eyes.

"I don't deserve my luck, in having such a lass as thee," he said.

Jimmy Thribble, Daffy Danny and the others played for all they were worth, and Joan and Seán McGilroy opened the dance as if it was one of those grand balls. They danced a type of jig, with the blood red sky behind them and a great moon rising like a yellow globe.

Joan had kicked off her shoes, and the dry grass that hadn't seen rain for many a long day was warm and dry beneath her feet. A soft breeze of evening blew sweet in her nostrils, and her hair whirled about.

Now Wilson the blacksmith was leading his wife onto their grass ballroom floor as proudly as McGilroy had Joan, and Jimmy Thribble was joining them with Sally Ridley and Jack Hooper with Kitty, and for a marvel, Marcie was honouring Tom. Hannah and Nat came back and she and another girl whirled about together. Joan noted her flushed cheeks. No doubt it was excitement at her first evening dance.

Then she remembered Timothy Yorke, and glancing round for him, saw that he had made off. That was a funny thing, for him to join in the forbidden marching, eager to keep in with the powers that be though he was, and then to walk away from some harmless dancing. Still, Joan supposed that he couldn't endure to make merry with those who had been ready to loot his shop.

As Joan whirled with McGilroy under a sky streaked with crimson, she couldn't spare any more thought for Timothy Yorke or those dark hints about those unlucky lasses the wicked fellow had trifled with, or anything else but the joy of the moment.

• • •

"Who was Hannah Lee?" The worlds seemed to tumble from Joan's lips of their own accord.

She and Seán McGilroy were picking blackberries near the edge of the stream that was slowed to a trickle, the sun hot on their heads and shoulders. Though she wore her bonnet, she could feel the heat beat down through it. A moment since, she was laughing at how with those long limbs he could stretch so far and get the berries out of reach to her.

Today though, Joan was a bit worried about her sister, who was feverish. Now Joan saw that becoming flush on her cheeks at the dancing must have been the start of it. She'd been poorly the next day, and had to go to bed in the afternoon.

Now Mrs. Wright blamed herself, for letting her stay out until that wicked night air came on. Hannah clearly wasn't up to withstanding it the way Joan and the lads were.

Joan was going to boil the blackberries up with one of her cures for her. Hannah often caught chills and colds. She'd be well enough in a day or so; their mother was talking nonsense about night air.

Of course, Seán and Joan weren't the only ones working hard to gather berries. Further back, brats sent to gather this free harvest squabbled over their spoils. Seán had already given a good few of his away to the squalling youngsters with the shortest arms.

There were adults among them searching the clumps of berries out grimly, when in recent years they had done it in fun. Then courting lads had stretched so far out over the brambles to get yet more for their sweethearts, that they had fallen into them, laughing and groaning at the scratches.

Joan and McGilroy had walked farther than any of the others. Then, they had spied a treasure trove of them growing in the middle of a bare patch of grass surrounded by a great tangle of thorns, and beaten down a way through. Now they were hidden from all view by the bushes.

At Joan's saying the name, 'Hannah Lee', McGilroy stiffened and turned to frown on her.

She was annoyed at herself for gabbling out, "Your cousins raised her name. They were teasing me about your being a light o' love."

"You shouldn't heed their chatter." He looked angry with her, and she thought that was a nerve.

"I didn't ask them. They took it on themselves to talk of her and another lass. The way they hinted made me hope you didn't treat either too lightly. They said Hannah Lee went into a decline."

He crossed his arms across his chest. "Her family were staying near the top farm a couple of years since. She were pretty as a picture: fairylike, with great eyes and golden hair, and a white skin with rosy cheeks. I mind she was nigh on as pretty as my Joan, if anyone could be."

Joan couldn't enjoy the compliment. She even wondered if he made it to soften her, though he spoke as if he was just saying what he thought. "What happened?"

"I was fond of her," McGilroy said. "She was a sweet lass. But I was in no mood to settle down, and at t'end of the summer, I wanted to be off. She took it quietly, but her brothers were wild, though I'd respected her and never asked for her. So, then, I had to fight' em, one after another. Fine, hulking lads, but clumsy brawlers. I made sure to put them down quickly, with as little damage as could be. I felt like a rat skulking off as I went on my way. Her family moved away soon after. A year later, I heard she had gone into a decline. She was always delicate, but I felt bad enough about her."

He looked at Joan, and then away. "Maybe I really did light up the day for her, the way you do me, though I couldn't see it then."

Joan sighed. The story hurt her heart. She could just imagine how that poor lass must have felt when the exciting McGilroy went away, never more to be hers.

She tried to be sensible. "Well, people don't die of broken hearts outside of stories."

They both stared unseeing at the wealth of blackberries in front of them, shining in the noonday heat. Then Joan spoke again, "Your cousins talked on another lass, who they said went crazed after you left her."

His eyes sparked like one of those fireworks that Joan had seen that time of the fair. "You gave them an ear long enough. I told you before, Joan, how I went on with a sight too many lasses. Some I courted respectable, and near thought I could care for, but something was always missing. I took up with light ones besides, but they were different. They knew the score."

"What of the lass who went crazed?" Joan insisted. Now her voice was sharp and her anger was rising to meet his: this was turning into a quarrel, she could see, but she wanted the truth.

"That was different." He looked almost relieved. "Peggy Price was a barmaid I was on with when I was working in Liverpool with Jimmy Thribble. She weren't the sort of lass a man of sense would take seriously; a sturdy, talking lass who knew how men are well enough, though I minded later how she'd get some fixed idea in her head that came out of nowhere.

"One night, I got fairly in my cups, though not enough to forget what was said. The next time I saw her, she held out I'd asked her to get wed, insisting she'd turned me down. So I laughed, saying I'd want some salt to do as much, when neither of us was up for that. Then she threw herself down on the floor, sobbing, and fought me when I tried to raise her.

"So t'landlady came over and hauled her up under her armpits and lugged her away, drumming her heels, while t'landlord came over, telling me to get out and not come back, and I wasn't sorry to go. Later, I heard she'd turned crazy."

Joan supposed that Peg had been a wench of easy virtue, and she knew how men looked on such unlucky females, while making use of them. Seán McGilroy had never made out he was anything but a wencher. These stories about two unlucky lasses who'd hoped to draw in that fast and loose rascal were about as different as they could be, one sad while the low tone of the other story was what Marcie would call 'bathos'. Both vexed Joan with him still further.

He moved towards her, but she drew back. "I feel sorry for them both," she said, staring at a tangle of bramble.

"Rightly," he said. "But I never asked for t'sweet one, and as for t'other… No more on it, now. My cousins like a bit of gossip, and you should take no heed of their chatter." He moved towards her again. It seemed to Joan, angry with him though she was, that he had never looked so handsome, with his dark curls and swarthy skin glowing in the sunshine.

Joan bit her lip. "I was riled with them for bringing it up, but they were warning me. Maybe they were right. Why should you be any different with me than to those two? It's vanity that makes me believe your fine promises."

He laughed. "Don't name t'pair of them together, or yourself alongside a whore."

"That makes you a whoremonger." The words were through Joan's lips before she could stop them.

McGilroy's eyes flashed. "Not another word on it, Joan! I'm weary of your scolding me over sowing a few wild oats, when I must be the only man in the world who would humour your wishes about adventure along with your cussed Marcie. You are an ungrateful baggage."

Joan looked on him another moment, and then turned on her heel. She knew she was acting like one of the heroines in one of Nancy's novels, and she didn't care. He started after her, but she moved swiftly, snatching up her skirts and jumping over the beaten down brambles. Naturally, they caught and tore at her skirt.

He was coming over to set her free, but she ripped her skirts away from the bramble, wrenching herself from his grasp. Still grasping her battered basket of fruit, she ran for home.

15.

Sacrifice

Joan trotted home, glowing with anger. When she opened the door, she sensed the fear in the house. Ben came through the open door to the stairs. "Mother sent me out before, looking for thee. Hannah's worse."

Fear clutched at Joan's own heart. Absurdly, it was mixed up with the story of that delicate lass who'd shared her sister's name and her fairylike looks. Hitching up her skirts, she took the ladder like stairs two at a time.

Hannah was in what was grandly known as 'a delirium'. It had been that way with Joan's older brother, though she was too young then for her to remember the details much. Now Mrs. Wright dreaded that her youngest daughter would go the same way.

She hung on Joan's every word, trusting to her all-too-clumsy healing skills. "We need that apothecary from the next village," Joan said at once. He knew more, from what she'd seen, than many a doctor.

"We haven't got the money, lass," said her mother.

"We have." Joan darted down take out the little cracked pot hidden away under the stairs that held the rest of her savings: her crock under the rainbow, you might say.

Mrs. Wright was too relieved to have the fee for treatment to take much heed of the fact that Joan had more savings than she had owned up to. Tom ran off to the next village, not trusting either of his younger brothers to sprint fast enough. This apothecary was less well known than Healey the 'quack doctor' but Joan and Marcie had learnt a lot from him. He was so eager to pass on his skill that he was happy to school a pair of young girls.

Meanwhile, Joan joined her mother in bathing down Hannah with tepid water. Mr. Wright, Nat, Ben and Tom - when he came back—worked on at the looms. They had an order, and they must eat.

Joan, standing by the bed and watching the apothecary's face when he first looked at Hannah, thought he looked grave before he put on the bustling, brisk face of the professional healer. She was sure that Hannah was too delicate for his liking. He left them potions. True, he spoke cheerfully, but no doubt he had spoken in the same jolly, bracing tones when Joan's elder brother had been mortally ill, if only she could remember.

Hannah began to talk nonsense. They boiled potatoes for dinner, with only a few herbs to add flavour to them, and ate them mechanically. When the evening shadows lengthened in the room, the women insisted that Mr. Wright and the boys go out drilling as usual. It would give them something to do, and they were no good at nursing.

Joan wondered dully what McGilroy would say to her father. Perhaps he didn't take their quarrel seriously. Or perhaps he was sulking and flirting with his tiresome Ridley second cousins. She was still too vexed with him to care, wretch that he was, swaggering about raising up dreams in girls and sauntering off again with never a care.

Then, Hannah murmured, "I looked for him to stay. When I saw him gang away down t'lane all speckled with sunshine with that gait of his, my strength went with him."

A superstitious dread filled Joan. It was as if that dead lass's spirit was speaking through this other girl who shared her name and delicate prettiness. She told herself that as likely enough, it was a line from one of Nancy Ridley's books. Hannah loved to go and sit and sew while Nancy read to them from one of those books she could get from that old dame with the whole library of twaddle on the top road, who trusted her with them. Still, she could not shake off her feeling.

Hannah looked fairylike too; her hair had a golden tint, unlike Joan's pale blonde mop, and her build was slight, her features delicate and her skin was—what was that grand word for seeing through something that her father had used—? Ah, 'transparent', that was it.

Over the next couple of days, as Hannah stayed in a fever, Joan and her mother took it in turns to sit up with her at night or sleep fitfully in a chair. Joan became wearier, and her thoughts became muddled.

She began to feel that she must choose between, not Marcie and her dreams of freedom and McGilroy, but between Hannah and McGilroy, because it seemed to her bemused brain that the price of Hannah's getting better was her giving up McGilroy, whose careless ways might even have brought about the death of that other delicate Hannah.

He sent a message of encouragement back via her father when the males came back from the drilling. Mr. Wright had forgotten most of it, and Joan didn't feel as if she cared anyway.

He turned up early the next day. Tom being nearest the door answered it and called up to Joan. Joan called down crossly that she couldn't come down and after some mumbled talk with Tom at the doorstep, McGilroy went away.

In so far as Mrs. Wright could take notice of anything but Hannah, she looked gratified. Joan didn't care about that either. Tom said that McGilroy wanted to talk to Joan but didn't want to press her now, when they had such trouble. Joan didn't even have the energy to say 'Humph'.

McGilroy must have gone out poaching after the drilling, as he gave Tom a rabbit, besides some broth from the Ridley women. Later Mr. Wright sat skinning the coney, his face the gloomiest that Joan remembered.

Later in the morning, there was another knock. Joan though it might be the apothecary, and hurried down. Standing outside the door, holding a pot of broth, was Marcie.

As Joan blinked in the bright morning light after the dimness of the cottage bedroom, Marcie put the pot down and held out her arms. Joan's tears came then, as they almost never did, as her friend held her. Nothing was said of McGilroy, and that was fine by Joan.

She had gone from wanting to talk about him all the time -aand fretting that she had nobody to talk about him with - to not wanting to talk about him at all. Tom was in the loom room again, and Joan remembered how she had never got round to asking him how things had gone between him and Marcie at the dancing the other night, in a time which now seemed far away.

She thought that things might even have gone a little better than usual; he was looking less downcast than normal when they stopped dancing together. Fool that she was, though, she'd been too taken up at the time with her delight in that rascal Seán McGilroy to pay much attention.

Marcie handed over more of their favourite herbal cure she'd made up.

"I thank thee. But it's not working," Joan said flatly

"Give it time," said Marcie. "Will your mother let me stay and nurse her?" Really, she meant 'doctor'. That was what she and Joan did. But as they were women, nobody called it that.

Mrs. Wright was so worried now that she eagerly took up Marcie's offer.

Later that day—Joan was beginning to lose track of the time, and didn't know when—the apothecary came again. Joan spied him through the bedroom window as he came up to the house. She saw him putting on a cheerful look before knocking at the door.

That decided Joan on what to do about McGilroy. It was that and the way that those words of Hannah's: *'I looked for him to stay. When I saw him gang away down t'lane all speckled with sunshine with that gait of his, my strength went with him'* which had been preying on her mind.

She took off the ribbon holding the pierced coin McGilroy had had given her, and went and got the blue beads and wrapped them in some torn cloth. She bid Tom give it to McGilroy when he called.

"What's in that?" he asked suspiciously.

"It's a secret,' said Joan.

He looked a bit relieved, but said, "Thou should give it to him thyself, sister, and I don't like the looks of thee; too pale and fraught by half. Lie down, and I'll sit with Hannah."

But Joan could not endure to desert her post in the sickroom. Instead, she laid her head down on the bed. Voices sounded in her mind as she began to doze. She couldn't make out the gist of their words, but sensed it was all about McGilroy.

She was awakened by Nat was shaking her. "Thy fellow is down at the door asking for to see you."

Joan scrambled to her feet, and swaying, looked down on Hannah. She thought her sister looked as if she were visibly sinking. The flush of fever stayed on her cheeks, and her eyes even looked sunken. That was surely a bad sign; Joan dreaded that her nose would get that pinched look she had seen on the faces of the dying.

"No change," said Marcie, who sat quietly nearby. Mechanically, Joan straightened her rumpled skirts and smoothed down her hair. Still, it didn't matter any more how she looked to McGilroy.

"I won't be long." She took up the coin with the ribbon and the threaded beads she had left on the window sill, and trod heavily downstairs.

• • •

Seán McGilroy flinched when he saw her. "My lass, you are wearing thyself out. Come out for some air for ten minutes." Before she could stop him, he put some potatoes down behind her.

She went with him down the road, heading towards the vegetable patches. He had made his declaration there in what now seemed a faraway time to Joan.

"I've made up my mind we couldn't suit," she said abruptly.

She saw anger, dismay, and a host of other emotions in the look he turned on her, but he masked it quickly. " Thou'rt too weary and taken up with worry to think straight now. If thou told me as much another time, I'd be angry enough with thee to say that thou could have your way, if this is about our having words t'other day. Still, thou'rt in a state, Joan, that's what it is. When thy sister is on the mend, all will seem different, and we'll talk on this again."

"I don't want to go on with you," said Joan, unsteadily, "And this time, Marcie has nought to do with it, for she has come round. But you're an overbearing fellow, who has no care for the female point of view. I reckon you think yourself mighty fine to go along only a little bit with those plans Marcie and I dream on. Those lasses you spoke on sum up how you are with us all. We'd never suit, save for having an eye for each other, and that's not enough for any with sense."

McGilroy's eyes sparked like stones being rubbed together, but he kept his temper. "I won't say hard words to thee, Joan, when thou'rt distracted with worry. It's best if I take thee back home now, and then I'll call tomorrow, to see how things are—"

"Please don't call tomorrow. There's nothing more to say." Joan rejected the look in his eyes, wrenching out of those strong arms which felt so right about her even now.

She'd known of a well-to-do old woman who'd been wild for poppy drops, getting so that she was fit to be tied if she couldn't take them. That dame had started with them just for fun, but over time they had taken over her life. Now Joan felt that McGilroy was like those poppy drops to her.

She took the half sixpenny bit with the lovely blue ribbon threaded through it, and the those fine blue beads the shade of the sky—very like his own eyes, in fact, what Marcie would call 'azure'—thrust them into one of those strong, long fingered hands and made off as fast as she could. He called after her, but she didn't turn. She must give him up, or Hannah wouldn't get better.

She met her father in the doorway, going out for a breath of fresh air. "What's to do, lass?"

"Nothing of any weight," said Joan. She only felt a sense of weariness over breaking off with McGilroy. It seemed impossible that she could feel anything else. She wondered dully how she would find it in the future, seeing him when he wasn't hers.

Mr. Wright saw more than usual. "I hope Joan, thou hasn't been falling out with that fine fellow. Well, it will all blow over. Thou'rt distraught, that's what thou art."

"I must see past his gaudy looks," Joan returned sullenly. She would have gone on, but her father stopped her.

"Yon's a fine brave lad who stands up for what's right."

"He's well enough with t'other men." Joan went on upstairs before her father could say any more. Her mother was standing up, her face working. Marcie held her arm. Dread clutched Joan's heart.

"The fever's broken," said Marcie.

Joan's dizzy vision focussed on Hannah. Sweat beaded her face.

"Heaven be praised," said Mrs. Wright.

Marcie pulled a wry face. "Perhaps Heaven guided Joan and me to use the herbs we did." She spoke briskly. "She will get much better now. The apothecary can stop plastering that terrible grin on his face when next he calls."

Joan spoke her thoughts without realising it. "Giving him up was the price." Marcie shot a look at her, so that Joan wondered if she had heard, though Joan had murmured the words.

Joan had lost Seán McGilroy—doubtful prize thought he was—and all her savings. Yet Hannah's life was worth it, though later she knew that she must feel bitter about her losses when her younger sister was tiresome and played on being her mother's good daughter in contrast to rebellious, naughty Joan, who now wasn't troth plighted and must stay on at home too, with no excitement to look forward to.

Besides, now, even in her befuddled state, she saw how unfeelingly she had spoken to McGilroy, thinking only of breaking things off quickly and only of her own feelings. No doubt it served him right, when he had broken things off with lasses he had been on with taking little enough care for their feelings. Still, that didn't make it right.

Joan went to collapse on the bed in the other bedroom. Marcie followed her and stood looking down at her. "Joan, what were you saying? Giving what up? I know you need sleep now, but I just want to say, I've been too hard on you these last couple of days. Maybe we'll work something out, like you say."

Joan muttered something in reply, she didn't know what. Then sleep overcame her.

• • •

After the cramped terror of those days in the female bedroom, going out felt strange to Joan. Her legs felt weak, and her chest felt tight with dread of meeting with McGilroy, which she knew she would, because she didn't want to see him; if she'd wanted to see him, he would be as elusive as a robin in late summer.

She didn't feel up to talking to anyone, so of course she met everyone. They all were full of questions about Hannah, telling Joan that she looked wan and peaked enough herself.

Turning into the footpath by the allotments, she came upon Seán McGilroy striding along vigorously.

"Joan…" For all the anger in their last parting, his face broke into a smile of pure delight at the sight of her, as if there was no better sight in the wide world. She couldn't but remember his words about her lighting up his day.

"McGilroy," she said. He smiled then instead of being angry, and she wished he hadn't.

"So we've come to your calling me by my surname again. Come hither, Joan, and let's get at ease with t'other again. I am happy that thy little sister gets the better of that fever."

It was hard to hold out against that smile. As he made to take her hands, she drew back.

Still, he wasn't angry; he coaxed. "Sweetheart, what is all this about: turning against me on account of tattle over my past, when I told you myself how I had been bad enough and acted fast and loose with enough wenches? But these tales my cousins hissed in thy ears were about years since. Besides, even with me out of the case, those lasses would have gone t'way they would have gone, the sweet one and the slut."

"But you helped them on their way," Joan's voice came tight.

The way he waved away that barmaid in Liverpool as a slut as if her easy virtue was all there was to be said of her, sparked Joan's spirits.

Everyone would say that these ideas of hers were foolishness. A woman who wasn't virtuous was a whore, and if luck came into it, and many a lass was saved the disgrace of a bastard by a lad taking her waddling to a parson, that made no difference.

But why was a man like this rascal never called a slut?

Joan could see in her mind's eye that lass in her rough inn, drawing measures of ale and mopping up spills, falling for the dashing stranger who swaggered in, giving off warmth that drew folks to him like a blazing fire in winter. Some careless word of his had led her not-quite-right head to seize on the idea that he wanted to wed her, for all her easy virtue.

They had been lovers. Joan had no idea how Seán McGilroy looked wholly naked, though she'd seen him without a shirt, digging in the heat in the Ridley's allotment, and she had gloated over his broad chest and muscular arms and hollow waist. She could imagine him naked beneath a cover pulled up to that waist, dozing beside the wench on a narrow bed in some attic room, with only a makeshift drape for privacy, and the wench gazing on him and thinking, 'He's mine' just as Joan did.

Just as I used to.

Though maybe, it had been a lot more sordid than that; maybe he had taken her by a wall, as Joan had heard coarse talk on.

And this was just as sad as the story of the innocent with her coming death in her fairylike face. Joan could picture her watching the handsome rogue who had made harvest time magical for her walk out of her life, he with only a shade of regret on features ruddy with health.

"This has all got nowt to do with me and thee, and thou'rt just making excuses to keep me off, my love."

Joan felt herself weakening under his look. He did indeed have a lure like the warmth of the sun.

I promised the heavens I'd give you up if Hannah got over that fever. Maybe she'll go into a decline herself if I go back on my word.

There was no point in explaining to him about the Hannah vow. He'd jeer at it as superstitious foolishness. Joan knew that she did indeed have a superstitious streak. Still, leaving aside all this, she just didn't trust this rascal to help her to escape from her life here.

Why, he had a way of trapping wenches into a worse version of their former lives—yes, 'version' was the fine word that Marcie or her father might use. He was a walking menace, this fellow.

"I don't trust you to help me and Marcie to break free from here into making our way with doctoring. I think you're one as keeps lasses down with fair, false words like those masters with all of us."

That was it: that was too much. His blue eyes blazed near alarmingly. He cursed savagely. "Then, vixen that you are, you may go to hell. I'll never lower myself to try and talk you round again. You're too demanding to be worth the effort, lovely though you may be. You're the sort of women who makes a man into a slave, and I'll not be yours or any wench's."

So that was it.

16.

STAVES

Tom and Joan stood by the front door, waiting to go with their father to the last drilling practice.

"McGilroy was drunker than I've known him," Tom said. "I walked with him back to the Ridley's, but he wouldn't go in for an hour, sitting on t'auld broken bench by the front door, and rambling on being a good-for-nothing, but some wenches liked him for all that." He shot a glance at Joan.

Joan shivered, though it was warm, and she didn't think she had caught Hannah's fever. She tightened her arms about herself.

Tom had told her at length how he thought her crazed to go breaking off her troth plight with a fellow she liked, and how this had spoilt things with Marcie just as he was melting her ice at last.

He went back to that now. "Thou hast done me an ill turn, Sister. I was just getting Marcie round to seeing that there might be something in McGilroy's plan for us lads to help you in these precious notions of yours, and now she says if thou hast broken off with McGilroy to keep true to thy word, then she can't be on with me."

"I'm sorry for that," Joan felt a pang for his disappointment. "But if McGilroy is a toper[47] on top of everything else, then any lass with sense would keep well clear of him."

"What d'ye mean, 'on top of everything else?'" Tom was indignant. "He's no tosspot in the normal way of things: you know as well as me it was down to fretting over you he drank too hard then, Joan."

"Maybe he's found a friendly barmaid in the Royal Oak," said Joan.

---

[47] Toper: a drunkard.

"Thou'rt a sourpuss, and thee and Marcie are too much trouble by half. I give over the pair of ye. Just so thou knows, McGilroy says he'll likely enough be on his way again after t'march, as there's nowt to keep him here now."

Joan bit her lip but said nothing.

Marcie herself had urged Joan when they went out gathering herbs. 'I don't want thee to break with Seán McGilroy over me, Joan. I was vexed and too hard on thee. If thou wants to get back together with him, I swear I won't hold it against thee. We'll do something to make our way with doctoring, and never fret about spending thy money on Hannah's care; thou'rt so skilled these days, we will make some more soon enough. Thou'rt not happy, Joan, and it troubles me."

Joan thought until then she was doing a fine job of acting bright and carefree.

Mr. Wright came out of the door, his hat at its most rakish angle. He glanced over at the church clock. "Time for t'drilling, lads and lasses."

Nat and Ben came over from where they'd been wrestling in the dust together. Joan saw that Nat had torn his shirt yet again and she would have to cobble the threadbare material together once more. The routine of household tasks, tedious before she met McGilroy, seemed to weigh on her unbearably. She jumped up as if to escape from it.

Mr. Wright turned to Joan. "And if thou hast any sense, my wench, do make it up with young Seán McGilroy before he takes up with another lass, wicked rogue as t'lad is. There's enough willing to take him on, if thou'rt too nice, or if he goes off again in disgust."

"Maybe I'm the one who is disgusted," Joan kept the dying embers of her wrath against McGilroy smouldering. That was a sight less painful than sorrow.

They fell in with Marcie and her father. Marcie's bright eyes were like a tonic to Joan. Perhaps a tonic was all she needed to stop things being so flat and dull. She must collect some herbs and dose herself, as well as Hannah. The same old scenes and faces near sickened her.

Widow Hobson shook a finger at them as they went by. "Ye are going on too proud, and that's the sin of Lucifer."

"Did he only have one?" Tom grinned.

"He did before the fall." The widow said. "'*Your pomp is brought down to Sheol, the sound of your harps; maggots are laid as a bed beneath you, and worms are your covers.*'[48]"

Marcie cut in, smiling again, but giving no Biblical quotes this time, "This isn't pride, Mistress. You mind you agreed that we must march to change how things are." She laughed as they left the widow behind, now lecturing Adam the blacksmith's wife on her low dress.

Ann looked sullen. Adam grunted, "Nobody has more of a care for his wife's acting modest than me." Joan and Marcie exchanged a wink. They grinned as he added, "But we don't have another fine one, and she's filled out since giving birth."

"Then she ought to wear her old modest one, if she must take place in these ungodly high jinks."

Joan stiffened as Timothy Yorke came up to them. She'd heard her father say that he had been missing from the drilling practice the last two times.

As he joined them, his smug look annoyed her. It was as if he had heard of her break with Seán McGilroy, and gloated about it. Unlike his mother, he seemed to have forgiven Joan's family and friends for saving his shop from looting. He greeted them all in a friendly way, and Joan reddened with vexation under the special look he gave her.

Perhaps he took that as maidenly coyness. "Joan, it is a fine thing how you and Marcie Royce here nursed young Hannah back to health."

"Doctoring, Yorke," said Mr. Wright, pausing in mid swagger to make the point. "They call it by that name, as if they think themselves men."

"The prettiest men in Lancashire," Timothy smiled winningly at Joan.

"That wouldn't be difficult," rapped out Joan, but Marcie's eyes flicked over to Tom, who sour faced though he might be, still looked fine enough with his hair lit up by the rays of the evening sun.

---

[48] Isiah 14:11

The Peterloo Affair

If Joan thought her brother looked well, as they came to the meadow she thought McGilroy made a sight to tempt any virtuous lass with his vigour and dark good looks. If he had been drinking too much it didn't show on him yet.

He greeted them all politely and began talking to Mr. Wright about the last minute arrangements for the march. Joan had feared that the magistrates would be able to find new grounds for cancelling it, as they had done only days since, when she'd been too taken up with worry over Hannah to take much heed of the talk over it.

The Ridley girls stared at her. Kitty was giggling quietly, as at the greatest of jokes.

Joan was making a point of acting carefree, joking with all she spoke to, but Sally came over to say, "You look badly, Joan. Fretting over wicked Cousin Seán's a waste of time, as many a lass has found out to her cost."

Joan said, "Fretting over Hannah might have been more like it." Perhaps she didn't know which Hannah she meant.

Joan began to wonder if she was indeed sickening for a fever herself; she had no energy, and it was all she could do to keep her mind on the marching. No doubt her mother would put it down to the dangers of being out too much of late as the dew fell.

As they went through this last practice before the great meeting at St Peter's Field, and marched, and about faced, and did all sorts of moves, she thought Daffy Danny did better than she, so long as he was tootling away on his pipe.

As they fell out and formed a circle to hear the last minute orders from the leaders, Timothy Yorke kept near, as dogged as a troublesome fly. Joan tried to keep on the other side of Marcie, who rapped back to his, "You yet look a little wan, Joan," with 'It must be the lack of cheap bread, eh?"

Jimmy Thribble and Jack Hooper, standing nearby, grinned as Timothy drew back. Jack tried for a piece of smooth flattery. "Any road, yon Joan has the fairest face of all t'wenches roundabouts, and a bit more fresh air will soon bring t'roses to her cheeks again."

Joan had to laugh at the picture this gave her, of all the wenches lifting their faces up for inspection, like men lined up for drilling practice.

Out of the corner of her eye, she caught a glimpse of Seán McGilroy, who overheard and stiffened a moment. Then he went on taking amiably with the people about him as he went over to the other leaders. On the way, he stopped to make a joke and link arms and do a half turn with Kitty Ridley.

Now, as the group leaders worked things out, they fell to disputing about bringing staves. Not the pikes that the word was the magistrates thought were being turned out by the blacksmiths for an uprising; just staves, which were used by most bodies with sense on a long walk. If they put their ankle out without one to hand, then they were in trouble.

All knew of the savage tactics of Deputy Constable Nadin and the government spy and bully, John Lloyd[49], who loved to beat and lock up agitators for not knowing their place. So Mr. Wright, Seán, Tom, the blacksmith, and Jimmy Riddle, Jack Hooper and both the Ridley lads among others said they must bring pikes; otherwise, they would have no means of defending themselves, as was an Englishman's right.

"Or a Paddy troublemaker's right," said Seán, raising a laugh.

Mr. Royce, normally so calm, was het up and speaking out against that. Joan thought he was talking through his hat—and unlike her own father, his had no holes in it from a kicking from the MYC.

"If they see us looking armed and warlike with stout clubs, there'll be trouble for sure. They'll ne'er let us so much as have the meeting. They'll stop us at the tollgate and read the Riot Act straight off, and send us on our way. We must be seen to be peaceable and unarmed. Word is, that's what they're saying over in Middleton. It's the only sensible way."

Seán McGilroy shook his head. As Mr. Royce stayed on his perch on the stool, he had to speak to the meeting from the ground. He was tall, but even so, he could scarcely be seen from the back of the crowd where Joan and Marcie stood. Joan found herself thinking of him as hers, as she had when she had admired him addressing the crowd before.

---

[49] John Lloyd was notorious for his use of torture in the Luddite uprisings, notably merciless in his treatment of Radicals and already had several notable Radical leaders locked up on the day of the Peterloo Massacre.

Seán said, "Master Royce, you are a wise enough man, and it's right enough we must not take weapons, like these pikes they think we've all got. But you're out, for once, about the staves. Even Samuel Bamford—who prides himself on being ever law abiding—holds out again' going to yon meeting empty handed. He holds there must be a guard of strong lads with staves, to keep those constables from charging us. They have signed up to back the magistrates and hate the very name of Radical, and would give a deal to charge the platform, take our banners and make a mockery of them."

"They must not do that!" Joan surprised herself by calling out among the other shouts from the crowd.

She glanced at the fine banner, sewn with such care by the women, where two of the young men from smaller villages nearby were holding it aloft. It stood fine and proud in the evening sunlight, and was green with gold letters saying, 'One Man, One Vote'. And if Joan now thought, *One Woman, One Vote wais more like it for a long term plan*, that was all in due course.

Beneath that was written, 'No Taxation without Representation'. That sounded well, but she hadn't really understand it until her father said as all food and other goods was taxed, in truth the common man had to pay for the running of the country without a say in it.

McGilroy glanced at her in surprise, before he went on, "There's women and children coming along—as they must, because they're suffering along of us. Still, I'm saying because of that, we cannot risk being set on, without so much as a blasted stick to defend ourselves. We're not looking for a fight, and we must keep quiet under their jibes, and even bear with a bit of shoving. But when such a law-abiding fellow as Samuel Bamford talks of the right for a man to defend himself and his, then we ought to think twice about going to yon meeting bare handed the way some would have us.

"After all, any man with a head between his ears takes a staff when he goes on a long tramp. Even yon special constables must know as much, though those boobies of Yeomanry Cavalry men are maybe too set up to put foot on the ground, save when they're too befuddled to ride."

There was a general shout. Mr. Wright let out a cheer, and Jimmy Thribble clapped his hands mercilessly, as if they had no more feeling than blocks of wood. From beside her, Joan heard Daffy Danny chuckle, tickled by Seán's words, and saying over and over, "Any man with a head between his ears!"

Marcie was looking at Joan keenly and a bit sadly, as if she was trying to puzzle out something about her.

Mr. Royce was speaking, but couldn't make himself heard as he tried to shout over the noise.

Tom, the glow of the low sun behind him lighting up his fair mane to the colour of a lion's hide, began speaking as the cheers were dying down. "Any road, a staff makes a rough walk smooth. I say we must take our staves that day. While we march orderly, they'll not be able to call us rabble out for a riot. We'll not look for a fight, since as McGilroy says, we'll have the women and bairns among us. We'd need our salt to do that in yon St Peter's Field, all closed in as it is. So I say, let's get our staves ready to beat time to t'music with, tomorrow. But leave those pikes yon spies has it we've all got stuck up—well, it's not manners to say what I near on did, with females present—so I'll say keep those pikes they say we have well hidden under our beds at home."

There was laughter and more cheers, loud enough to show who had won the dispute. But Mr. Royce spoke up again, angrily, and a couple of the older men shouted agreement.

In her surge of enthusiasm, Joan turned to Marcie and anyone else who might be listening, "Our Tom knows when to get his word in."

Then she saw that Marcie was still looking on her in that same odd way, and remembered how each of them had given up one of those speakers.

Now Marcie said, "Joan, what was it you said just after Hannah passed the crisis of her fever? Something about, 'Giving him up was the price.'"

"I was rambling. It's of no account," said Joan.

But now they had a vote about the staves, with the women voting too. Joan, Ann Wilson and some others voted for taking them. So did Marcie, despite her father's scowl. Nancy Ridley and some others voted against. Sally and Kitty Ridley voted both ways, giggling at Marcie

148

THE PETERLOO AFFAIR

when she called them to order. Meanwhile, Jack Hooper and Jimmy Thribble tried to rise the numbers in favour by voting with both hands.

There was a tie. It was agreed that people must do as they thought fit about taking a walking staff, but they must not use it for aught else, save they were set upon.

Now Mr. Wright and Seán McGilroy were giving the last directions. Mr. Royce was sulking and left it to the others to go over how the leaders would be wearing laurel sprigs in their hats, where they were to gather after the meeting, and so on. The stoutest lads would lead the procession, two carrying the banner.

Mr. Wright turned to Daffy Danny. "And thou'rt to the fore, with the lasses after thee and all, so we count on thee to play thy pipe for thy life, Danny."

Danny flushed, nodding his head so hard, it looked as if it might come loose. Mr. Wright warned them again about not rising to the bait when there was taunting from fellows who knew no better on the road, or shoving and jeering from the constables or the Yeomanry Cavalry as they got to St Peter's Field.

"And if we're stopped on t'way, and they read yon Riot Act, even then, we must not retreat in disorder. Then we must turn about, and march back. We'll still have our meeting in a place on t'way, or maybe with Sam Bamford's lot in Middleton."

Jimmy Thribble shouted out, "We hear you, master. No brawling."

Seán McGilroy answered him quick as a flash, "Tomorrow we just go and hear t'speakers. It's next week we take over t'world, seeing as Boney fell short."

Most laughed, but Timothy Yorke muttered either to himself or to Joan, "Arrogant fellow."

Well, McGilroy wasn't Joan's any more, for her to be vexed over that. She ignored Yorke. But now, the enthusiasm that had surged through her during the speeches seeped away, and she looked flatly on the great march, and all her tomorrows.

Once, her father had been to see a play by that Shakespeare, and come back quoting a speech about 'Tomorrow and tomorrow and tomorrow and all our yesterdays'. Joan didn't know about all her

149

yesterdays, but now she clearly saw her tomorrows as all drab and grey without McGilroy lighting up her days for her, and no tonic would help that.

∴

When they got in, Mrs. Wright had slices of bread ready on a plate. She grumbled about, 'That good-for-nothing fellow who got round our lass to go marching before she saw what a worthless rascal he was, and set her about raising a bunch of foolish females to march along of the men on yon foolish jaunt tomorrow.'

Joan was annoyed that her mother thought she had no ideas of her own. Then, before she could give one of the pert answers that had earned her many a tap as a bairn, Mr. Wright broke his rule of keeping a lordly silence while his wife muttered complaints. "Hush thee, Martha. The lass had Radical notions from her father, long before McGilroy came by them. Anyhow, thou knows he's added many a rabbit to our table."

"He has, and it might be better not to take what he's stolen from the squire's grounds," Mrs. Wright retorted. Then, no doubt recalling her rule of never criticizing 't'master' before their children, she closed her lips tight.

Mr. Wright said, "Those grounds were taken from us by those former enclosures, wife. I hope tomorrow we may go with your blessing."

Mrs. Wright bit her lip, and her eyes went bright. She did something Joan had never seen her do before. She stepped fast over and kissed Mr. Wright before them all.

"You'll all go with my blessing, though I think there's little enough to be gained by it but worn out shoes and dusty clothes, a big thirst and a turning back before you reach town. But you all deserve a holiday, I'm thinking, and I wish you success."

Then she stroked Joan's head as she used to when Joan was a wee lass. So again Joan held her tongue about coming by her own ideas, so as not to spoil the good feeling between them all.

That night, in the close room, still warm from the heat of the day, with the cracked plaster on the walls, and the rag rug over the boards,

Joan waited until her mother and sister were asleep. Then she began to weep.

After a few minutes, Hannah began to stroke her arm. "Thou'rt sorry about breaking off with McGilroy."

In a fit of great weakness, Joan, between sniffs, told Hannah of her vow. The rest of the story she judged to be too improper. Their mother, a heavy sleeper, snored on.

When she reached the end of her tale, Hannah amazed her by whispering, "But that's silly to stick to that daft vow. I'm not even called Hannah really."

"What do you mean?"

"Our mother was still weak from the birth, so Grandmother Wright took me to be christened, and had me named Caroline after herself. Mother was so vexed she always called me Hannah anyway."

Joan had once heard that story, and forgotten all about it. Now, the childishness of keeping to her vow did make her give a snort of laughter, so that Mrs. Wright stirred in her sleep and said, "Hush."

Then Joan sighed. "It isn't only that, though. It was other things thou'rt too young to know about. You said things in your fever about, *'I looked for him to stay; when I saw him gang away down t'lane all speckled with sunshine with that gait of his, my strength went with him.'*"

"Did I?" Hannah sounded embarrassed. "Well, it came from a story I made up about an old maid and a talking cat."

"You used high falutin' enough words." Joan gave a sobbing laugh, so that their mother mumbled again.

But Hannah was already asleep.

151

17.

Holiday Jaunt

Joan thought over her sister's words on waking the next morning to the usual cooing of the pigeons. It would be yet another hot day, as the pink sky had promised last night.

Before that reminder, Joan had almost forgotten that Hannah wasn't really Hannah at all. Then, there was the absurd fact that those sad words she had muttered in her fever had really been from a story she'd made up about a cat.

Did that make a difference to Joan's feelings about that other story of the other, fairylike girl who faded away after Seán McGilroy left her? Or the blithe way he'd waved away the one of easy virtue as 'a whore'?

It did bring home to Joan how there was no sense in her bargain with Heaven, which wasn't supposed to go in for bargains, anyway. Still, it didn't alter the fact that McGilroy was a trifler, and if he had seemed to value Joan more than the ones who had come before her, she couldn't be sure he would keep feeling that way.

Besides, Marcie was right when she said there were no adventures for lasses when any lads came along, and she'd kept aloof from Tom.

Anyway, it was too late. Joan had rejected McGilroy too heartily for him to want her any more, even if she abandoned her pride and told him she was sorry. After this march, he'd be on his way; he'd said as much to Tom, and he'd never lingered so long here before.

Let him: they were all better off without him.

Joan turned as she realised that Hannah wasn't in the bed. Only her mother lay across from her on her back, breathing heavily, her silvered plaits spread out.

Hannah came back into the house as Joan reached the foot of the stairs, carrying the water bucket. Joan fussed, "That's too heavy for thee, thou'rt still not strong yet."

Still, she was pleased to see that the colour was coming back into Hannah's cheeks. In fact, her eyes were sparkling with mischief. "I'm well enough, and it's a long hike for all of ye to Manchester. I saw Marcie at the pump."

Joan was too busy fretting about her shoes to dwell on Hannah's words. Her fine ones, which her mother had tried to sell not long since but found no buyer, did for a short walk, but rubbed on a long one.

Her workaday ones had holes in the soles. One of the last jobs the cobbler had done before he took to his bed was to patch them. The holes were coming back now, and it was only because of the drought these weeks past that Joan hadn't got wet feet. Besides, they would spoil the effect of her lovely white best dress, so prized that it would be the last thing her mother sold, folded neatly in the battered chest upstairs. Joan must wear those fine shoes, padding them with cotton waste. She could always go home barefoot.

She felt a stirring of excitement as she went to put on that dress after their usual skimpy breakfast of oatmeal porridge and weak tea.

She gloried in the dress, the feel and the swish of it. She left her long wavy light hair falling loose about her shoulders. Though she began to see that she might be suffering from what the females in Nancy's novels called a 'broken heart', life yet had its excitements, and the roses had come back to her cheeks, besides Hannah's.

Marcie came in, wearing a dress of faded yellow with a bonnet to match. Joan thought she and Hannah exchanged an meaning glance.

"What are those funny looks about?" Joan wanted to know.

"Nothing." Marcie smiled. "Thou'rt a picture in that dress, Joan. It makes thee look more than ever all fairylike." She turned to Hannah. "Now, what's the grand word? Ethereal, that's it."

It was what people said of Joan besides her sister Hannah—who wasn't really Hannah—and McGilroy had said of that other Hannah, on whose account she couldn't enjoy that praise any more.

"But we must hope you're not so wanting in sense, as to pine away over a lad," Marcie went on, and now Joan saw that Hannah must have told her that story. After all, before their quarrel there had been no secrets between Joan and Marcie.

Before Joan could answer, there was a knock at the door. Timothy Wright stood there in his grand clothing, with a touch here and there of red, which Joan thought matched his cheeks.

"You look a picture, Joan." His eyes were full of an admiration she could do without.

"A picture of what?" Nat came up behind them in his best blue jacket with the elbows mended so well it hardly showed. Tom and Ben followed him, both of them finely turned out too. Joan thought that even if Tom hadn't been her brother, she would have thought him handsome. All over again, she wondered at how Marcie could hold out against him so long.

Mrs. Wright came out to greet Timothy Yorke as warmly as Joan herself didn't.

Then Mr. Wright, the mending to his hat hidden by the laurel sprig stuck in it, led his group to join the marchers on the remains of the village green, the bit that hadn't been taken over by the squire's family.

There was so great a crowd gathered that Joan started. Half the people from the neighbouring hamlets were there, and strangers among them.

Seán McGilroy was talking to a group that included the blacksmith, who for some reason was carrying, not one of those pikes the informers insisted he was turning out as fast as he could make them, but a staff and his wife Ann's shawl. Still, Joan had no interest in the looking at the blacksmith, being too busy trying not to look at McGilroy.

He was looking as jaunty and glowing as ever, wearing a fine shirt, with his crimson kerchief knotted about his throat, and a hat with a laurel sprig which the leaders wore. At the sight of Joan, his eyes widened. Looking quickly away, he came over to speak to Mr. Wright, giving a brief word of greeting to the rest of them.

"McGilroy, there's something I want to ask you when you've a moment," Marcie called out to him. He nodded, while Joan wondered what that could be. Then she turned to wave at her mother and sister as they joined the crowd of those waiting to cheer the marchers on their way.

Old eagle-eyed Widow Hobson came out shaking her stick, with many Biblical quotations. The voice which had scolded the village for forty years was turning into a croak. It didn't deter her.

"And yo' tell them rich folk as says you have no right to speak out, that they're in the wrong of it, letting us starve: *'For I do not mean that others should be eased and you burdened, but that as a matter of fairness your abundance at the present time should supply their need, so that there may be fairness.'* [50]"

Some nodded solemnly, while others smiled.

Joan's father had those he saw as the bonniest lasses grouped directly in front of the banner and the players. He counted Joan among them—as he would never have done a year or so hence—along with Ann the blacksmith's wife and others. Joan was only glad he had kept from saying so outright. The Ridley girls, who were in the bigger group behind, would never have forgiven any of them for their not being picked as belles themselves.

Daffy Danny gave a sudden blast on his pipe that made them jump.

"Wait till we're fairly going, Danny." Seán McGilroy waved a finger at him.

Then their Committee—as they grandly called it—Mr. Wright, Mr. Royce, Tom and Seán McGilroy, stood before them to go over the instructions one last time. McGilroy was insisting that the women must keep close to the men, just in case of trouble. Sally, Kitty and Nancy called out jokes and giggled and Marcie's would-be sweetheart and Joan's one-time sweetheart joked back. It was all part of the holiday jaunt feeling of the day.

But Joan remembered McGilroy being uneasy about trouble to come, back in that other time when they had been together. That gave her an uneasy feeling; still, likely enough that was just her finding it miserable to have to see this fellow now he wasn't hers, and she couldn't gloat over him any more.

---

[50] Corinthians 8.13.

The young lads in the crowd joined in the joking. They were eager to met with the others on the road into town, and made guesses about who would have the finest banner. Meanwhile children scampered about among them, happy for the day's jaunt, though it would be a weary walk for the smaller ones. No doubt they would end up riding home on parents' and older siblings' backs. Ben had forgotten to act grown up, and was playing chase with some of the others. A few of the women had nursing babies tied to back or hip.

Suddenly, as Hannah stood waving her handkerchief, her face twisted, as if she was fighting back tears. But now the leaders shouted for all to fall in, their little band struck up, and they were off among shouts and cheers.

They marched along the lanes through the sunlit fields, with cattle on either side staring. Some sheep bleated at them, and the wags called out, 'Yes: Hunt and Liberty!"

Soon their ordered ranks broke up a little. Girls danced along the sides to the music, and people dodged in and out of the ranks. Joan and Marcie drew to the back of the group of belles in front, as the women in the group behind kept shouting questions at them.

Sally Ridley called out, "They're back together, those two. So close, it fair makes you wonder about 'em."

"What do you mean?" Joan challenged her, and Sally went on giggling but would not say.

Marcie said, "Is that a sally?"

Kitty nearly fell over laughing. "That's a good one, that is!"

Sally said, "Marcie and Cousin Seán are both dark as pitch, they're alike on that."

"And you won't say what you mean," Joan's temper was rising.

"He's got the proper bits, which Marcie don't," spluttered Kitty, "And Joan didn't like him making too free with them."

Joan felt like a banked up fire, smouldering underneath and ready to blaze. "That's none of your affair," she snapped.

"You'd think the pair of you were keen on yon cousin of yours yourselves, to hear you go on," said Marcie. "Your blather minds me, I've got to ask him something." She slipped out of her place, heading towards the leaders.

Joan thought how she would like to pull both Kitty and Sally's noses, just as she had Kitty's ten years back.

Suddenly, Jimmy Thribble and Jack Hooper were mincing along among the women behind. Jimmy said in a treble, "They say I'm fair enough to march with t'lasses." Jack sneaked an arm about Nancy Ridley's waist. She slapped it away. Jimmy Thribble tickled Sally's.

"Here comes thy new sweetheart," Kitty called as, Timothy Yorke appeared on Joan's left.

"Joan, I'm not happy with the arrangements."

"What arrangements? Our hair?" Joan laughed.

He shook his head. "Your mother urged me to look out for you, when we get to St Peter's Fields."

Joan caught sight of McGilroy, talking to Marcie in the front, turning about to see her laughing while Timothy Yorke urged something on her. He scowled.

Joan, who'd only been laughing at her own quip to put Timothy off his prosing, was ruffled further. In the short time since Joan's break with McGilroy, her mother had clearly been scheming to get Yorke together with her yet.

"It's no laughing matter," said Timothy. "You must take care and keep close to me when we get there. There'll be a great crush, and you're a delicate wee thing."

"I'm not, and it's kind of you, but my father will be there after all," said Joan, adding, as Marcie slipped back to join them, "Besides, Marcie's the best of guards."

Jack Hooper shouted some jest to Timothy Yorke, buffeting him on the shoulder, while the Ridley girls tittered. After a bit more of that, Timothy fell back. Joan sighed with relief.

It was a long enough walk. The sun soon burnt through the mist, and the heat beat down on them. Their feet sent up clouds of dust on the dry roads. Soon, the hem of Joan's fine dress was soiled with it three inches up, besides her shoes. She would normally go barefoot on such a long walk, but she wanted to look as fine as anyone. This pair rubbed if worn for a few hours, and she was main and glad that she had stuffed pieces of cotton waste inside to protect her toes.

In each hamlet they passed through, they got a cheer from bystanders, even if it were only the old men out on the village bench. They soon had word that the Middleton group, led of course by Samuel Bamford, and the Rochdale people had joined together in a group of many thousands, with the last of them ahead by some half an hour. Great crowds were moving in orderly fashion on Manchester from all sides.

Their little group got a warm greeting from most, though not all of the people they passed. She gloried in how she and Marcie had got the women to turn out, with a good part of them marching.

Some stared to see these marching women, and some respectable housewives hissed things such as, "Boldfaces! Go home to your cooking and cleaning and mending where you belong, sluts as you are!"

Joan told herself that they must hold their tongues, though she would have liked to call back, 'There's nigh on nowt to cook and mend.'

"Shameless baggages: look at their faces." A stout man in fine clothes waved a stick at them.

Joan saw the comely wench, who as belle of the next hamlet, was walking by her, open her mouth to answer them. She shook a warning finger. "Remember: keep silence."

"You cheeky brat; who do you think you are scolding?" The lass grumbled as they went on.

If anyone else shouted out, the sound was lost in Joan's ears by the music of the band. She saw that people had joined them from places along the way, and they moved on as a great wending snake. Her heart swelled again. Truly, Danny had never played so well, nor any of the others, or so many miles gone so lightly.

At first, Joan's father and the other leaders hurried the pace of the march, eager to catch up with the people from Middleton.

But now they were thirsty in the heat and the dust of the road, and many men called out for a halt for a draught of ale, so they stopped at the tavern in Harpurhey.

Tom bought some weak beer to Joan, Marcie and the boys. "It's thirsty going, eh, my flowers? Not wilting in this heat? Mind you wenches stick close when we get to the square, for they say it's the greatest crowd ever today, with half o' Lancashire turned out."

Joan tried to picture that many people in her head and failed.

Marcie smiled, not seeming to mind Tom calling her a flower. When they looked on each other like that, Joan could see that they belonged together. But they weren't together, and as Tom said, that was largely down to her.

Have I done the wrong thing?

It was too late now. Anyway, it was for her and McGilroy—he wasn't going to take her back—not an arrogant so-and-so like him—but maybe she could do something about Tom and Marcie. She'd urge Marcie after the meeting.

Joan, keeping a wary eye out for Timothy Yorke, saw Seán McGilroy coming towards them, only to be surrounded by a group, all asking questions at once. Then she saw Yorke looking round for her. To Joan's relief, he was stopped by a serving man who began disputing with him about something. Perhaps he had been mistaken for somebody else. Timothy's cheeks were redder than ever as he raised his voice in denial.

Mr. Wright came over too. "That young Yorke's all over a dither over thee, Joan. Of course, thy fathers and t'others have your safety to the fore, but he thinks he knows best."

They formed into ranks and marched off again. Joan was pleased that her shoes didn't hurt her feet yet with this padding.

They were still out of sight of the Middleton group when they came up to the toll gate where the road branched between Newton and Collyhurst. Here it was that they'd thought to be met and turned back by soldiers and a magistrate reading the Riot Act. However, only a single horseman watched them from the side of the road.

"Good takings today?" Mr. Wright asked the stunned looking toll booth man.

"Near all o' the county must have passed this way. Yon Middleton friends o' yourn took the Collyhurst way, and then turned back to double up with Henry Hunt's group."

They took the upland road towards Collyhurst. The leaders sent back word that the gully-like road through Newton would be too clogged with people to make a good route. Joan knew that many Irish weavers lived in Newton, who, so her father said, were dealt with worse by the putters-out of work than any other group. At least half of McGilroy would feel right at home among them, so he'd be sorry to miss them…Well, that was no affair of Joan's.

Finally, they were coming into Manchester town, with those tall buildings that cut off the sunlight from the narrow streets. They came up to other groups of marchers, calling out greetings. They had many cheers from passers-by showing no alarm at this great turn out of people in holiday mood.

Joan exchanged a smile with Marcie, glowing again that they had played their part in this.

Still, they had some hisses and taunts shouted at them besides. Joan heard her father calling to the hot headed ones among them to keep order. As they went on, she saw Jack Hooper catch hold of Jimmy Thribble, and Tom and others bid the men who were shouting back to hold their noise.

Soon, the streets were so packed with people, that the leaders led their group down some side lanes. Then, taking a wrong turn, were walking for some time out of their way in back alleys, until at last they came to Piccadilly. Then they were turning into Moseley Street with its great houses. Pale faces were watching from the upper windows. Here there was no cheering: still the band played on as merrily as ever.

Joan saw that the residents were in fear of such a crowd, and she said, "Let's wave," waving herself. Many of the wenches about her, proud as the belles of the parade—even if they were now dusty ones—waved too. But there were no answering waves from the folks above in their grand buildings.

They went past the left side of St Peter's Church, and were greeted by cheers again as they marched onto the field. Joan gasped at the dense crowd already here. It grew by the minute as more and more groups of marchers arrived. The sun had moved a bit from directly overhead; she thought it must be past one o'clock already.

There were bright banners raised above the crowd all about, embroidered with legends about 'Hunt and Liberty' and—she had to spell this one out—'Universal Suffrage'. Joan was taken with the fine sound of that. It was the sort of term her father would use when holding forth about changing the lot of the common man.

The heat beat down. The great number of bodies, all giving off heat too, added to it. It was sweltering, and felt airless, for all the breeze that whipped many of the words from the speakers on the makeshift hustings away before they reached the ears so eager to catch their meaning.

Mr. Royce and the leaders were organising their group, urging the women to keep to the middle.

Joan, not being tall, could only make out the speakers' platform by going up on tiptoe, though sometimes she caught a glimpse through the crowd. She stared at the black flag of the Lees and Saddleworth Union, the one led by Dr Healey. It put her in mind of the flag of a pirate ship. At first she thought that the image on it to be a skull and crossbones, but then she saw that it was a heart and two clasped hands. Indeed, the legend on it said 'Love'. The other—she had to spell this one out too—said, 'Equal Representation or Death'. Up on poles above the crowd were those red caps Joan's father had said were caps of liberty, which was some symbol to do with freed slaves.

Then she noted the double line of constables, leading all the way from the platform to a house nearby. Their faces were as grim as the mood of the great crowd was festive. She saw a group of men she supposed must be the magistrates, gathered by an upper window of that house, gazing over at the platform. It gave her a turn, but she tried to dismiss it. After all, it made sense that the authorities had to keep in touch with the platform and to have an easy way to it through the crowd if need be.

A great shout went up, nearly deafening Joan. She and Marcie both clapped their hands over their ears. She caught a glimpse of Timothy Yorke moving away from their group, back towards the church. Perhaps, with his sharp hearing, that noise was too much for him. It was as well to give him the benefit of the doubt.

But Joan felt misgivings for other reasons.

"Here's Hunt!" Now Joan made out the words, and cheer after cheer rang out.

'Orator Hunt' as they called him stood on an open carriage with blue and white hangings, slowly moving through the crowd to the platform across the field, where the crowd was most dense. He was a tall man, and well made, though not handsome in the way of McGilroy or Tom. From her glimpse of his face from a good few yards away, Joan thought so, anyway. He was very gentlemanlike in his ways, bowing to left and right, doffing his white hat.

There was a group of men in white shirts about the carriage and some other people in the carriage itself, among them a woman, finely clothed and great with child. Another man dressed as a gentleman, with an ill look, had a few words with Hunt, and then held on to side of the carriage as it went on, with the crowd parting before it.

The cheering went on and on, like the noise of the sea Joan knew from that time when she had near died of fever, and been sent off to stay with a distant cousin who lived in the village of Wallasey, near where the River Mersey joined the Irish Sea.

Again, Seán McGilroy made towards Joan's direction, she supposed heading for Tom, who was standing behind her. He was stopped by Sally, who fell against him, gasping loudly. "Oh, there's no air."

He caught hold of her as she sagged at the knees, and she leaned against him, her head against his chest. "Bear up, my lass, it's not so bad as that. Breathe deep."

She hung on to him. "It's all very well for you; you don't lace[51]."

He patted her shoulder. "You'll do well enough, Sal. It's nerves at the crush. Breathe out, that's the thing."

"I'm fainting." Sally was hauling on him, wheezing. For someone half conscious, Joan thought that she was making enough noise.

Suddenly, the terror of being closed in and unable to breathe that Joan sometimes had in the stuffy bedroom back home was on her. The hot pangs of jealousy shooting through her made things worse. She refused to compete with Sally, anyway.

Now Jack Hooper was saying, "A fine idea, that," and seizing hold of Kitty Ridley.

Turning her back on them, Joan was through the gap he made in the enclosing circle of males. She broke free of their group, looking for some opening in the crush.

---

[51] A corset was tightly laced.

She knew that this went against what had been agreed, but she'd made her special promise to keep close to McGilroy when they were together. She was free now. Sally could faint on him all she liked. Joan wanted to get some air.

She thought she heard Marcie's voice call her name, but pretended not to hear.

Then she groaned. She'd caught sight of that young menace, Ben, moving further into the thick of the crowd. She guessed he was making for the platform to hear better. Slight lad that he was, he could worm his way through the crowd with ease. Joan shouted after him, but if he heard he took no heed.

She shouted then to her father, but her voice was drowned in another cheer. Usually, Ben followed Nat about; for once he went off on his own.

Suddenly, she was taken with the wild notion that something terrible would happen if she lost him now. It was a mad thought, and must come from this feeling of panic surging though her as well as Seán McGilroy's earlier talk about having a 'bad feeling' and wanting to keep her close.

Whatever set her thinking that way, she went struggling after that pest of a younger brother through the crowd, breathing hard and fighting down surges of dizziness and senseless terror.

Though Joan was slight herself—the more from all the going without they'd been doing of late, for all her ex-lover's presents of potatoes and rabbits—she couldn't slip through the crowd the way that weedy lad could. She kept bumping into people, and having to say a sorry here and there, while all the time Ben was getting further away from her in the mass of bodies.

The heat and the stench of sweat made her dizzier. People couldn't help but sweat in this heat and crush, fine clothing or not. Joan sweated herself, strands of hair clinging to her forehead.

With a start, she saw the burly, paunchy form of Nadin, the hated Deputy Constable, strutting up the aisle. He'd been pointed out to her once before as the brutal swine who liked beating suspects. The sight of him among the jolly crowd, swaggering along that double row of stony-faced special constables, batons to hand, sent a shiver down her spine.

Some of the crowd shouted things like, 'There's old fat belly Nardy Joe.'

For a second, she thought how her father and Seán had been right to speak up for taking something to use to defend themselves, should they be roughly used by the officers of the law, who saw them as rabble got above themselves, and set to riot.

She thrust the thought aside. Fretting would do no good. Where was that boy, drat him? There he was, the monkey, right up close to the platform, staring up, open mouthed.

With one last squeeze, Joan came up to him. She was angry enough to slap him, but couldn't in this crush without hitting someone else. "Ben, thou lummox, why did thee not keep with the others as Father and t'leaders said? We'll never get back to them through this. It's near hot enough here to kill."

Ben made a jeering noise. "I wanted to see and hear what goes on. Thou needn't come fussing after me as if I was a babby. We'll find them easy enough at after, and if not, I know my way home, any road."

Joan turned to see Seán McGilroy, his face cold and blank, thrusting his way after her. As he came up the mask vanished. He was furious. "Thou daft wench, what did we agree about keeping close?"

Her anger rose to meet his, though she knew she should be grateful that he came after her. "You look out for Sally; I was looking out for Ben."

Ben said hotly, "Thou'rt a dafty, Joan."

McGilroy seized hold of him and took Joan's arm. "Nadin's up to something, strutting up and down. Back now, damn the pair of ye."

"Damn you yourself for an idle whoremonger!" She shook free his arm. Now they were brawling in public. Joan's mother would be horrified. People turned to stare. One man laughed, and one woman hissed, "Shush!"

And now Marcie came swimming her way through the crush of bodies. As she reached Joan she said, "I saw you go burrowing into the crowd after this pest. I know you've never liked a crush."

It came to Joan that minding suchlike things about someone was one of the best ways of loving.

Joan and McGilroy stood red faced, avoiding each other's eyes. Now Joan felt bad about what she'd done; still, she'd had to go after Ben. "Let's try and get back to our group."

Then Tom was squeezing up to them, saying easily, "No chance of getting through the crush now, daft happence as thou'rt. I saw thee come after this rascal. Ben, one of these days, I'll murder you."

"You lasses must keep safe with us men, seeing you can't get back to our group," said Ben airily. Joan forced a laugh, trying to ignore the knot of fear in the pit of her stomach.

Marcie shrugged. "Like enough not. We must bide until the field clears, and a thirsty enough wait it'll be."

McGilroy was scanning all about, as if seeking out an escape route for them. Marcie turned a glance on him like a question, eyebrows raised, but he missed it. "I'd like us all together. No help for it now. You got your staff, Tom?" Putting aside his brooding, he nodded towards one of the buildings in the roads leading off behind the hustings. "We're near a tavern, anyhow." He smiled on Ben. "Enjoying yourself, youngster? You don't get a day's jaunt often enough."

Joan wouldn't look at him. Instead, she turned to watch Henry Hunt's procession coming up to the hustings amongst deafening cheering. He still bowed this way and that, waving his white hat. Joan had to wonder what a grand gentleman like that, in his fine coat with the brass buttons and his glossy top boots, could know of Lancashire folks who worked in cotton. Still, it was good to have such a man on their side, with his knowing his way about parliament and the laws.

Hunt got on to the platform, and a great shout went up from the crowd. He was followed by the unwell-looking gentleman and the others. There was a woman up there, too, but Samuel Bamford, who she'd heard speak before, wasn't among them. Joan was sorry that young Bagguley and those other workman leaders had all been clapped in gaol for 'sedition'- whatever that was—and so couldn't take their place up there on this great day.

Tom was talking to Marcie. Seán McGilroy was pointing out people to Ben. "Yon's Mrs. Mary Fields, the President of the Manchester Female Reform Union."

Joan looked with awe at the woman he pointed out. One day, she wanted to be like her. It must feel grand to be up on the platform among the men and the cheering.

Now McGilroy was chatting to the couple of raw-boned young men next to them, and Joan caught their shout that the sickly-looking man up on the platform was a reporter from a grand newspaper called *The Times*. Joan looked on that man with some wonder, too: fancy knowing enough to write for that newspaper, though it didn't seem to be doing much for his health. It was a fine thing, too, that they had sent him here. Surely that meant that grand people down in London were taking notice of them after all, for all the petitions that had been turned down.

These knowledgeable lads talking to McGilroy were gaunt as nature had never meant them to be, besides downright ragged in this outing where anyone with good clothes left was wearing them. Joan thought that things must have gone very hard with them.

Next to Joan was an old man, who pointed to the leader of the women's union. "Yon flaunting quean is right shameless, up among the men."

The sturdy young women with him, perhaps his granddaughter, laughed. He was clearly deaf, not hearing as Joan shouted that it was a fine thing. He shook his head. "Shameless harridan."

Joan yearned, saying to Marcie, "It must be fine to be up there."

Ben heard, and his face fell. "Don't do that. T'other lads plague me enough about my sister getting the women to march. I had to scrap some of them over it."

McGilroy heard that and laughed. "That's my lad."

Joan knew how he felt, remembering how as a young lass she'd been teased so often about, 'Your old man's a Jacobin: Father says they're traitors.'

Tom, catching that too, said, "Yon other lads are fools, Ben. You tell 'em so from me."

At that, Marcie turned a smile on him. She looked so lovely, with her dancing black eyes and plump red lips parted, her glowing skin, and her dark hair all tumbling down her back and the bodice of her dress tight across her high, full bosom, that it took even Joan by surprise. Maybe it was those smiles that kept poor Tom enslaved.

Tom said something to her. Not wanting to spy on them, Joan turned away, and a movement above the crowd caught her eye. Looking up, she saw a thing that made her smile. A fussy-looking man in the clothing of a gentleman was leaning out of the upstairs window of a house maybe a hundred yards away, reading from a paper.

He leaned out so far that it seemed that he might tumble, but so great was the noise below, not a word of what he had to say could be made out by the crowd. His lips moved soundlessly. Certainly few others even saw him.[52]

Most of that great mass would not be able to hear one of the men on the platform, either, as he shouted that he proposed Hunt as chairman. Then Hunt called for quiet. He had an air about him. It was amazing how now the voices stilled, all straining to hear his words.

"Gentlemen," began Hunt in his great rich voice, "Fellow countrymen, I hope that those in front of me this day, will now exercise the all-powerful right of the people; and if any person would not be quiet, that you will put him down and keep him quiet."

He said how happy he was to speak to so great a meeting, and how the delay the magistrates made only served to double their numbers. Joan was already drawn in by his fine words and voice, when one of the men on the platform took his arm, whispering something to him.

Hunt was annoyed. "Sir, I will not be interrupted. When you speak yourself, you will not like to experience such interruption."

Then came the cry from those in the crowd near Mount Street: "Soldiers!"

---

[52] The magistrates insisted the Riot Act was read by Mr Ethelston. If so, his voice was lost in the noise of the crowd..Instead of an hour being allowed for the crowd to disperse, the magistrates sent the troops in at once.

18.

Peterloo

Seán McGilroy and Tom Johnson, ex-soldiers themselves, turned about as sharply as game dogs. Now Joan saw the blue uniforms of the Manchester Yeomanry Cavalry, their dark shako hats making them tower further above the crowd on their tall horses.

McGilroy shouted to Tom something that might have been, "Get ready!" As Joan seized hold of Ben, McGilroy and Tom pushed the girls between them. "Keep hold of us, whatever you do."

Marcie somehow sounded calm. "It's madness to try and break up this crowd, and they've not even read the Riot Act."

Then Joan remembered the man whom she had thought looked so funny, reading something out of a window. A great jolt of fear gripped her heart. "My God: that man at the window was reading it, and none heard!."

Hunt called out in his strong voice, "Do not be alarmed, friends: They seek to frighten you. Hold firm: see, they are in disorder already. Give them three cheers."

That cheer went up.

Whether the volunteer force took it for a jeer, Joan had no idea. But the cavalrymen shouted back themselves, the shout that urges a charge.

The crowd all about them swayed, as if pushed by a giant's hand. Screams and shouts cut the air.

Deputy Constable Nadin and a group of special constables came at the platform from the aisle made by their fellows. Above the noise, Joan heard Nadin shouting at Hunt, "Sir, I have a warrant for your arrest," and Hunt's reply, "I willingly surrender myself to any civil officer who will show me his warrant."

There was tumult about the platform as Nadin led Hunt away down the aisle of special constables. Other leaders were dragged off the platform, while some jumped into the crowd to be borne away in a rush of fleeing bodies.

Joan could see glimpses through the crowd of Yeomanry Cavalry galloping through the mass of people, knocking them down like skittles and riding over them, rolling in the saddles and lashing out with their sabres. The shrieks and groans terrified the untrained horses. They reared and bolted, knocking people aside to land on top of others and trampling on growing piles of the injured. People shoved and scrambled to get away. Panic broke out all about.

Joan stared, unbelieving. This couldn't be happening: it was too horrible.

McGilroy drew out a stout cudgel from inside his clothing, gripping Joan with his other arm so hard that it hurt. Tom seized Marcie as he had never dared at those dances on the green. Joan and Marcie caught hold of Ben. Covering them as best they might from the buffeting from the surging crowd, McGilroy and Tom thrust them away from the platform and towards the nearest lane leading from the field.

They struggled towards that escape route, Tom holding Marcie, and McGilroy gripping Joan fiercely. Both the girls kept a pincer hold on Ben. Joan well knew that if they let go, he would be trampled to death. If any of them went down, that would be the end of them.

Joan had lost sight of their neighbours the talkative youths, the lass and the old man, but she saw the old man's stick carried along among the crush of people. She snatched at it with her free hand, as if seizing it for him could be of use to him now.

The MCY men set about the banners around the platform, cutting them to ribbons. A woman tried to jump down and her dress caught on one of the broken poles. As she hung there a cavalryman slashed across her exposed body.

Those who held the colours struggled away, the militia chasing after them. Even in her horror, Joan found time to wonder if the militiamen were maddened with drink. Certainly, their eyes were glazed, their faces reddened; still, it might be bloodlust that had befuddled their heads.

She remembered McGilroy telling her of the Battle of Waterloo. Now she was in a just such a slaughter herself. She and Marcie were at last in an adventure, and one that she could have done without. It was likely enough to be their only one.

They could not get through to the lane—the surge of the crowd drew them away from it. Joan fought down panic. One of the broken poles that had fallen into the crowd was carried towards them as on a tide, and Marcie snatched it up.

Joan glimpsed one of the special constables hit furiously at a young man[53] standing nearby. Even over the uproar, she heard his shout:. "I'll break your back!"

The youth was knocked towards a cavalryman, who raised his sword. The youth held out a stick. He might have picked it up or he could have been one of those, like McGilroy, who thought it best to bring something with which to ward off attack, if needed. The cavalryman slashed his arm. He fell and was lost to view as another horse trampled over him.

The cavalryman rode over the crowd, cutting to left and right with his sabre. Joan knew from her father that soldiers dispersing crowds were supposed to ride forward slowly, using the flats of their swords to push people apart. Someone should have told these MYC men that. People struggled away as a one cut his way towards them. McGilroy thrust Joan behind him and the cavalryman slashed at his head.

Quick as a flash, Marcie burst from Tom's hold to block the blow with the broken piece of pole from the hustings. The weapon flashed as it splintered the wood. Marcie was left with the broken stump in her hand, while McGilroy and Tom hit out with their staffs. Joan, her blood up, still holding Ben tight with one hand, struggled to reach round McGilroy and lay into the militiaman herself with the old man's stick.

---

[53] This was John Lees, a Waterloo veteran from Oldham who died of his injuries a couple of weeks later. Many witnesses at the inquest gave damaging evidence of the murderous violence of the Yeomanry Cavalry, and the inquest was closed by the authorities on a technicality.

The MYC man yelled furiously, "Fight back, would you, damn your eyes? I'll have you know I'm a soldier today."

Their eyes locked briefly. Now, Joan knew him; even as he fought to steady his nervous great mount, enough to get in another attack. It was Mangnall, one of the cavalrymen who had come with Mr. Harrison on the day of the threatened bread riot.

She saw that he knew her too, glazed as his eyes were. He was the dark, gaudy one who had identified McGilroy. Even in this split second, she cursed fate for bringing them together on this packed field. His lips tightened as he raised his sabre again.

Suddenly, over the din, a voice shouted: "For shame, gentlemen: forebear: the people cannot get away." Close by, an officer was beating down the raised sabres of the frenzied soldiers with his own. Mangnall hesitated, swearing and lurching in the saddle.

The officer turned away, shouting at another group of cavalrymen to stop. A woman was thrown forwards, a baby in her arms. A cavalryman raised his weapon to strike at her. Joan and the others, trapped in the mass some feet away, could not move to help her. They yelled their fury. She raised her arm to protect the baby, but was knocked to the ground. A man bent to raise them.

"Bless him," Joan sobbed. She tried to close her eyes against seeing these horrors, but they snapped open again.

She saw other cavalrymen rushing at the special constables. They raised their batons to show who they were, but the soldiers cut at them unheeding. Blood sprayed.

A backwards rush bore Joan's group away as lightly as if they had been sticks thrown in the rindle swollen by autumn rains. Joan's feet were lifted wholly off the ground. Tom and McGilroy were holding them tight. Even through her horror, Joan felt that despite everything, in his arms was the place where it was right for her to be. Ben was howling aloud. It was only through biting her lip that Joan kept from joining him.

"Don't fret, we'll get out." McGilroy sounded almost cheerful they were swept along on the human tide. "You'll have some story to tell folks now, eh?"

Joan sensed that he was braced to get his feet down as soon as he could. She knew that when this flow stopped, they mustn't fall; there would be little enough chance that they would get up again if they did.

Next to them, another baby, held close in its mother's arms, didn't wail, for all the panic all about and the terror in her eyes. The infant had that look of calm she had seen before on babies' faces. Joan could not bear to look at it. She turned her head and tried to reassure Ben, though the breath caught in her throat.

McGilroy said something to the mother, though what he could say to her by way of comfort, Joan could not think. He thrust his club in his waistband, and took the woman's hand. That recalled to Joan a form of catch they had played as bairns, when all those tagged held hands and joined in the chase.

Ahead of them, a young girl was slipping down into the crush. Joan pushed her upwards with one leg, trying to keep her upright. Marcie, seeing, thrust with a leg too. Somehow they raised her again. But then a large man calling on his God fell into her. With a scream, the girl tumbled under the mass of bodies.

Joan stared at Seán McGilroy, as if it was the first time. For sure, it might be the last. She saw his dark ringlets, all in disorder, his hat with the laurel sprig in had it gone. She noted the sweeping brows and eyelashes as black as his hair. She saw his bright blue eyes and the tanned skin, as dark as any Spaniard. She marked the beads of sweat on his brow, the ridges of his jutting cheekbones, and that straight nose, a mite too short, and his mouth, a bit too wide, but all as regular as might be, fitting together like pieces of a jigsaw puzzle. She saw his strong throat, the red kerchief pulled loose, worn proud as any gentleman's stock. He looked wholly beguiling to her. She knew it, even now, when they faced a danger that might be the end of them.

Whatever happened, she could admire him now. She wouldn't let herself, when he stood up for her father (where was that father now and Nat now and all the others?). Then, she refused to let her heart admire him as she'd said her thanks. She had refused to melt, when he'd kept back the crowd from setting on his enemy, Timothy Yorke, and his family. She'd been grudging, that's how she'd been.

Yes, he had been careless with lasses' feelings, and she had been right to take him to task over it, and be wary of him herself. But she'd taken it too far: making her fear for Hannah her excuse, she'd brought sorrow on them both.

It was all too late now, but she let her heart show in her eyes as she looked at him. But he wasn't looking at her. As a male caught up in a battle, he was wholly intent on that.

Some people nearby were groaning and bleeding, one or two were praying, while one matron, her cap gone, blood clogging her hair, sobbed again and again, "Margie, come to Mammy!"

The movement slowed. "Make ready to run!" Joan called to Ben, as she and Marcie held him up. McGilroy and Tom and were shouting the same thing. Joan's feet hit the ground, and she nearly fell backwards. Once again, McGilroy saved her from falling, his arm strong about her waist. He and Tom grasped the woman with the baby too. Their group kept their feet, while all around, people went down. Joan heard their screams as they were trampled underfoot.

The mass parted like waves hitting the shore as some more Yeomanry in different uniform rode on them, sabres raised. Now Joan's group were on the edge of the crowd.

"Run," McGilroy roared again. The group whirled their way out from the human stampede, spinning to a stop in a sheltered spot between piles of timber left from some building works and the wall of a building. Joan saw that rush had taken them right over the field, as far as the Friends' Meeting House.

Other soldiers appeared. Joan hardly took in that these must be the Hussars. These professional troops[54] were calm, their horses reined in, and they seemed to be trying to part the crowd with the flats of their swords instead of hacking their way through.

Now people were fighting back against the cavalrymen. Joan saw that some had jumped over piles of timber stacked by the wall of the Quakers' Meeting House, and were picking up stones there, hurling them at the MYC men.

---

[54] These were the 15th Hussars, who came from further away in Byrom Street, and arrived when the carnage had begun.

Nearby she saw a young woman, blood running down her face, hair flying and bonnet hanging by its strings, holding by one hand an apron weighted with stones. She was hurling them at a cavalryman who came after her, sabre drawn.

Then a stone caught the cavalryman square on the head. He fell from his horse, dropping like a stone himself. Another horse trampled over him. Joan had a terrible glimpse of his face disappearing under one shoed hoof. Any cries he made were lost in the other shouts and groans all about.

Thinking alike, Tom and McGilroy seized the arms of the woman holding the baby, and hoisted her up onto the pile of timbers. As she scrambled down the other side Ben had already gained it.

"Joan," McGilroy made to lift her, both hands round her waist. "You lasses too." Joan saw by the battle-lust in his eyes that he and Tom would stay to fight.

"Not without you."

She saw Ben at the other side of the timbers. "Go on!" she screamed after him. "Get into the open streets."

Despite her words, McGilroy hoisted her up on the timber barricade. She caught a glimpse of how the crowd had thinned. Some had taken refuge in the Quaker's Meeting Hall or the nearby houses. Some had escaped into the surrounding lanes.

She saw a flash a shot cracked high above their heads, coming from one of the buildings behind. In this frozen moment, Joan wondered if it was the soldiers or someone maddened by the slaughter. She forgot it, as one of the MCY men rode at them, sabre raised. It was Mangnall again.

"Damned filthy Mick Radical!" Again, he aimed his sabre at McGilroy's head. McGilroy parried the blow with his club. Splinters flew. The blade stuck in the wood.

As Mangnall wrenched his weapon free, Joan stretched over to bring the old man's stick cracking down on his wrist, while McGilroy leaped up to jab his splintered stave into the side of Mangnall's belly. The cavalryman howled, nearly dropping the sabre and rolling in the saddle. The horse wheeled away from them, caught up in a new surge of people rushing from the middle of the field, while Mangnall called hoarsely to another MYC man nearby: "It's that Irish bastard!"

That MYC man turned, and his eyes narrowed as they focused on McGilroy. Perhaps he was one of those revellers McGilroy had defied in Manchester weeks since. He rode straight at them.

Joan wobbled on the pile of planks, striving to regain her balance.

"Poxy whore!" The MYC man cut at her.

McGilroy leaped between them, reaching up with his damaged stave to stop the blow. The blade knocked the club from his hand and the cavalryman slashed at his arm. Tom jumped to parry the blow with his staff, knocking the sword aside. Joan lashed out with the walking stick again, but missed and toppled off the wall to land beside them.

Face distorted with rage, the man jabbed downwards at McGilroy, who twisted away. Still the blade ripped down his shirt. Joan regained her balance and lashed at the MYC man's arm as he made that thrust. She must have done him some hurt, for the force of the blow shot pain up her own arm while he flinched away, swearing. She saw Marcie leap to stab the jagged stump of her own stick into his thigh. He shouted, lurching sideways. A savage joy rushed through Joan.

The horse's flank bumped against the wall. It reared, its massive, metal-shod hooves waving above Joan and McGilroy's heads. They were under the cavern of its great sweating chest, the odour strong in Joan's nostrils. Its whinny sounded loud in her ears, shrill among all the other noises of agony and grief.

McGilroy thrust Joan away from that massive belly. The tang of its sweat mixed with that of blood in her nostrils. Warm drops fell on the skin of her arm. She saw a growing red stain on the side of his torn shirt.

Hooves thudded down, missing them by inches, and then they were free. The horse bolted into the open space before them, the MYC man swaying in the saddle.

"Over!" Joan didn't resist now as Tom and McGilroy pushed her and Marcie up on the stack of timber.

She scrambled back up—and in this moment of fear and flight, she found time to be thankful for her rumpskuttle[55] climbing days. She

---

[55] An old term for 'tomboy'.

turned to help McGilroy climb up, wounded as she knew he was, but he was already following Tom up beside her. They stumbled over the barricade of planks and down to the stony ground beyond.

Others came after them. A horde of people ran or hobbled towards the streets behind. Many lay on the ground, too badly hurt to flee. A man staggered past Joan, blinded with blood running from his scalp, while a woman sat dazed, her gown torn to ribbons, her bare white breasts covered in gore.

As they stood, gasping for breath, Ben joined them, eyes wide and wild. Joan had a moment to dread for her loved ones and her neighbours. Fear squeezed at her heart for McGilroy as she turned to look over his wound.

He pushed her hands away. "No time for that now- it's only a scratch. Out of it quickly. There'll be troops all about. I must look to you, hoping the others are safe."

Joan glanced back over the piles of planks, looking in vain for a sight of those others, half expecting to see the MYC men after them still. Out on the field, the tumult of charging riders and fleeing people raged on, though already, the crowd had thinned.

The sight that met her eyes horrified her more than anything she had seen today, and she groaned aloud. She would never forget this. It was like McGilroy's description of the battlefield after Waterloo. No: Joan thought it was worse: these were civilians.

The wounded or dead lay on top of each other in the piles where they had been thrown by the cavalry charges. They were tangled together, some deathly still, others moving an arm or a leg. Men, women and children lay as if they had been cast on a refuse heap for human beings.

Charging about these piles of damaged bodies, the cavalrymen went on riding down others. She supposed they yet saw themselves as breaking up an unruly mob with necessary force. Amongst them she caught sight of an officer yet trying to control a group of maddened MYC men attacking the fleeing crowd. In the buildings above, pale faces watched.

All about, there was a litter of shoes, hats and other torn pieces of clothing. Broken musical instruments, ragged pieces of the banners, and broken splinters of pole lay in pools of blood. On one torn piece, Joan could just made out the word, 'Liberty'. Next to it lay the crushed body of Jack Hooper's dog, lying on its back with its paws up in the air, just as if it were playing dead.

19.

Defeat

Behind the piles of planks, people were rushing to the safety of the open streets.

"Joan: Ben!"

It was her father's voice. He, Mr. Royce, and Nat were struggling against the thinning crowd. As they joined them, Joan saw that her father held his left arm stiffly, his torn sleeve bloodstained. Nat sported some cuts and torn clothing and limped slightly.

Mr. Royce, unhurt, reached out and touched Marcie on the shoulder, as if reassuring himself she was really there. "Thank the Lord that thy brother's still at the harvest at thy uncle's."

Tom drew aside McGilroy's slashed shirt to look at his damaged side. "I'm thinking thee needs t'infirmary my lad, and my father here, too."

Joan, in her role of healer, took a quick looked at that torso she had once gloated over, though as his former sweetheart she was shy. She winced. "He speaks true."

McGilroy's said, "To be taken up? This is only a scratch, and make no mistake, they'll blame us for today."

Joan realised how she was shuddering as she urged him. "Then you must let me bind it for you as soon as may be."

She went over with Marcie to look at Mr. Wright's arm.

"One of those pretend soldiers came after me, hacking at the banner. I would have saved it, only another came on me from the side." His arm was cut, though not deeply, and it pained him to move the shoulder. There was no time to fashion a sling now: they must escape from town quickly.

For the first time, Joan realised that one side of Tom's golden wavy hair had been shaved off close in their fight with the two cavalrymen. It looked silly enough, though if she hadn't been shuddering already, she would shudder now at how near that sabre cut had come.

"Then you and the lad aren't hurt, Joan?" Her father sighed his relief. "I feared thee squashed flat. Thank God Hannah kept away today."

"I'd never allow that, Master," said Seán McGilroy, urging them on, full of himself yet, though wounded. "I must find out if my cousins are safe."

Joan realised that she must look a sight herself, if Marcie was anything to go by. Her friend was walking stiffly, her bonnet gone, her hair tangled, her gown torn and her face swollen from unheeded bruises.

Mr. Wright told McGilroy that he hoped none of their village had been badly hurt, though he hadn't seen Jack Hooper or Jimmy Thribble or Wilson the blacksmith after their group had been forced apart. McGilroy's male Ridley cousins said Sally, Kitty and Nancy had left for the haberdashers along with their youngest brother soon after they had got to St Peter's Field.

Joan was thankful for that. McGilroy would never have left the town without them.

Now they were caught up in the fleeing crowd again. There were other Yeomanry Cavalrymen about, still harrying those fleeing the scene. Two stood jeering and waving one of the captured banners.

Tom burst out, "The cowardly sods!"

Joan read the carefully embroidered great letters on the banner: 'Women's Union'. Her heart burned.

McGilroy said through gritted teeth, "Armed with only our good consciences', eh? Damn that Hunt's[56] eyes."

The crush around them broke up, with people running down the different routes. Shouts and cries still came from every side, showing that the chase went on yet.

---

[56] Unlike Bamford, Henry Hunt insisted that the people should attend the meeting wholly unarmed, so as to give no excuse for an attack.

They paused for Tom to give McGilroy his coat to cover his bloodstained clothing. This way they hoped to make less of a target for the MYC men. Joan was fretting to bind his wound and fashion her father a sling by tearing up her petticoat.

They came on Jimmy Thribble and Jack Hooper. Jack Hooper was leaning on Jimmy and clutching his side. Joan saw tears in his eyes as he muttered, 'The bastards killed my dog.'

Jimmy Riddle was unhurt. He jollied Jack along. "Brace up, my lad, thou'rt all in one piece," as he brandished his cracked bugle. They too said that he'd seen the Ridley girls leave the field with their younger brother before the trouble began. Jimmy had a good laugh at Tom's new haircut, while Joan told Jack that his chest should be bound up.

Tom and Joan each held one of McGilroy's arm, and tried to hide his slashed clothes and bleeding side by walking close. Still, his blood dripped on the ground. It was too risky to stop and bind up at his wound, and she feared how bad it might be.

Her father walked on McGilroy's other side. "Never fear, this rascal will get t'better of a cut or two in no time. Look out: there's more of yon swine."

They tensed as a group of MYC men came galloping towards them, but then they abruptly turned off down an alley, no doubt spying some other prey.

Joan's group hurried on. All about, dazed and bleeding people staggered along. Joan yearned to help them, but she had to think of her own. There was one good thing about today: Marcie and Tom now went hand in hand.

They reached the toll gate where the roads parted. A great crowd of people was forcing its way through. Some threw down sixpences and shillings, not waiting for the change in the outwards rush, as if pennies were a trifle to them. Others simply barged their way through. The toll keeper made no effort to stop them as he stared at the tide of battered humans, their mood so different from that of the morning when the world had seemed to be opening up before them.

• • •

The inn at Harpurhey was the meeting point for the march home. Here they at last came on the rest of their group, who set up a cheer when they saw them. The tale had been that McGilroy was dead and Mr. Wright either cut in two or under arrest.

As Mr. Wright led his group up to the yard, he looked as if he would have loved to wave his hat at them, like Henry Hunt, if only he had it still.

Again they narrowly missed the Middleton group. Samuel Bamford had marched them off, holding up in defiance their fine green banner.

"I only wish we still had ours, though I know you put yourself at hazard to save it, Master." McGilroy seemed more worried about the loss of their colours than the blood from his side dripping into the road. Even here, he wouldn't sit down, but went about, checking on what he seemed to think of as his troops.

Joan caught him leaning dizzily on the wall a minute later, and told him boldly that he must let her bind his wound.

Still he wouldn't have it. "Look to t'others first. There's some worse than me. I don't like the look of Jack Hooper or Ann Wilson." Then he paused, smiling, for all his pain. "As you take on so about me, Joan, maybe you will hear me when I ask you summat I've been wanting to all day after what Marcie told me—only things got in the way."

Joan's face caught fire and her breath came fast. "Of course I will." She sighed like to some foolish heroine. Her look must tell him her feelings.

Those bright blue eyes of his were as tender as they'd ever been as he said, "There's no time for our own matters now, but you must hear me later."

"Yes," she murmured, with her heart in her own, "But I'm feared for you now, bleeding all the long way home. That's a nasty gash; let me bind it up."

"I'll live to plague you all," he smiled.

Joan smiled back. Marcie came up, and Joan forced herself to leave him as they went round the side of the building to tear up their petticoats for bandages.

Normal things didn't seem to matter any more, so they hitched up their skirts without a care in the world, whatever their fathers might say. Joan was relieved that she'd forgotten to put on her good petticoat. Her mother would be cross enough over her ripping up this worn one, so threadbare it was easy to tear.

Marcie's was much less worn, the Royce family having done better than the Wrights these last years, and the two of them had to struggle to rip it across.

McGilroy had again joined Tom and Mr. Wright in jollying people along, menace that he was. Joan saw that she and Marcie must treat some of the others before he would let them do anything for him.

Most were only scratched and bruised. A few, like Jack Hooper, complained of pains in their insides. That worried Joan and Marcie, who knew that crushing could do lasting damage. They bound Jack's ribs, while some matrons nearby clicked their tongues at such improper goings on. He was another spare, muscular type. Joan dreaded that soon enough he would lose all that strength. Still, she spoke cheerfully to him, as did Marcie.

Ann Wilson the blacksmith's wife was another they were troubled about. She had pains in her back and abdomen. Adam Wilson was carrying her home, raging that for all his great strength, he hadn't been able to keep her from being hurt in the crush. Joan was only thankful that they had left their infant at home with Ann's mother.

When they got home, Joan and Marcie would make up poultices for her back pain, but they urged her to see the apothecary, seeing that he might know some treatment they didn't. They said the same to Jack Hooper, who snorted. They put Mr. Wright's arm in a sling, planning to make poultices for him too.

Tom went to get McGilroy and the other wounded a nip of gin each as just the thing for cuts, while Mr. Wright and Mr. Royce went for jugs of ale.

Only then would McGilroy let Joan and Marcie see to him. As they undid his waistcoat and shirt, Joan's knees went weak at how stuck fast by the blood as they were; they had to pull them off the long gash. She never thought of herself as squeamish. Now she felt his pain as he winced. The wound looked deep to her, and she longed to smear some of their soothing herbs on it, dreading its going bad.

For all her worry, she couldn't help thinking all over again how nice he looked bare to the waist, but for that wound, with his broad shoulders and chest and hard muscles and hollow waist.

"Does it hurt to breathe?" Now Joan remembered tales of pierced lungs. Tom said, patting McGilroy's shoulder, "Never fear, I've felt over his ribs. That made you grunt, eh?"

Joan feared that the sabre might have cut through the ribs, though if he breathed shallowly now, it was more through the pain. She knew how that was from others she'd treated. As the shock wore off, the pain set in.

She and Marcie finished binding the wound as tightly as they could. Then she saw Timothy Yorke standing looking at them. She went fiery red. Then she saw that he was bleeding from a cut to the head, and seemed dazed. She had wondered vaguely where he had been, supposing that like the Ridley girls and youngest boy, he had left St Peter's Field before the trouble began.

"Sit down and rest a bit," she urged McGilroy, forcing herself to follow her father over to Timothy.

Mr. Wright, feeling much better for the sling, was already regaining his spirits. "Why, young Tim, you found no friends on yon field, I'm thinking. Does that gash need binding? T'lasses will see to it."

Timothy said, "Had I ever been in Nadin's pay, as some tattlers made out, those fellows would never have used me as roughly as they did back on that field."

Joan thought of those MYC men slashing wildly at the special constables, but said nothing.

Timothy glared at them all, his gaze roving over to rest on where McGilroy was getting up again. "I heard that McGilroy chap was dead for a certainty." He made no effort to hide his disappointment that he wasn't. "He must have as many lives as a cat, so I wouldn't trouble too much about him. Nay, Mr. Welch, I thank thee for your offer. Your lass has enough to do, caring for that fellow above all the others."

Joan supposed 'that fellow' made a change from 'that ne'er do well' or 'that good for nothing'.

183

"The lasses do love a wounded hero," said Mr. Wright. "And I hear from Tom how fine McGilroy acted back on the field. You can't keep up with yon rascal."

Joan went fiery red again. Mr. Wright laughed and shook his head. "I had four of those MYC after me myself at one time, for they knew me well. Though I say it myself, I near unseated two, though as a modest man, I don't like to boast."

Timothy Yorke muttered something, turning away. Joan let him get on with it. His injury hardly looked serious, though she supposed his pride was bruised, both by her concern for McGilroy and how badly his supposed friends in the Yeomanry Cavalry had treated him.

Daffy Danny came up, weeping. Mr. Royce put a hand on his arm. "Did thee get hurt, lad?"

The bruises were already coming out on Danny's face, arms and hands, but he could tell them nothing of how he came by them. All he would say was, "They cut my pipe in two."

Jimmy Thribble, standing by, made a coarse joke. The other men told him to mind his tongue in front of the wenches. Joan tried to find out more, but all Daffy Danny would say was, "They cut my pipe in two."

They made to set off again. McGilroy and Tom had those of their band who still had instruments play again to keep up their spirits. Others said it was foolish, for it might yet draw some MYC men to them.

McGilroy stood up in front of them, taking no heed of his injury. "We must not crawl away like beaten dogs. It wasn't us who did wrong. If we let them get away with what they did today, we let them get away with anything."

"That was murder. Even t'government we have cannot let them get away with that," insisted Mr. Wright. "Aye, they'll pay for what they did today."

Mr. Royce shook his head. "Yon magistrates will have sent 'em in, and they'll turn the law about to have it on their side, you mark my words. We'll be the rioting rabble; those MYC will be the ones upholding the law."

McGilroy's eyes flashed. Joan guessed that he was thinking how, if he'd gone along with what Orator Hunt, Mr. Royce and some of the others insisted on—as so many had—he'd have had not so much as that cudgel to defend himself and others with against those cavalrymen.

Joan took his arm. "Can anyone lend Danny a pipe?"

Nobody could, of course. Most of their band's instruments had been lost under the horses' hooves and the fleeing feet. It was a stupid thing to say, but she said it to stop McGilroy from getting into a row with Mr. Royce. She knew that was the sort of thing that matrons did to keep the peace. Well, today, she felt she had aged so much she felt like a matron herself.

• • •

They did have some music on the way home, from their last two pipes and Jimmy Thribble's damaged bugle. He blared cracked notes upon it as he helped Jack Hooper stagger along.

For all McGilroy's and Tom's hearty words, defeat hung heavy in the air about them. The wounded limped along at the back, save for McGilroy, who insisted on leading them. All the lasses' dresses were covered in dust and some were torn and stained with blood. Some had hurts, and many had lost shoes. None of them danced. George the blacksmith carried his wife, at first in his arms, and then on his back, all the way home.

All about, in the fields lining the roads, was a sight that made Joan want to wail outright. There were people from other towns and villages lying down, too badly hurt to walk further. It looked as if the fields had grown a crop of torn humans overnight.

Joan's group could do nothing for them, save take some of the children to carry home, if they came from nearby. There were too many of them, and they had to look after their own injured.

She had to keep herself from looking at those sufferers by the wayside all the way home. It was too painful. She began to see why funny things happened to the inside of veteran soldiers' heads, so that they ended up all warped like Ned Pritchard. By her side, Marcie flinched over and again.

That bitter walk home, with the August sun beating down on them, seemed to go on forever to Joan.

It was a strange thing, but at first, Danny marched with the band, his hands held and his fingers moving as if he still had his pipe. Joan thought that he heard the tunes in his head. Then slowly, he stopped, as if the music had too. While he had been playing his make believe pipe, he had marched as well as ever, but now, he fell out of step, and took to stumbling along anyhow. No-one had the heart to call him to order. Anyway, it would have been a waste of time.

Joan's heart contracted as she saw Seán's blood trail start again on the road under her feet. She bit her lip, but he marched on as if he didn't feel it, until he started swaying. Marcie followed her as she squeezed her way through to him. "That bandage needs redoing."

His eyes were dazed. He let the girls to draw him away to the side of the road.

"Ne'er worry: I'll take over," Joan's father said, swinging his good arm bravely.

With Ben helping Nat to limp along, and Jimmy Thribble blasting notes on his cracked bugle, still supporting Jack Hooper with one arm, with Timothy Yorke scowling at the group at the side of the road as he went by, with Daffy Danny crying again, and the injured hobbling behind, the others marched away from them down the dusty road.

Adam the blacksmith stopped beside them to take a rest. Ann sat down by the road. Joan did not like her pale look, but she could do nothing for her until they got home to her herbs, and maybe not even then.

Marcie helped Joan tear some more off her petticoats—with a fine flash of leg, so that McGilroy joked hoarsely, "I'll try not to look at thee."

She forced a laugh. They peeled off his blood-soaked shirt and waistcoat to bind up the injury once more.

"You've messed the road up enough." Tom told him. "Yon Nadin will be after thee for that."

Joan couldn't joke. Besides her fear for McGilroy, she dreaded the MYC men they'd fought would come after them, what with them having a friend in Mr. Harrison out here. She could even see them saying that McGilroy and Tom had attacked them and have him dragged off to gaol, and her father too, before their wounds were properly tended.

It was as if the people had lost all the rights they'd gained. As like as not, the government would go and undo that *Habeas Corpus* law again, and lock up every known Radical leader they could find.

She knew they'd even done it to Henry Hunt, landowner as he was, beating him besides, so the word was at Harpurhey. They had dragged that *Times* reporter Mr. Tyas off to gaol too. Apparently, Samuel Bamford was still free, and Dr. Healey, though Joan thought they'd be rounded up soon enough.

She remembered playing in games with the Ridley girls, years ago. Then, the sisters hadn't liked Joan winning at catch or whatever it was, so they'd kept on making up new rules, and saying this or that wasn't allowed, and she was out of the game, and a dafty not to have known. This was how things felt to her now in real life.

Still, there was no time to worry about that now. As soon as they got home, she must make up poultices for McGilroy and for her father and the others. She must see what could be done for Ann Wilson and Jack Hooper and even Timothy Yorke if he let her. As they set off again, McGilroy leaned on Tom and Joan, and they helped him along. Joan thought they would never get home, but at last they were coming into the village.

Waiting for them was Widow Hobson, standing in exactly the same place where she had seen them off this morning—a lifetime ago. Tom groaned. Seán McGilroy was too dizzy to take it in. Joan saw Marcie brace herself for a scolding laced with scripture.

The widow held up her hands at the sight of them. Then she said, "*Do not rob the poor because he is poor, Or crush the afflicted at the gate.*[57]"

• • •

---

[57] Ezikiel, 22:22

At the Ridleys, Sally, wearing a new ribbon she had bought when she and Kitty had skipped away from the meeting, took one look at her injured cousin and shrieked aloud. Certainly, with his shirt dyed red with blood, his hair damp with sweat, dazed and held up between Tom and Joan, he must have looked shocking enough.

Kitty Ridley joined in: "He's dying!"

"Don't fash lasses, he'll live," soothed Tom.

The Ridley lads strutted in after them. "We came through all t'fighting unhurt. We showed those MYC cowards summat, eh?".

Mrs. Ridley hurried up to take a look. "Thank the Lord for that. The girls heard there was fighting at t'meeting, and so their young brother took them straight home from t' haberdashers. We guessed our Seán would be in t'thick of it. He needs a doctor, that's plain."

"Not one who's hand in glove with those MYC," slurred McGilroy.

Tom frowned. "They'll like enough have taken up yon Dr. Healey from Lees, or he's about seeing what's to be done now, or I'd go and get him straight. We must rely on Dr. Joan's herbs for now."

While Mrs. Ridley and Tom took McGilroy upstairs, Mr. Ridley, kept at home as he was by the rheumatics in his foot, wanted to hear all about how things had gone wrong. Joan left Marcie to tell him, while she dashed off to search out some herbs.

What with the drought, many of the plants were half dried already, but that didn't matter for Joan's poultices as she added water anyway. She rushed about the meadow in a panic, scarce noting that she passed by poor Daffy Danny.

He was sitting with his back against a tree, rocking to and fro, and making a sorry noise. Joan was too worried about McGilroy to do more than say, "Ne'er mind, Danny; you'll get a new pipe in time."

Back at the Ridley's, Mr. Ridley still had Marcie trapped, telling her about what everyone should have done, and what he would have done, had he been there. Joan wondered that she could bear it. At least Nancy had made her some tea.

Tea—when there was any—was what Joan always turned to in times of trouble, but now, when Nancy offered her a cup, she said, 'Thank you kindly. I'll have one later if I may."

"Tom brought your pestle," said Marcie, holding it out, and Joan hurried to beat the herbs into a paste. Before that, she washed her hands, using some of the well water. She'd found that if she bathed her hands before treating wounds, then they didn't go bad half so often. She didn't know why that was, but she did it.

Mrs. Ridley tut-tutted and said it wasn't proper for Joan to treat McGilroy with him naked under the cover.

"Ne'er you mind, I'm like a eunuch for now," muttered McGilroy, who'd revived a bit since getting his head level with his feet. That was another medicinal thing Joan had learnt from practice.

She didn't know what a eunuch was, but supposed it was a bit like Ned Pritchard, whom she'd overheard saying thought a smoking a pipe better than a strumpet any day of the week.

Joan insisted that they couldn't trouble about notions of decency now, and so Mrs. Ridley stood guard while Joan treated the wound.

Meanwhile, Marcie told the girls about their adventures. They kept well away from the bedroom as Joan tended the injury. Fond of their cousin though they might be, they didn't want to see open wounds and gore. The Ridley lads were torn between joining in the talk of the horrors of the day with their father and Marcie below while boasting of their own bravery, and watching McGilroy bite his lips as Joan worked on him.

Joan talked away about foolish things to try and distract McGilroy from the pain a little, the way she always did when treating someone with a wound. Meanwhile he cursed his male cousins, who asked if his insides might come tumbling out. A detached part of Joan noted again what a nice torso he had.

As Joan was doing up another bandage—more of her petticoat—Mrs. Ridley cut in to scold McGilroy for having no more sense than to get into a fight with the MYC.

"It was more of an ambush," he said between clenched teeth. "If they'd just gone for the men, it wouldn't have been so bad, but they went after women with bairns."

Mrs. Ridley was ever ready to look on the bright side. "It can't have been as bad as the Battle of Waterloo, anyway."

"It was worse."[58]

"Thank heavens the girls had the sense to keep out of it, is all I can say," said Mrs. Ridley.

McGilroy said hoarsely, "Would you let me have a minute alone with t'doctor, Mistress?"

"That's not proper, and you said t'troth plight was off," said Mrs. Ridley. Joan thought sullenly about certain former lodgers at the Ridleys'.

"Take 'em all out for me a minute," urged the pale but determined McGilroy. His older relative softened and shooed her sons out of the room before her. "Mind, but two minutes."

"Got to get thee now, while thou'rt softened towards me," he told Joan, winking. "Ne'er heed some wild vow thou made, when thee was befuddled with weariness and worry. Wilt thou be mine again, Joan, and not hold my past against me? I was wrong to treat lasses so lightly—but I meant what I said about not knowing before what it is to have someone light up my day."

"Of course I will," Joan's tears spilled over. "Thou saved my life today. I was wrong to break things off over what thee can't undo and a few hasty words. I've so longed to undo that, and thought thou'd never want me back. I know it's thee for me or nobody."

"Thou saved my life and all, fearless hoyden as thou'rt. We belong together. Thou'll get thy adventures, never fear."

Joan had to gulp. "Thou saved Ben and others. Don't dare go fading away from blood loss, or getting an infection or summat. We need men like thee to fight for our rights. That matters more than all. Not grand folk who don't really know—though they can help."

"I'm thinking we all need women like thee, but I need one exactly like Joan Wright above all," he said.

She leaned over to kiss him, taking care not to put any weight on his damaged side. His dry lips were different enough for her to draw back worried. The fever that usually came with wounds and blood loss was setting in already.

She said in concern, "We must bathe you down in tepid water."

---

[58] One of the last things that John Lees, the Waterloo veteran said was that he felt in more danger at the Peterloo Massacre than at the Battle of Waterloo.

"Before that, look what I've got in my waistcoat pocket," he said.

Joan went to where the torn and bloody waistcoat was hanging on a chair. The bloodstains made her wince again, but she soon found the blue ribbon with the half coin that she had returned to him.

She glowed, and her tears flowed as she put it round her neck. "Thou kept it."

He sighed. "And my half, and those beads waiting for thee. I couldn't bear to give up on thee."

Mrs. Ridley, true to her word, bustled back in, her lips tight.

"I'm going to wed this lass," said Seán—never more McGilroy to Joan.

"So it's on again." Mrs. Ridley shook her head.

Joan mopped her eyes with a bit of her torn petticoat. "I'm right glad he speaks true, but fever's setting in. We need to bathe him in tepid water."

"You shan't do that, lass, that's not right." Mrs. Ridley shouted down to Kitty to warm some.

Soon, Sally Ridley came up with it. "You must be on your way to see to your father and t'others. We'll take care of Cousin Seán."

Joan fought down low thoughts about how Sally had kept well away when it came to treating the bloody wound, but was ready to minster to him now, and about how as like as not, she'd not quite given up on Seán as an admirer. She told herself she should be glad that there were women on hand to nurse him, men so often being hopeless at it.

Besides, Sally was right; she had to get home to tend to her father and then there were the others. She was puzzled what to do about Ann Wilson and Jack Hooper. She and Marcie would try poultices and draughts, but she feared these would do no good.

So, she rose to go, leaving some instructions for Mrs. Ridley about Seán's care on her way out.

Seán caught her arm. "Thou'rt to be mine, my lass. First thing I do, when I get over this fool scratch, is to make thee give me a date to be wed."

"I just might," she said.

And for all the horrors of the day, her lips turned up in a smile.

20.

BROKEN AND MENDED

Seán was truly in a fever by the next day, and talking about fighting booths in fairs and what he'd seen at Waterloo all mixed up with what had happened on St Peter's Field.

Soon though, he got the better of that and started to regain his strength, recovering from the blood loss too. He was, as Mrs. Ridley said, as strong as an ox and set on mending fast to make sure of Joan. Joan knew he was recovering when the Ridley wenches started driving him mad, cooped up as he was with their tattle and their squabbling.

There wasn't much else to smile about for a while after that. Joan's father's arm wasn't broken, yet for all Joan's poultices, it was slow in mending and stiff afterwards. He couldn't do his weaving without help for many weeks.

Tom and Nat had to do what weaving there was. That was, when Tom wasn't courting Marcie. But there was little enough work. It had all dried up like the streams in this drought, after that terrible day in St Peter's Field.

They used up Joan's savings. It was that, or give up eating, which would have saved all their problems, had they been able to do it years since. They scraped along on those savings, and on the little weaving jobs Tom and Nat could get.

Joan tried to help out in the workshop, but she had to keep running off to the Ridleys' house to tend to Seán, and the other injured all about besides. Of course, none of them could afford to pay her save Timothy Yorke, who refused any treatment from her anyway.

Mrs. Wright was so horrified by how nearly she had lost them all that she put up with Joan's renewed troth plight to that rascal McGilroy. Besides, after what was starting to be called 'The Peterloo Massacre'

Timothy Yorke began acting strangely and not doing any work. If there was anything that Mrs. Wright couldn't abide, it was idleness.

Friends often called in when Joan was tending to the sick. That was how they got word that Samuel Bamford and Dr. Healey and the rest of the Radicals had been carted off to gaol charged with 'sedition' or 'treason', it wasn't clear which. Henry Hunt was charged, too.

Joan heard how that *Times* reporter, John Tyas, who was no Radical, and whom they'd arrested by mistake, they let go. She also heard he wrote such an account of what he'd seen at St Peter's Field that *The Times* gave him the sack.

Within a couple of days, word was out how the government had nothing but praise for the Yeomanry Cavalry, and of how the Prince Regent sent a letter from his yacht, saying what a fine job the magistrates and the part-time soldiers had done.

Meanwhile, lots of the young men all about were fired with rage. Now they really were making weapons and sharpening scythes, wanting to fight the troops. There'd been riots round the New Cross part of Manchester on that terrible day after St Peter's Field had been cleared, with a man shot dead.

Many were just waiting for the word to rise up. But as time wore on, with nearly all the Radical leaders in gaol, and those who were free still holding out against force, slowly all the fury was replaced by a bitter despair.

Mr. Wright thought he'd be taken any day, too. For all his stiff arm, he went round with a special walk and a fine speech ready for the constables. Joan thought that he saw it as a snub that they never came for him.

Joan and Seán heard that the young fellow they'd seen beaten, cut down and trampled that day was still alive, though deadly ill. John Lees was his name. He was a spinner from Oldham. Somehow, he'd managed to walk home, all those seven miles.

Joan winced at the pain he must have suffered. It seemed he was a Waterloo veteran, too. Somehow, he merged in Joan's mind with Seán over that, so that she fretted over him like a brother, stranger though he was.

And thinking of brothers, one of the few things that made Joan smile as she ran around trying to get things done, was Marcie giving in to Tom inch by inch. She was so stubborn, that wench—and Joan knew she was bad enough for that herself.

And she had to laugh over the haircut that MCY man's sabre had given Tom—as it was that, or cry at the thought of how close he had come to having his head shaved off instead. She snipped off the other side to match, and now it was short and spiky. Marcie, who'd always made fun of his golden curls as better suited on a girl's head, was sad over that. Joan knew that's how she'd feel over Seán's ringlets, were they cut off.

And in a way, Marcie's surrender was too hard a thing to be a joke, when for her, as for Joan, it meant giving up on at least part of those schemes for independence they'd dreamed about.

Still, that was extra difficult for a working lass. If only they had funds to fall back on, it would be so much easier.

Even then, what a woman must never do was fall in love with a man, and first Joan and now Marcie had broken their vow in doing exactly that.

Yet for all that, they would not give up on their plans and schemes. "We'll find a way for you to have some adventures yet," said Tom and Seán, too easily. But Joan knew that she and Marcie must shift for themselves about finding a way of coming by them while still being with these two.

But that was for the future; the present was hard enough. All about their charmed circle, there was enough unhappiness, what with the hard times and the fear. The mistrust between people was as bad as before, or maybe worse.

Everyone scowled on those thought to be informers. Ned Pritchard sneered, "Massacre, they call it? There were less than twenty killed. That's no massacre. You were lucky it wasn't more, going there marching so cocky, looking for trouble."

Jimmy Thribble rounded on him so hotly that Ned jumped backwards. "Damn your eyes for a nark, Pritchard, shut thy mouth or I'll shut it for you. That is the figure the authorities boast on. If you'd seen those heaps of people lying in the field, and along by the lanes all t'way home, you'd talk more sense. They'll be hundreds dead in t'coming months down to what was done to us that day. But they're too scared of being blamed for being at yon meeting to go to t'infirmary or ask for help, so they'll die quiet, and be no part of those official figures you blather of."

Ned Pritchard quailed and slunk away.

Joan, standing by, nodded. She knew how worried Jimmy was over Jack Hooper, who was getting no better, suffering from pains in his inside. She feared for him herself. Nothing that she and Marcie could do for him helped him.

The well-to-do sympathizers set up a relief fund—and hundreds were seen by the committee. No idlers these, but folks so injured they had no choice but take charity.

'Professional beggars,' said Ned Pritchard, but out of the hearing of anyone who might hit him for it. Joan thought that for every professional beggar, there were fifty like her father and Seán, too proud to ask for help.

Like Jack Hooper, Ann Wilson didn't get the better of that crushing. As the days went by, she seemed to get worse, and her legs got weaker. She took to lying on her sofa. Joan felt helpless as she made up herbal draughts that did nothing for her.

It was the same in the villages all about. People were suffering in just the same way from being crushed or trampled, while many had infected gashes. Joan and Marcie did their best to treat them, for as Jimmy Thribble said, few of them dared to go to the infirmary, as that would be to admit that they had been at the meeting, and they couldn't afford to pay for an apothecary.

Some seemed to be damaged inside their heads. Timothy Yorke was one. Since that day on St Peter's Field, he would scarcely say a word, going about like a tallow-faced, tight lipped sleepwalker. Joan overheard Mrs. Yorke say to a neighbour—not to Joan, she still wasn't talking to her—how he couldn't sleep at night, and if he did drop off, he'd wake up screeching like an owl.

Had he been one of the informers, or just too friendly with those who enforced the law? Nobody really knew.

Joan wondered if, without those tale bearers' wild stories, those nervous magistrates might not have sent in that half trained militia to do slaughter that day. They would never know that either.

Once, Joan had tried to talk to Timothy as one human being to another. He'd glared at her. "You won't win me over with your smiles. You must be a boldface to let such a good for nothing fellow as that McGilroy come about you."

"Never mind about that. We're all troubled about you, carrying on so strange and hiding away from everyone."

He said nothing, staring at her blank faced. Joan waited, but he said no more, so she took herself off.

As for poor Daffy Danny, he was more than ever away with the fairies. Before, he'd helped out his parents a little. Now he went about taking to himself, and wouldn't answer if anyone spoke to him. At least, unlike Timothy Yorke, he did some talking, only it was to himself.

As Joan ranged about the meadows looking for healing herbs, she often came on him shambling along chattering to himself, the words flowing from him, as if he couldn't get enough said before bedtime.

Once she came on him unseen. He was standing tall, speaking out proudly, and waving his arms:

Rise, like lions after slumber
In unvanquishable number!
Shake your chains to earth like dew
Which in sleep had fallen on you:
Ye are many—they are few.[59]

That sounded good to Joan, like real poetry, not sloppy stuff. She tiptoed away, and found a pen and rooted about for a bottle of ink left over from when her father had run those classes. Happy days, those had been, when people could think of something other than where their next meal was coming from.

---

[59] Words from the poem by P B Shelley on the Peterloo Massacre, 'The Masque of Anarchy', written soon after the massacre, but not published until 1831.

She found a piece of paper to write upon. It was an old picture of Joan, a bad drawing edged by flowers done by some lad with poor enough taste to shove it under the door for her last year. She'd forgotten to throw it out, and now she wrote down those words on the back of it.

Somehow, it felt wrong to tell anyone but Marcie. Marcie said the poor fellow was picking up someone else's thoughts, some poet's, by the sound of it. Joan supposed that explanation made about as much sense as any.

Still, Joan was too busy to think much about it, what with helping out in their workshop, going over to aid Mrs. Ridley in nursing Seán, and searching for edible plants. Their vegetable patch was nearly bare. Desperate folks had raided it.

At last, Seán was properly on the mend, and calling on her to come for his first walk out since he'd been wounded. She wore the blue ribbon with the half coin and the blue beads he'd returned to her.

Walking slowly, with his side still being stiff, they went to the bank of the rindle where they'd sat before, only weeks since, when they'd still been young and foolish. Joan hoped that maybe they could be like that again when those visions of Peter's Field faded.

She thought they had got old heads, after what they'd seen. Then, when she looked at Seán, with his olive skin still pale from blood loss, but still with those wicked blue eyes and curling black locks, she thought that she could be young and daft again already. And from the way he looked at her, she could tell he was as silly about her in return. She smiled.

But then he dashed her spirits.

"I just heard from Jimmy: that other fellow, John Lees, he's dead. His father wants an inquest. Any fair-minded jury must return a verdict of murder, if they're let to. But I'm guessing that yon coroner will find a way of tinkering with the case."[60]

---

[60] When it became clear that the inquest was going in favour of a verdict of murder, the coroner, who had tried to overrule most of the statements from witnesses, first adjourned and then found a technical excuse to close the proceedings.

Joan's throat hurt. She had to swallow, and spoke flatly. "So what we hoped for when we set out that day - it's all come to people killed and maimed for nowt."

Yet, Seán wasn't cast down, though she could see how moved he was. It took more than running him through with a sabre to keep him out of spirits for long. "We'll get there in the end, my lass: they can't stop us in the long run. But for now, they'll do all they can to stamp on our heads, because they're scared of us not knowing our places."

Joan supposed this terrible 'They', the government, Lord Liverpool and Lord Sidmouth and Lord Castlereigh and all those, would do the taking away of that *Habeas Corpus* thing that everyone spoke of and worse. Like as not, they'd make it against the law to be a working man or woman and say anything but 'God save the King' and 'God Bless Our Betters.'

She thought of her father, struggling to work with his stiffened arm, with all the men with two arms fighting for work, and so little to eat, and the growing Nat and Ben going hungry, though, thank God, they hadn't left their mischief behind on St Peter's Field, and her savings all whittled away, and her mother sourer than ever, and Hannah scared into trying to be the good girl even more.

Then there was Ann the blacksmith's wife, and Jack Hooper, and the people with hurts come by that day all about, and Timothy Yorke and Daffy Danny and all the others.

Her upper lip shook, for all she tried to keep it firm.

Seán put his arms tightly about her, as he hadn't been able to, since the gash on his ribs. She could feel how his strength was returning. "Whatever comes, I'll look after thee. I won't let my lass or hers go hungry, never fear."

"I must look after myself," Joan spoke quickly, but she said it nicely. This moment wasn't to be spoilt with too much awkwardness from her.

He took her chin between finger and thumb. "Thou looked after me on yon sick bed. We must look after each other. In a day or so, I'll be back to getting in rabbits again for dinner."

"Thou must not, yet: take care." She was anxious, but he laughed.

"Then give me a date to be wed, and then I might listen. And it can't be after this autumn. Thy father's agreeable."

She could believe it. Things were bad enough for her father to be glad to get her off his hands. She felt even her mother was ready to put up with it, for all she snorted when Joan and Tom and Ben and Marcie said how Seán had saved her on St Peter's Field. All she said over it was, 'Don't dare turn Papist. Though yon fellow's godless, his father was one.'

"Maybe Tom will never be able to wed Marcie till the cows come home," Joan said now, "Though Nat's getting of a size to do Tom's work."

"I'll think a way out for them; I always do," he said. "I was doing some thinking when I was laid up. I've got a few schemes."

"That must have hurt worse than that gash." Joan laughed for joy to see him on the mend and arrogant as ever. It would stand him in good stead, with these hard times ahead.

So Joan, knowing nothing of the Six Acts[61] to come that would silence Radical protest, or of so much suffering that lay ahead for her people, or of Ann Wilson and Jack Hooper and so many others all dead within months of the wounds that they'd come by at the Peterloo Massacre, turned a happy face on the future. She knew somehow that whatever came the way of Seán and herself, they'd make a fine team facing it together, the way they had on St Peter's Field…

…And she and Marcie were still set on having some adventures and keeping some independence yet.

…But above everything, they wanted to help their own people: not just their families, not just the locals, but all the people like them who the rich thought should get by on nothing, with less to look forward to.

Joan was proud of how their cures had kept infection from Seán and the others. She and Marcie were going to keep on with those, learning all the time, and might even get a living through it in time. That would be a fine thing, though they'd never call a woman 'Doctor' the way that they did Healey.

Wedding Seán would be a fine thing, too. They'd find a way to keep their bairns well fed. They were lucky that there was that farm in

Northamptonshire he would come into. They might all be able to do many things with that.

She put her hands on his shoulders, and said, "Thou'rt truly are a rascal, talking me into wedding thee so stupidly early. Thou wants to tame me, that's what it is."

Before he started kissing her, he winked and said, "Thou? I stand about as much chance o' that, as that lot in government stand in keeping us rabble beaten down for long."

THE END

Lucinda Elliot was born in Buckinghamshire, and brought up in various parts of the UK in a series of rambling, isolated old houses which her parents were renovating in the days before this became fashionable. After living and working in London for many years, she now lives in mid Wales with her family. She is a classic English literature and history geek and is addicted to tea. She loves a laugh above anything.

Printed in Great Britain
by Amazon